Weather, or not . . .

On-camera, Forest Hill was the personable, often zany weatherman for ABC-TV in New York. Off-camera, he was a sophisticated meteorologist with a deep interest in his work, which often left him with too little time for his personal pursuits.

Now it was different: he had just been overwhelmed by the most exciting and fulfilling sexual experience of his adult life. Jenny Wells, who was only twenty—half his age—claimed she loved him. And Forest was afraid he loved her, too.

But the pleasures of their lovemaking were overshadowed by confusion, even suspicion. Should he tell her about the bizarre weather patterns he had discovered? And, was their meeting really pure circumstance, or was he being set up? After all, she *was* General Wells's daughter.

Forest wanted to trust Jenny. He needed someone. There had to be somebody he could tell. *Everyone else he had told had been killed!*

Leonard Leokum & Paul Posnick

WEATHER WAR

PINNACLE BOOKS • LOS ANGELES

WEATHER WAR

An original Pinnacle Books edition, published for the first time anywhere.

First printing, August 1978

ISBN: 0-523-40229-5

Printed in the United States of America

PINNACLE BOOKS, INC.
2029 Century Park East
Los Angeles, California 90067

DEDICATION

To Murray and Gail Bruce,
for their faith, hope and charity,
and to my father for his inspiration
and love.

L.L.

To Charlie Werther,
who always believed.

P.P.

ACKNOWLEDGMENT

To Joe Witte, CBS-TV meterologist in
New York, for his helpful advice and
technical assistance.

WEATHER WAR

MONDAY

JULY 3

SAN FRANCISCO, CALIFORNIA

Darlene Edwards felt like she was going to explode out of her skin. As she sat hunched over the wheel of the '67 Volkswagen, she picked at the pimple on her chin, hoping it would break before she did. She inspected her finger for a trace of blood and, finding none, licked it anyway. The front seat of the car—the floor, even the dashboard—was littered with wrappings from McDonald's and Burger King and Pizza Hut. But there was nothing left to gnaw on but herself.

"That son of a bitch." She looked out again quickly, down the almost-deserted street, afraid he might appear and catch her hating him, and yet desperately anxious for him to arrive. They had to get away from here and before the storm broke. She looked up through the little hole they called a sun roof. Above her, the sky rumbled but didn't stir the air, and sitting there gasping she felt herself swelling with unexpelled breath. Darlene farted

1

slowly and felt no better. She fanned the air with a wax-paper wrapper that once had held a cheeseburger, licked her fingers, and waited for James Grotz, the most evil man in the world.

"Her Jim." And Susie's, and Jenny's, and Mable's and all the rest of his stable, that she knew of. She didn't mind the hooking that much, she thought, clenching her thighs just a little, or his pimping, she thought, relaxing them again and feeling the almost permanent ache on her pubic bone. It was the other part that made her scared and angry and always hungry and getting fatter still. Gas stations, 7-Elevens—just little jobs at first. For peanuts and beer and a bottle of scotch, and a quick sweaty bang once she'd driven them to safety—on another side of town, in an alley, an old dirt road, anywhere.

And now, always just once more into the street to hook, into the car to drive, just a little more scratch for this or that, or anything that came into his wanting head.

And now he wanted a bank, that stupid shithead. A bank, for crissakes. He'd get them both killed. The sky above her lowered its stomach, and she could hear the gurgling inside it. Darlene reached down and turned the key in the ignition, waited for the motor to turn over, and then turned it off again. Where the fuck was he?

She wormed her eyes down the street once more toward the bank and inched a finger into

2

her nose, and then suddenly it was too quiet. And then it was too loud to bear. It started with a sputter of coughs and pings in the distance that she wished were backfire but knew wasn't. And then the storm opened and offered the world its own violence.

The street went black as she saw him come running from the door, his front foot ahead, his back one sidling to let him see over his shoulder. Like an ugly evil bug, he came at her in the darkening, a gun in one hand and a too-small bag in the other. The sky boomed again and she remembered to start the motor, though this time she couldn't even hear it. Again the sky slammed fist into palm, and suddenly he was beside her on the seat yelling, screaming into her ear and punching her with the gun as he tried to jerk the car into motion. But she couldn't hear a word.

The first bolt of lightning left a jagged crack in the sky for a moment, if you were looking, and lit the artificial night of the city.

Inside the Volkswagen, Darlene Edwards and James Grotz felt nothing. The stroke heated their narrow chamber to 30,000 degrees Centigrade in a few ten-millionths of a second. When lightning hits a tree, it makes the sap boil and turn to steam, until the tree finally explodes from the inside.

It was the same for Darlene and Jim. Their blood came screaming out of every hole they owned, out of every pore. And then they exploded, victims of a freak, hit by lightning

3

right in the middle of downtown San Francisco.

And although nobody thought it was a shame, it still made the papers. After all, the odds against it were a million to one.

TUESDAY

JULY 4

ALLIANCE, NEBRASKA

The white man slept and the black man wept. Neighbors all their lives, and their families going back a century, they lived to prove the other didn't exist.

It was hailing in Box Butte County, raining stones the size of fists, on both sides of Federal 385. On his side, the black man had been squeezing the land for sugar beets and clothes and honor and dignity and anything else he could get out of it. And now his crop was gone. The protective leaves were being shredded, the plants crushed and his eyes, which, when he was very young had shed tears, were now frozen dry with pain as he watched. But a lump the size of a fist was sitting under his heart, weeping.

The white man had opened his eyes at the first rattle on the roof, as always, alert to any change, any threat to his kingdom. Thousands of acres of wheat surrounded him, connected by the tendrils of his desire. His house encased him, testament to his heritage and ability. Machines and servants attended him, subject to his whim. And the United States of America stood behind him, goddamnit, insuring him. He had land the United States government paid him to leave fallow. He had crops he was paid not to grow. And if, by some irritating quirk of nature, the weather destroyed what he did grow, why then there was money in that too. And so he turned over, eyed his wife, and went back to sleep.

WEDNESDAY

JULY 5

ST. LOUIS, MISSOURI

In the clubhouse under the stands, all you could hear was the humming of the air conditioner and the chatter of bodies without minds—jock talk. But lying on the training table, a beer in one hand and his other arm being gentled by the trainer, Bucky Bently could tell from the TV on the wall that it was still raining. And it made him feel good.

"Two days before the All Star Game and who's rotation comes up? You guessed it." Bucky lifted his head just high enough to pour down some more beer, and then belched loudly. The beer was already warm. He dropped the can onto the Astroturf carpet and turned his head to watch it seep into the rug. In three minutes they'd call the friggin' game and he could get on with it. Shower, shave, blow-dry, and suit-up for real life, without the wife. On the road and a star.

On the TV you could see those die-hard, 1,500 mother-humping fans still sitting out there, hunched under sheets of plastic like some transparent worm, waiting for the rain to stop, for the game to start, any game . . . waiting for Bucky to feel the fear. God, Bucky loved the rain.

At 8:37 the umpires officially declared the game rained out. At 11:37 Bucky Bently came for the second time into what's her name, rolled over, and passed out a happy man. Outside, it was still raining.

THURSDAY

JULY 6

15 miles south of SUMMERSVILLE
22 miles southwest of NETTLE FENWICK,
WEST VIRGINIA

They had gone too far, climbed too high. They were too young, too innocent, too much in love. And now, sitting curled against each other, high on the side of Mt. Lookout, they knew they were in trouble. Their clothing was too thin, and they hadn't brought enough with them. A stolen afternoon out in nature's country was all they had wanted, so they weren't dressed for night and cold; they had no tent or food; in fact, they were as good as naked.

Earlier, with the afternoon blanket of warm filtering rays through the pines, it was erotic to feel the fingers of air blow across nipples until they were hard, and watch each other's skin ripple like the surface of a lake, with prickly bumps running cold in channels of hot flush.

The clothes they had strewn across the glade in their private abandon were now clammy against their skin. Nylon panties and a rayon shirt, wind breakers that didn't, and bobby-socks gone thin and bunchy in shoes what were never meant for nature. And it was dark without a star, and getting darker.

They cuddled, huddled, squeezed each other's skin as if to wrench a calorie out by friction alone. They would have made love again for warmth but were too sore and too afraid of freezing some private part, some cavity, some extremity that didn't need to be exposed to this devil cold.

Finally they slept. And it wasn't until seven days later that they were found. Dead. Frozen. Thawed. And, finally, decomposing in the once-again sun.

FRIDAY

JULY 7

WESTCHESTER, NEW YORK

The thirteenth hole at the Leewood Country Club was one of the toughest par fours anywhere. Four hundred and twenty yards. Most of which twisted steeply uphill. Zanetti walked to his drive on the level part of the fairway, but in 94-degree weather even level ground felt like it was uphill. He gazed through the haze in the direction of the green, thinking that he had never been on in two. As a matter of fact, he had never seen anyone else make the green in two either. After he wiped the sweat off his forehead, he flipped the towel to the caddie, who exchanged it automatically for a four wood. Addressing the ball deliberately, Zanetti wiped each palm on his pants to get a better grip. The ball sat up perfectly in the recently mowed grass, and the strong sun seemed to illuminate the ball's whiteness as it grew larger and then smaller again in his vision. He blinked a bead of perspiration out of his eye. He was feeling a little wobbly, but in the instant when he could have stepped away from the ball, he started his backswing. Just as the club arced into its resting place at the top of his swing, the bolt of pain hammered into his chest. Zanetti froze momentarily as the club tumbled out his hands and his mouth opened wide, reaching for a breath he could not catch. As his left knee buckled and sank to the ground, he could hear the faint but shrill voice of Marie berating him. "You're sixty-three years old. What are you trying to prove playing golf in this weather? What do you mean you didn't take a cart? Are you crazy or . . ."

CHAPTER ONE

In the control room of ABC-TV in New York you could see several faces of Roger Moss delivering the six o'clock news. And you could see one face of the sportscaster straightening his tie, one face of Lydia Baily catching a last puff on her cigarette before she went on, and one camera was on Forest Hill, the weatherman, setting up the big weather map. If Roger hadn't been delivering such a racy human interest story, you would have had to look at Forest, because as a weatherman he went all the way. Today he was dressed in an 1890s bathing suit and a rubber swim cap, and beneath the big board was a sandbox and beach chair, from which he would deliver today's weather report.

But Roger was in the middle of a hot one, and even the crew was interested. "So, Miss Annette La France, who you might remember about a year back was elected Miss Wall Street by popular acclaim, an award based, perhaps, somewhat more than less, on her unique and generous physical endowment . . ." The camera cut to film of the lady in mention displaying an enormous chest, proudly parading down Wall Street as throngs cheered. Back to Roger. "Well, today, in Central Park, at Bethesda Fountain, Miss La France, impelled by who knows what, but certainly in reaction to the beastly hot wave inundating this city, decided to bare it all and take a dip. It seems this was fine with everybody, and soon a rather large cheering section formed, urging Miss La France on to other swimming feats, like the breast stroke."

Roger never broke a smile, but off camera you could hear muffled laughter. "The problem began when some of New York's finest arrived and decided that something here wasn't entirely legal. After she refused to emerge from the fountain, the police waded in after her. And in their wake, a bit of a riot ensued." Now the camera cut to film of a swirling, milling mob of people, police, and, somewhere in the middle, a naked lady whom everybody was hoping to get a glimpse of. However, through the magic of television and film editing, the TV audience was denied the pleasure. "Finally she was subdued and taken, wrapped in blue, to the precinct house, where she was booked for indecent exposure and inciting a riot. Twelve people were injured, two policemen are in the hospital, and a horse was stepped on in the proceedings. The horse will be fine." Roger looked cadaverously at the camera. After all, his ability to keep a straight face was making him almost a quarter of a million dollars a year. "And now," he intoned, knowing full well that this was an impossible act to follow, "here's Forest Hill with the weather."

It was only the six P.M. news, nothing to get excited about. It happened every day, on every network, but there was still tension in the air. The news was big business and the stars brought viewers, and viewers meant ratings and sponsors, and sponsors meant big money. Forest Hill had become a star, the first weatherman in the history of television to be the main attraction on the news. His style was part stand-up comic, part country boy. Every show was different and zany and people tuned in to watch him as much as to find out what the weather would be like tomorrow.

So now, lounging in his beach chair, he didn't worry about following a story about a naked lady, he just went into his act. "Hot! Hot! I'm so hot." Forest removed one strap of his bathing suit from his shoulder. "Aren't you hot-hot out there, folks? Do like I'm doing, take off your clothes. Get comfortable. This isn't over yet. And who is to blame? Not me. I told you it was going to be hot, didn't I?" The stagehands and cameramen answered back, "Yes, Forest. You told us." Forest leaped to his feet and ripped off the other strap of his bathing suit, leaving him bare to the waist. Catcalls and wolf whistles rang out in the studio. Forest ignored them and slogged through the sand to a map of the country.

"Now, I tell you what I'm gonna do. I'm gonna promise you some relief. You see this storm?" he said, pointing to a black balloon near San Francisco on the map. Forest took the balloon and moved it across the map until it was over the New York area. "Well, this guy should get here tonight, and we're gonna get rain."

Forest broke into song. "It got its start in San Francisco. . . ." Then he stopped, consulted his watch, and announced, "four days, ten hours, and seventeen minutes ago. And ever since then, it's been snaking its jolly old way across the country, chasing this warm front through Nebraska, Missouri, West Virginia . . . and well . . ."

He paused and looked up. Then he rolled his eyes and said deliberately, "I said, we're gonna get *rain* tonight between seven and eight o'clock. And since I'm never wrong—almost— take your umbrellas with you." At that moment, it began to rain in the studio, buckets of water pouring down over Forest, turning his sandbox into a mud pile.

Forest looked up at the water pouring down on him and then at the TV audience, winking as if some giant joke were being perpetrated on him.

"That's not rain. I told you it would start between seven and eight. This is just water from a common, ordinary garden hose." Forest stepped out of his sandbox and started to walk off the set, camera three following. And, indeed, millions of viewers discovered with

16

Forest, the stagehand holding the upturned hose causing the deluge.

The chatter in the control room was immediately replaced by an atmosphere of alert concern, as Forest departed from the script for the who-knows-how-many-hundredth time. The director slid his fingers into position above the control panel. With Forest, he had learned to expect the unexpected.

"Ah ha," Forest intoned, "a rain machine." He grabbed the nozzle from the startled stagehand, and turned. Camera one quickly scanned the chaos as Forest proceeded to hose down the entire six o'clock news team, causing Lydia Baily's coiffure to undo, and sending everyone except Roger running for cover. He sat there stoicly, water dripping down his face, as if he were waiting for the child to finish his tantrum. In the midst of the laughter and the "Jesus Christs," a wise technician turned off the water at its source.

"And tomorrow the rain will be gone and it will be hot again. Hot-hot. I tell you." Forest dropped the hose and smiled. "Until tomorrow then," he waved. "Sunny days." He then began to take off the rest of his bathing suit, and only the quick reflexes of the director prevented 20 million viewers from seeing his firm white buttocks.

The six o'clock news was over. The big lights were out, and stagehands were mopping up the mess Forest had created. But nobody complained. It was their job, and they were glad to

17

have it. Forest, wrapped in a terry-cloth bathrobe and with a towel over his head, became an entirely different man. Well built, blond, good-looking, he was nothing like the clown who delivered the weather. And in fact, Forest Hill was a serious man, a trained meteorologist who did his homework better than any other weatherman on the air. His predictions were almost always right, and he was proud of it. There could be no doubt that weather was his life.

As they walked down the winding corridors toward their offices, Forest Hill and Roger Moss presented a complete picture of opposites. Off camera, Roger was a madcap, a boozer who chased women, always laughing, always on. Forest, who was usually serious, was even more so tonight.

"Roger, let me ask you a question. Do you really think that bit about the lady with the tits was a news story? Or was it a weather story?" Roger looked at him quizzically.

"I'd say a bit of both, old boy. You aren't jealous, are you? I mean your rain dance was certainly a hell of a show stopper." Roger displayed no anger toward Forest for having hosed him down. Roger knew he had come out of it looking fine, and he was well aware they were both in show business.

"It's not that, Roger. What I want to know is, what's the special ingredient that turns a weather story into a news story?" Roger looked at Forest again, and saw that he was

18

asking this in a more general sense, and thought for a moment.

"The weather becomes news when it has human interest, I'd say. When it affects people, directly, specifically, or humorously. The elder statesman has spoken." Roger was making fun of himself but Forest didn't laugh. Instead with a distant look in his eyes, he thanked Roger and left to go to his own office. Roger watched Forest Hill go, shoulders stooped, lost in thought, and wondered what was bothering him.

Forest was wondering the same thing. Sitting at his desk, still in his sodden bathing suit and bathrobe, he was trying to figure out what the hell was wrong. He looked around the room at the familiar equipment which usually gave him so much enjoyment. The three clocks for Pacific, Eastern and Greenwich time stared back at him blankly, their sweeping second hands revolving mindlessly. On one wall neatly hung charts for: stability, snowfall, rainfall, max. temps, min. temps, temp. change, five-day, and QPF—quantitative precipitation forecast depiction. They told him nothing he didn't already know. The four teletype machines at the end of his office chattered intermittently. Forest almost didn't hear them anymore.

He swung his chair around to face his desk and stared at his clasped hands. He certainly wasn't bothered by the story about Miss Tits; he had no professional jealousy with Roger. Then he considered for a moment his repulsion for himself, his job—his act. He knew he hated

19

himself for being a buffoon and demeaning the importance of the weather, but no more today than yesterday. So what the hell was it? Lonely, divorced, bored, making too much money, and not able to justify his existence to himself, he sat brooding.

His assistant, Micky Leary, came in without knocking. She never had, from the first day she had started working for him five years ago. She was a thin woman, without the curves most men associate with femininity. Now in her forties, she had assumed the protective coloration of the working girl. She wore her hair up in a bun and dressed sensibly, which some people would call plain. But her eyes were alive and there was warmth and humor in her face.

Micky looked at him sitting there and her heart went out to him. On some days she felt like his mother, and on others, she wished he would see her as a woman. But there was always something about him, something about knowing the serious, caring, slightly lost side of the famous person, that made her go soft inside. And she had never let him know, nor would she. A person who'd been around for as long as she had, and had the scars to prove it, doesn't go asking to get stepped on again. And still . . .

"Well, well, well, who do we have here? If it isn't Mr. Florence Chadwick and Little Egypt all rolled into one. He swims, he strips, and he moons the audience, right on the six o'clock news. And all those little kiddies watching, too.

20

Have they called you upstairs yet, boss?" Forest turned to her smiling. She did him good.

"Fuck the brass, Mick. They don't care about anything but ratings. The phone will never ring. You can bet on it." And they both laughed, because she had broken his mood, and they both knew it was true.

"Here's the data you wanted," she said, coming across the room and putting the papers on his desk. "And for God's sake, will you please get out of those wet clothes. Preferably while I'm here to watch, cutie." They started to laugh again, but Forest dove into the papers, spreading them out across his desk and comparing one chart with another, and left her laughing alone. She watched him for a moment, seeing how quickly he synthesized the information and marveling at how hungry he was for it. But then she felt left out.

"Hi there, remember me? I'm your trusted aide, Micky, who has been busting her ass all afternoon to get you that mess of numbers." Forest was finished reading and now knew what was bothering him. The knowing made him feel better and, at the same time, worse. Because now Forest Hill knew he was scared.

"I want to ask you something, Micky. And don't laugh at me."

"If people like me stop laughing, you're out of work, boss."

"I'm serious, damnit." He glared at her.

"OK, I'm serious too." She glared back, mocking him.

"Do you know what makes a tornado? I

21

mean, let me put it this way. Do you know what conditions are necessary for a tornado to be formed?"

Micky shrugged. "Sure I do. Severe thunderstorms. A cold front moving in on warm moist air. Right?" Forest smiled at her, pleased.

"Right you are, my girl. Very good. But specifically," he got up and began to pace the room, acting it out for her, "you need a layer of warm, moist air near the ground, and another layer of warmer air on top of it, holding it down." To see and hear him describe it, she thought, was like hearing someone else describe a hot-fudge sundae.

"Now, the sun heats the earth, and the ground heats the bottom layer until it's hot enough to rise, and the cold front comes along and plows under the warm, moist air, giving it an extra shove, and before you know it you've got this column of hot, wet air bubbling up to forty, fifty, sixty thousand feet, like a giant chimney." He grinned diabolically and moved toward her, his arms waving.

Micky retreated. "I got you, boss." He kept coming.

"And then the winds go to work. A high jet wind blows across the top of the chimney, venting it, so the hot air can keep rising. Another wind pattern at twenty thousand feet curves in and starts the chimney spinning in a counterclockwise direction, and the rising air keeps condensing, feeding heat back into the system, and the air starts spinning faster and faster, sucking more air in from all around it, until you have this violent, explosive, twisting mass, and then . . ."

"Then?" she asked. Forest ran at her at full speed, stopped, and then leaped into the air right in front of her.

"Then a fierce mother funnel drops down and varoom . . . you've got a tornado!" He looked expectantly into her eyes. "Well?"

"Well what?" Micky asked. Forest exploded at her with an intensity he had never hinted at, even to her.

"Goddamnit! What the hell have you been doing all afternoon? Can't you see it?" Micky bowed her head against the onslaught, afraid tears might come to her eyes, afraid she might strike back at this blind, self-centered sonofabitch, afraid she had missed something.

Then she lifted her head, gathered herself, and spat back at him. "See what? I don't see it! What?" She found herself screaming at him. He grabbed her by the arm and dragged her to the desk. He pulled one of the charts out of a pile and spread it in front of her It was a weather map of the United States, accurate as of the six o'clock news.

"See this?" Forest said, tracing his finger across a storm line that covered the country from California to New York.

"Sure boss. That's the storm you've been tracking for three days." He patted her shoulder gently.

"Good. Now, would you point out to me the area you have been investigating all afternoon?" Micky leaned over the chart and put her finger lower on the map, at the edge of the Oklahoma-Kansas border. Then she peeked at him and flinched, as if expecting him to lash out at her.

"Now, Micky, what happened in this area yesterday? What happened to the little town of Garnett, Kansas?" To her ears, he sounded rational again, although mocking, and she decided not to run for it. She summoned up an answer.

"Well, boss, it seems to have been blitzed by a tornado. Nothing left but tumbleweed." She paused, and then rushed on. "And you asked me to get the data—confirmed national and local readings on the weather conditions in that area. And I did. And there . . ." she jabbed at the pile of papers on the desk, "there it is. Highs, lows, temperatures, fronts, wind speeds, cloud formation . . . for a five-hundred-mile radius. There it is. And why the hell are you yelling at me?" Micky Leary was as close to tears as she would ever want to be with this man, and Forest couldn't help but see it. But he was being driven by something more compelling than her pain.

"Did you read the data, Micky? Did you just compile it, type it, and deliver it . . . or did you read it?"

"I don't know what you mean, boss. Of course I read it." He stared at her.

"Well?" She didn't have the answer, and something in Forest sagged inside. "You don't see it, do you? There was a tornado here, wiping out this little fucking town. Wham bam

24

and everybody's dead. And from all the data, from all the sources available, there is no possibility of a tornado occurring in that place at that time." Forest started arranging the sheets of paper next to one another on the desk. "What do you see in yesterday's satellite photographs?

"Clouds over the entire area."

"Heavy cloud cover," he prompted. "And what about the day before yesterday?"

"Same thing," she said, looking at him confused.

"Well, how much of the sun's heat do you think those clouds would reflect back into space?"

"About eighty percent?"

"That is an excellent guess. So tell me, how in the hell did the air and the ground get hot enough to get the whole thing moving? How could there be . . ." Forest walked away from the desk and stood by the radar scope, looking at it but not seeing it. "How could there be a tornado, Micky?" he whispered.

She looked at his back, hating him the way you can hate only someone you love who has hurt you, and wondered what to do. She had no answer to give him. If she had, she would be doing the weather reports herself instead of being trapped in the perpetual limbo of being his boy Micky.

"Well . . . maybe it was just a freak, Forest. You know, Forest, freaks do happen." It was all she had to say, all she could squeeze out without dissolving, and then she ran from the room.

It was a long time before Forest brought himself back. He had to wrench himself away from the mesmerizing screen, with its overview of the planet, back to this room and this time and his dilemma. Seeing that Micky was gone, he went to the door and closed it. Then he went to his desk and sank into his chair. He couldn't keep his eyes off the charts laying there in front of him.

"Maybe it's a freak," she had said, "a tornado that couldn't happen."

"Sure," he said to himself, "a freak. Just a freak." And then he opened a drawer of his desk and pulled out another folder of charts. "And that's two! And that's three!"

CHAPTER TWO

Rain came to Manhattan in torrents, as predictably as Forest had promised. But as he emerged from ABC, Forest scowled at the black skies relieving themselves onto the streets. Ordinarily he would have been pleased with his accuracy, but tonight it was an empty triumph. Standing under the canopy, he watched the pedestrians scurrying for cover, jacket collars pulled up to their ears, sodden newspapers—the everyman's rainhat—hanging limply on their heads. Gusts of wind-driven rain blew umbrellas useless and the traffic added insult to the abuse from below by hurling cascades of puddles upward. Everything was perfectly normal. It was raining in New York and the city was grinding itself into a tangle.

But no matter what they say, rain doesn't fall equally on all men. With a flick of his wrist, Forest activated his umbrella. It was a carbon steel, precision-tooled instrument that

opened like an unclenching fist in his hand.
There was no other umbrella like it in the
world. It had been custom made, by Streets of
London, from his own design, and it was truly
marvelously effective. Closed, it fit into the
palm of Forest's hand; open, it flexed gently
against the wind—any wind, even a hurricane
attack. The bottom rim of the umbrella diverted water from his legs, and, striding securely
beneath its cloak, Forest made for the Silver
Cloud Rolls-Royce, waiting to take him to the
party. Almost magically, the door opened, the
umbrella folded itself back into his hand, and
Forest tucked himself into the corner of plush,
dry comfort that stardom and money bring.
There would be no taxi meter ticking on his
ride, no bus crush of sodden passengers steaming next to him, no anxiety about how to get
from here to there when nature is acting up.

The sleek, metallic gray car cruised inexor-
ably through Central Park, as the few remain-
ing ocean ships still do somewhere at sea, and
Forest gazed through the window at the
bedraggled children escaping the outdoor rock
concert they had spent hours waiting to see.
Some still tried to stay dry—under trees,
bushes, or by running—as if they could escape
the onslaught by being very thin and sliding
between the drops. The others—the realists,
the slow, the fat, and the tired—plodded
through the mud, too wet to care anymore.

Forest watched and wondered why he had no
impulse to press the electric button on the door
until his window was wide open to the stream-

ing wetness and scream into the night, as he had done so many times before, "I told you so, you dumb jerks. I told you to take umbrellas and raincoats, or to stay at home. I told you! I told you!" But he didn't. He couldn't anymore. It was as if there was no joy anymore in just being right about something so simplistic as when it would rain. Anybody with half a brain could make predictions if they wanted. Once, he had wanted to, with all his energy and intelligence, and he had done it better than anyone else. And now here he was, riding in his reward, alone. A glass partition shielded him from the nameless driver provided by the network, and he was on his way to the last place he wanted to go—a society party, very rich, very chic, very avant-degenerate.

The elevator door opened directly into the penthouse and Forest was confronted with a living tableau in which every figure was totally conscious of how his or her pose affected the perfection of the image: a bent wrist; a slouch; a backward tilt of the head, which still featured the profile; creased trousers that wouldn't cross all evening; and an acre of decolletage precariously and artfully balanced between tan line and nipple. There wasn't anything that Forest hadn't seen a hundred times before, but tonight he found himself observing it, and the impact was disturbing. Tonight he wasn't part of it. Forest took a breath and plunged in, heading for the bar, summoning his public personality as he swam.

"Sunny days, Mr. Hills."

"That's Mr. Hill, Fred. Forest Hill. You're getting so old you can't even remember my name." The old black bartender chuckled gently to himself and shook his head, enjoying the ritual. Forest gazed fondly at the reassuring old face with the magic, twinkling eyes that seemed to have seen everything, including most of the depths to which Forest had stooped, staggered, or fallen. And yet, Fred never seemed to judge him and always welcomed him genuinely. For a moment Forest wondered whether the bartender's welcome was a reaction to him or if he treated everyone that way.

"I would like two Saharas, Fred. That's a vodka martini with gin instead of vermouth. On the rocks, please." Fred didn't blink. "That's a very dry drink, Fred. In fact, you might say it's wry." Forest shared a grin with Fred and turned to survey the field.

"You expecting some heavy company, Mr. Hills?" The bartender put two tumblers in front of Forest and chuckled again. It was an alien sound in the artificial babble and shrillness of the party.

"No, Fred, just the opposite. I'm trying to avoid any kind of contact—banter, middle, or heavyweight." Forest paused and poured part of one of the drinks into his throat. "Sometimes pretense is the best defense. And this is my diversion." Forest clinked the two glasses together in a mock toast, drank again, and then turned away from the bar into the crush of the party. And because he knew Fred so well, he knew he only imagined that round, soft voice calling "Sunny days" gently after him.

Forest elbowed himself politely around clusters of people—faces and reputations he knew, didn't want to know, and couldn't remember. And he smiled as he went, avoiding eye contact, but not offending. Across the room he could see a cocktail trio performing, but, caught as he was in the belly of the festivities, they were like mimes swaying in the distance. It was a little too crowded to both drink and walk, but Forest was afraid that if he stopped he would be trapped into a conversation. Two drinks were no defense against this crowd. He could smell the grass, hear the drunks, and feel the sweat on even the very rich, and he knew there was coke around and probably everything else illicit, illegal, and titillating to people who have no real fear of being caught. Crime, he realized, *is* in the streets; when you get off the elevator at the penthouse, it becomes chic.

Forest looked up and saw that he had reached an impasse, a solid mass of bodies separated from their cliques and seemingly not caring. They were a wall, swaying gently and clinging to their vertical territory. He felt a hand stroke the back of his right leg, above the knee but below the buttock. Then he felt his right cheek being pinched, not painfully, but clearly with fingernails.

"Selina?" It was a question with an expectation mark.

"Of course, darling. Who else would dare to

31

be so intimate with the great Forest Hill?" Forest couldn't run. He couldn't even walk. In fact, he was wedged in so tightly that he was being forced to have a conversation with his ex-wife without being able to turn around and look at her. He could feel her breathing on his neck and he resented it.

"How are you, Selina?" He felt her lean forward, pressing against him.

"You want today's highs and lows, or do you want a five-day forecast?" Forest felt something go numb inside him and he tried to get one of his drinks up to his mouth. But it was like being trapped against a vile body at rush hour on the subway, with no escape possible until they opened the doors. What they once had together and now didn't ran up and down his spine and he shuddered away from her body pressing against him.

"Be well, Selina," he muttered. "It was nice not seeing you." Then he bulled forward, quickly sliding through the wall that had been holding him up, and left Selina's clicking talons reaching for his ass in a momentary empty space.

There was a bitter taste in Forest's mouth. Though he tried to wash it away with the rest of his first drink, he knew it wouldn't. Selina always affected him like this these days and, although he tried to, he couldn't entirely avoid her. They met mostly at parties and usually she was flaunting a new boyfriend or a new lover, but never a new husband. At first, during the separation and right after the divorce,

it had been Forest's ego that had been wounded. He had hated to think of her touching or
fucking someone else, much less making
love—as if she were even capable of the emotion. But lately he had discovered that he
didn't really want her back. In fact, he didn't
want any kind of relationship with anyone, not
if it could make him vulnerable to that kind of
hurt. Perverse, vindictive, shallow Selina—she
had walked all over him and here he was still
paying for it. And it bothered him that it was
his money, truly hard-earned these days playing the clown, which was allowing her to do it.
Alimony is such an indignity when you don't
care anymore.

Forest sighed and looked around the room.
Now that he had dealt with the one person he
hadn't wanted to meet, he was free to look for
the one person he needed to talk to, his brother
Arthur. They met at parties like this because
Selina and Valerie, Arthur's wife, had gone to
the same schools, as had the hostess, Marissa,
and over the years their social lives had somehow become entangled. It was a kind of mini-
Jet-Set boredom. Arthur and Valerie had flown
up from Washington for the party, and Forest
rationalized to himself that that was why he
came to the party too. But tonight maybe it
was true, because tonight he really needed to
talk to his brother. There was no one else in
the world he felt he could talk to.

"Stinking party, don't you think?" Forest
looked down to see an incredibly innocent face
staring up at him. He looked at the clean,

scrubbed skin surrounded by actual yellow hair and then he peered into the bright blue eyes confronting him. She seemed perfectly serious.

"I don't know what you mean, little girl. I was having a wonderful time."

"Bullshit. I've been watching you since you came in. You're trying to get drunk." There was no accusation in her voice, rather an understanding of his need to insulate himself against the occasion. Forest glanced at her discreetly. She was very young, very attractive, absolutely short, and positively endowed with breasts that didn't go with her otherwise elfin frame. Despite himself, he was attracted to her.

"I guess I should be flattered—I mean, that you've been watching me so carefully."

"Not really." He looked at her and saw that she wasn't being snide, just honest. "There's nobody to talk to here, just deadheads and middle-aged druggies. Everybody is so rich, so well dressed, so suave, so plastic, So I watch for signs of life. You looked like you were suffering or something." Forest nodded his head in acknowledgment and smiled ruefully.

"You're very perceptive, little girl. You're right on both counts. I had hoped it didn't show quite that much."

"Oh, it doesn't," she answered quickly. "Only if you care enough to really look. Believe me, in this crowd your secret is totally safe. They wouldn't notice if you had a heart attack and died standing up. Was that your wife you were talking to?" Forest gulped. Jesus Christ, she was fast and to the point.

"My ex-wife, if it makes any difference," he said, involuntarily scanning the crowd. All of a sudden he felt uncomfortable. He was about to turn away when a burly arm wrapped itself around his shoulder, immobilizing him.

"I see you've found my little Jenny, you old letch. Has my brother been molesting you?" Arthur's booming voice was filled with good humor. He gave Forest another bear-hug squeeze, just for good measure. Forest managed to wriggle free, grinning affectionately at his brother. Arthur Anspacher was a giant of a man and, although he was in his fifties, he still had the hard, firm body of an athlete. As a major in military intelligence he didn't have to wear a uniform, but he invariably did because it made him more comfortable. To look at the two of them it would be impossible to tell they were brothers.

"I was not molesting this little girl, Arthur. She was working me over, and doing a pretty good job of it." Jenny refused to wilt. She looked at the two of them appraisingly.

"I didn't know you had a brother, Arthur. And I certainly didn't know that I was talking to him. In fact, we haven't even been introduced." Forest realized it was true. They had been chatting along happily on a no-name basis.

"Forest, this is Jenny Wells. She's General Harlan Wells's daughter. You remember him, he's in weather, too, at the Pentagon. Jenny's my little darling. My protegé, so to speak." Arthur's voice rose merrily above the party noise. "She's working for the summer at Goddard—you know, the space-satellite computer center." Forest bristled despite himself.

"Arthur, for Christ's sake. I'm a meteorologist. I know who General Wells is. Believe it or not, I even know what Goddard is. Give me a break and tell Jenny who I am." Forest grinned sheepishly and Jenny grinned right back at him.

"Right. You're right. Sorry. Jenny, this is my brother, Forest Hill, the famous TV weatherman." Arthur jabbed Forest gently in the ribs. "Your ratings must be slipping, buddy, if I have to introduce that famous face of yours." Forest and Jenny appraised each other again. What had been a simple attraction with a touch of flirtation was now suddenly complicated by family, mutual interests, and careers. They surprised each other by both catching themselves looking to see if that changed anything between them. Apparently it didn't. Nothing died. But for Forest, it wasn't the moment for anything to be born, either. Now that Arthur was here, he realized that what was bothering him took precedence over everything, including manners.

He broke eye contact with Jenny and turned abruptly to Arthur. "Isn't Valerie here, Arthur? Because if she is, perhaps young Jenny could talk to her while you and I have a little chat on the terrace."

Jenny's eyes burst into flames. "I am per-

36

fectly capable of taking care of myself, Mr. Hill. Even amusing myself. I'm sure I'll even find some other . . . person to talk to." She spun on her heels and walked away, as if she were feeling rejected but wasn't willing to show it. Forest watched her go and registered that there was a redheaded personality in that blonde head and tucked the information away. He took his older brother by the arm, as if his mere six-foot frame could move that bear, and tried to steer him toward the terrace.

"I need to talk to you, Arthur. Right now. Right here. It's important and I need a few minutes of your time."

"Goddamnit, Forest, why are you so anti-social? This is a party and you're several drinks ahead of me, and that is a wonderfully attractive young woman. She may a little out of your age range, I'll admit, but I think she likes you. You certainly got her mad."

Forest was clearing a path while he hung onto Arthur's arm. "I like her too, Arthur. And I didn't mean to make her mad. It's just that this is more important." Suddenly he felt Arthur lurch. Forest looked back to see if he had lost him, but Arthur had merely reached out to grab a glass of champagne from a passing tray.

Forest slid open the glass door to the terrace and they stepped outside. It had stopped raining but everything was still wet. The city sparkled after its bath and the air was clean and cool, as Forest had promised. Forest closed the door behind them, hoping no one else would notice how much nicer it was here, outside the artificial air-conditioned atmosphere of the party. Somewhere below, a siren wailed and Forest realized that in New York fires start even in the rain.

"Nice night, lovely view, am I in trouble, or are you?" Arthur laughed and downed the glass of champagne in one gulp.

"I wish it were that simple. I think we're all in trouble."

"Uh oh, philosophy. Just wait here and I'll be right back. This sounds like a discussion requiring a tray full of drinks." Arthur moved toward the door, but Forest blocked him.

"Will you stand still for a second and listen, you big lummox." Arthur apparently heard the determination in Forest's voice. He shrugged, put his glass down, and clasped his hands behind his back.

"Okay. We'll talk first and drink later. But this better be good." Forest nodded quickly, the excitement beginning to bubble inside him. He had Arthur's full attention and he was about to say out loud what he had been thinking, dreaming, and worrying about for over a year. He began to pace, knowing that Arthur was waiting impatiently, but he wanted to present it correctly and fairly, without offending his brother. Finally he turned to Arthur.

"Arthur, I really don't know how to approach this. You're in intelligence so I don't know if I'm asking for information or telling it to you, but here it is. I believe that there's something wrong with the weather. Something seriously wrong. There are things happening that shouldn't." Forest paused, choosing his words carefully. "I'm afraid that something has thrown our whole weather system out of whack . . . and that we're on the verge of an outbreak of weather disasters we may never recover from."

At first Arthur said nothing. He had the ability to listen and give himself time to absorb information before reacting. "I see," he said finally, keeping his voice neutral. "Am I to understand that you are forecasting the end of the world?" Forest listened for sarcasm but there was none.

"No, I'm not. Not yet anyway. What I am saying is that if this trend continues it's going to become unstoppable very soon. And once that happens . . . yes, it will be the end of the world. At least as we know it. A chain reaction will be set off that will wipe civilization from the face of the earth. The oceans will shift. There'll be ice ages and droughts and holocausts the likes of which this planet has never seen. And it might take another ten billion years for it to rebalance itself."

Arthur unclasped his hands and walked to the edge of the balcony. He leaned on the wall and stared into the night. "Not a pretty picture you're painting, if it's true. But why are you telling me this?" He turned his head and looked at Forest seriously. "What does it have to do with me, and what do you want me to do about it?"

Forest, taking a cue from his brother, tried

to keep the emotion out of his voice. "Arthur, I believe the freak weather we've been having," he said evenly, "is directly related to the weather experimentation being done by the military." Arthur's head snapped around and Forest could see that Arthur was ready to interrupt. Forest put his hand on Arthur's arm to stop him. "I believe this because there is no other rational explanation. I know because I've investigated all the others. They're trying this over here, and that over there, and they don't realize what they're doing. We live in a closed system, Arthur. Everything affects everything. We get our goddamned oxygen from the rain forests in South America. Did you know that? Well, I'm not sure the military does.

"And the reason that I needed to talk to you is because you have access to information that I don't. I only know about the experiments that have been made public, but I don't know about the others. And I'm sure there are others."

"Jesus Christ, Forest." Arthur took Forest by the arms. "Have you gone crazy? You're walking around preaching doom, predicting the end of the world, and you don't even know what the fuck you're talking about. Jesus Christ!" Arthur was fuming. The color had risen in his face and he looked as if he was ready to explode. "And why in God's name does everybody try to blame it on the military? Well, it just ain't so, little brother. In this case, you haven't got a leg to stand on." He held his palms up expansively. "Not guilty!"

Forest had rarely seen his brother so angry.

He realized that he had hit a raw nerve and that if he wanted any help at all he would have to calm him down.

"Arthur," he said softly, "don't get so excited. I'm not accusing the military of anything. I'm not saying they're doing it on purpose. I'm not even sure they know what they're doing or what the effects are. That's why I'm talking to you. I just want to know what the experiments have been so I can pass on the dangers to the proper authority. I'm trying to help, Arthur, not make trouble." He faced Arthur with quiet determination. "Someone has to do it, you know. Someone has to pay attention. I just happened to notice it, that's all."

Arthur grinned awkwardly, ashamed now at his outburst. Forest had given him time to calm down and compose himself. "Look, I'm sorry I blew up. We've just been getting a lot of bad press lately, and I think most of it's unfair. So I'm a little sensitive. But, on the other hand, you've got to admit your story is a little hard to swallow on the first bite. I mean, shit, the end of the world . . ."

"Forget the end of the world, Arthur. I'm sorry I ever mentioned it. Let's just talk about some unexplainable disasters and the military weather experimentation program." Arthur shook his head in defeat and boosted himself back onto the brick balcony wall. He smiled at Forest, any trace of anger gone as if it had never been there.

"Okay. I can tell you everything I know, because it isn't classified. Remember that, Forest. All this information is available at the library. And if there were anything that was classifed, I would know it. That's my job." Forest leaned against the wall, ready to listen. He stood quietly but his pulse was racing.

"Basically, there were two areas—trying to make weather and trying to stop it. Neither was very successful. In 1962 the navy and the Department of Commerce initiated a project called 'Stormfury.' Its purpose was to see if they could diminish the impact of hurricanes by using a plane to seed storm clouds with silver iodide outside the eye wall. The idea was to build bigger clouds outside the eye, until they had replaced the eye wall. By increasing the size of the eye, they could reduce the force of the winds by fifteen to thirty percent." Arthur began to demonstrate with his arms.

"It's like an ice skater in a spin. When his arms are tucked in to his sides, he spins faster. When they're spread out, he slows down. Well, anyway, there were tests in '61, before the project started, on . . ."

"Ester?"

"Yeah, that's right. And in '63. And in '69. That was . . ."

"Debbie."

"Jesus, what a memory you have. Now, what was Ted William's batting average in 1941?"

".406. What happened?"

"Not enough. The navy scrapped the project in 1972. Then, of course there was 'Project Cirrus.' There, they used planes to seed hurricanes in the Gulf of Mexico. Well, some asshole sprinkled about two hundred pounds of dry ice into a little lady they called 'Mimi' after she had already dissipated and was heading out to sea. The next thing they knew, Mimi had changed her mind. She had completely reversed her direction, and, having grown to her original force, hit Savannah, Georgia, like General Sherman before anybody could even open an umbrella. Cute?"

Despite himself, Forest had to smile. "Very cute."

"We also had research projects to diminish hail. That was in 1966, 'Project Hailswath.' One for lightning, 'Project Skyfire.' 'Project Whirlwind' for tornadoes and 'Fido' for fog."

"Zilch?"

"About as effective as cancer research. For all intents and purposes, they've been scratched." Arthur jumped down onto the terrace.

"What about the other half?" Arthur looked puzzled. "You know, making weather?" Arthur laughed.

"We call that, 'Nixon makes rain.' You remember Nixon, don't you?"

"You mean Vietnam?"

"And Laos and Cambodia and as much of the rest of Southeast Asia as we could piss on. We started that in '66. You might have read about it in the Pentagon Papers." Forest could hear derision in Arthur's voice.

"I read it. That was the Department of Defense Operation . . ."

"Popeye. It was disguised under lots of code names. Would you believe 'Project Intermediary Compatriot,' 'Project Smiling Sam,' or 'Project Rubber Duck'? Anyway, it was supposed to turn the Ho Chi Minh Trail to mud and screw up the Commies' main supply route. Which it did, along with drowning the rice crop and starving the people. And despite everything we did, we still lost the fucking war."

Forest looked at him quizzically. "You sound vaguely disgusted about the whole thing. That's not a very military attitude."

"Drowning peasants, or their crops, isn't my idea of how men should wage war. That's war on civilians, and I don't like it at all. But I guess I'm a little old-fashioned." Forest smiled.

"No, you're not. You're just too humane to be working for a war machine. They're animals and you're a teddy bear."

Arthur's shoulders went up. "I'm no teddy bear, Forest. Don't you believe it for a minute. I'm just a different kind of animal." Arthur looked in at the party and then back at Forest. "Well, that's it, kiddo. The whole sordid story, from failure to embarrassment. Sorry, but there's nothing there to support your theory. You may be having lousy weather, or having a hard time forecasting it, but you can't blame it on us."

Forest could see that Arthur was tired of the discussion and that he wanted to rejoin the party, but Forest couldn't let him go yet. "Arthur, wait a mintue. That can't be all there is. I have documented evidence of weather that's

44

out of sync. Something is causing it. Maybe you don't have all the information, or maybe you're not telling everything you know, but I know there's more."

Arthur took a threatening step toward Forest and then restrained himself. "If you weren't my brother . . . do you know what you're saying? You're telling me that either I don't do my job or that I'm lying. And that's a little heavy coming from a lightweight TV weatherman."

Forest could contain himself no longer. Arthur had finally pressed the one button Forest couldn't handle. "Don't call me that, Arthur. I'm a meteorologist. A scientist. I did my homework. What I'm talking about is true. You're just too stupid or too deep in a rut to be able to understand it."

Arthur stepped closer to Forest, towering over him. "I'm not stupid, you clown. I don't go running around like Chicken Little screaming that the sky is falling before I have any evidence. So why don't you get off it." Arthur turned and started to walk away, but changed his mind and came back to Forest. "But if you don't believe me, why don't you go talk to General Wells at the Pentagon. Why not let him make a fool of you? But don't use my name."

"I wouldn't use your name to curse with. But I'll tell you this. You think I'm just a jerk reading the weather on TV, but I'm a very good forecaster, and I see rain in your future."

Inside the penthouse, Jenny had found Valerie, and after enough chitchat they had de-

45

cided to get the brothers off the terrace. As they worked their way toward the glass doors, it was with some amazement that they witnessed Forest emptying his drink onto Arthur's head. Then they watched him come storming into the room, bulling his way across it, jostling, pushing, elbowing, and yelling at the top of his lungs, "Sunny days, you all! Sunny days!"

Arthur stood stoicly on the terrace as the part-gin, part-vodka martini dripped down his face into his collar. He finally realized that his brother Forest was very upset about something.

It's a fact. Ask anyone. Ask Arnold
Ginsberg, the Bar Mitzvah boy. Ask his mother
and father. Ask even the accountant of the
synagogue who, by the way, can tell by looking
at the parking lot the size of the take. Ask if it
wasn't a disaster of the first magnitude.

Hot you could understand. Maybe even very
hot, for such an occasion. But that it should be
so very hot outside, and so very much hotter
inside? Well it was. A veritable heat wave of
proportions that made the baby-man Arnold
schpritz a silk shirt and a $200 suit so badly he
couldn't wear it even once, but had to. And
that, mind you, was before the air conditioning
broke down and the chicken liver statue began
to run under foot, and aunts and maidens and
vice versa began to faint.

In fact, it was a tragedy. You could see enve-
lopes coming unsealed in pockets, and crisp
check paper wilting as the glorious figures, the
perfection of several zeroes standing next to

47

each other, began to drip and blur inside blue suits of every color.

And if the truth were to be known, even if it were never to be talked about, none of them ever recovered. Especially Arnold Ginsberg, the boy-man.

CHAPTER THREE

Forest awoke slowly to find he had all of Saturday on his hands and the dregs of Friday night on his head. He winced at the fraudulently cheery sun that was beginning to bake his Riverside Drive apartment and he made his eyes small. As he turned his head slowly, the clock told him it was nearly noon. His head told him he had a hangover. He reached out instinctively to turn on the weather radio by the side of his bed, but he stopped himself. Not today, thank you.

As he showered, shaved, and dressed, Forest was hit with a wave of confusion, indecision, and self-doubt. He had expected scepticism from Arthur, but nothing like that bruising attack on his scientific credibility. It was damaging to his ego that even his own brother couldn't see past his TV personality. But there was something inside Forest that wouldn't let go; he was dented, but not broken. Facts are facts, and there is a reality with laws of action and reaction. He had avoided looking at it, but Forest couldn't forget his briefcase sitting on his desk. The charts and data in it made him feel like the briefcase was a ticking time bomb; the only problem was he didn't know how to dispose of it.

Forest went out; the pressure of being in the same room with his problem was just too much. At first he just wandered through the hot city streets, teeming with the poor who couldn't afford to escape the city for the weekend. He had breakfast-lunch at a hotdog stand and kept walking. Some people go to bars and lose themselves, and some to the movies. Forest found himself in front of the Hayden Planetarium, and that's where he spent the day. He slipped away into a magically reassuring overview of life: solar systems, galaxies, nebulae, stars being born and dying millions of lifetimes away. The great domed ceiling above his head became a telescope into the universe.

When evening came, Forest stayed to watch the laser show: swirling lights and shapes moving to Mozart and Bach and then embracing and dancing to jazz and the hustle. By the time it was over and Forest had left, he felt as if he were paralyzed. His neck was cramped from tilting it up toward the ceiling and he was sure he would never stand up straight again. It had always mystified him why the seats weren't soft and able to tilt back, but he supposed it was the price one had to pay to experience the beyond. And it certainly kept the audience awake. Forest felt better. He went home and slept.

SUNDAY

JULY 9

DAYTON, OHIO

Harry Wexler wasn't drunk. His bitchy wife had seen to that. She had managed to start their nightly fight before the party had barely started. Now they sat in stony silence as Harry tried to pick his way along Riverfront Drive in a horrendous fog that had rolled in from nowhere. It was the first time Harry, or for that matter anybody, had even seen fog in Dayton in the middle of the summer.

Harry squeezed the steering wheel nervously. The density of the fog kept changing and he had to stare hard to keep the car on line. He wished there were somebody in front of him so he could follow their lights, but apparently no one else was dumb enough to be driving in this kind of weather.

Elise said, "The night was perfectly clear on the way in," her voice somehow indicating that the fog was also his fault. He was trying to drive slowly, but his anger agitated his foot. Suddenly the road was gone, Harry was peering into the blanket of white, trying to find it again, when Elise began to scream, but he never had a chance to find out if she was screaming at him before their car hit the water.

CHAPTER FOUR

The phone ringing beside his ear woke Forest, and he didn't have to look out the window to know it was going to be another beastly hot day. It was early, but the sun's reflected glare on his white sheets was already blinding. The phone didn't stop ringing, so Forest answered it.

"Forest, old man, I hope I didn't wake you." It was Roger Moss. Forest sighed and lay back, one hand looking for a pillow to prop his head.

"Hell no, Roger. I was just vacuuming the apartment and didn't hear the phone. Of course I was sleeping. It's nine A.M. Sunday morning," he grunted with mock ferocity. But Forest was smiling to himself; he knew what was coming. Roger was the closest thing he had to a friend and they spent a lot of time together, so Forest knew what a Sunday morning call always meant. Roger was a weekend father.

"It's like this, Forest. I've had Linda with

me since yesterday and I'm about to O.D. on Sesame Street. Even now, Big Bird is prancing through my living room at full volume and Linda is dancing along, crushing Rice Crispies into the rug. If I don't have some adult companionship and a drink very soon, I will certainly be arrested for trying to force my ten-year-old child back into the cavity from whence she came." Forest said nothing. He was trying to keep from laughing aloud at the picture of America's most distinguished and honored newsman being terrorized by a small female child. On the other hand, you had to meet the child.

"Do you get my meaning?" Roger growled.

"Oh, I get you all right. You want us to have brunch at the Plaza together, but you want me to meet you as early as possible to hold your hand until the bar opens. Is that it?"

"That's it on the nose. How did you know, old boy?" Roger was being very pleasant.

"Because we've done this before. A number of times." Forest looked around the room at the ceiling and walls that would soon need painting, at his silent weather machines, at the clothing thrown over chairs and strewn across the floor, and out the window at the humid, baking heat.

"Well?" Roger asked.

"Sure. I have nothing else to do. I'll meet you in the park at 12:30 and we'll have brunch. But you've got to promise me one thing, and I'm not kidding . . ."

"Anything. Anything."

"Please don't leave me alone with . . . her. I mean it. Not for a minute, you understand?"

"I promise," Roger answered instantly, relief and elation in his voice. "I give you my word on it." Forest chuckled.

"Yeah, well we all know how much that's worth, don't we?" When Forest heard Roger's cavernous laugh, he hung up.

As he entered the park at Central Park West and 72nd Street, Forest could hear the drums and feel the throbbing in the air. There was no question in his mind that Central Park had literally become a circus on weekends—a spectacle more fantastic than any single mind could invent. An older man and a younger lady dressed in matching purple tie-dyed jump suits rode by on their bicycles. On the back of their bicycles were large wooden containers into which they put the dog droppings they scooped off the street. Around them, however, were thousands of dogs of every breed, leashed and unleashed, and their owners, all totally unconcerned about the problem.

Forest passed mimes and magicians, jugglers and clowns, a yoga class, a boccie game, and even stopped for a moment to watch a handsome, half-naked black man playing Schubert on a tin drum. A steady stream of ten speed bicycles flowed in one direction, and runners panted past in the other. Every now and then, rented horses cantered through the crowd with Sunday riders perched precariously on their backs. Forest ended up following a highly colorful Puerto Rican gentleman most of the way down the mall. The man was carrying a combination radio-tapedeck which must have weighed at least thirty pounds, and following behind him were two small boys, each carrying a separate speaker. The effect was astounding and the music was infectious.

Forest found Roger and his daughter on Fifth Avenue, just outside the entrance to the zoo. Little Linda seemed content for the moment. From her right wrist rose a balloon with a Mickey Mouse head floating inside. From her left wrist rose a replica of a 707 airplane. She was trying to eat a raspberry Italian ice from a white paper cup, but the balloons were making her somewhat spastic. Her face was changing color, but since it matched what she had already dripped down her dress, Forest thought it really didn't matter.

Roger, however, looked desperately grim and in need of help. He was clearly suffering from parental overexposure, and plainly resenting being forced to endure it in public. They immediately set off down Fifth Avenue toward the Plaza and, as always, Forest was aware of people's faces lighting up with recognition as he and Roger passed. But, strangely, fewer people seemed to be aware of them when they were together than when they were alone. Roger had commented on the phenomenon long ago, and compared it to finding Robert Redford and Cary Grant sitting together eating hot dogs on a park bench. He had reasoned that it was more than the average mind could accept.

58

Forest had always wondered which of them Roger saw as which.

From outside the fronds that ring the open room, the Palm Court at the Plaza is an anachronism: marble tables, linen napkins, and Muzak provided by ancient, but still live, musicians. But inside the circle there was much more going on. Roger chose this particularly expensive place to have Sunday breakfast because he inevitably ran into ladies he could not meet elsewhere. At first Forest had refused to believe that any of the encounters could have been planned; Roger wasn't that good an actor. And yet, every time they came here it happened. Forest eyed Linda nervously and prayed that today would be different.

Forest and Roger ordered drinks and then fiddled with their fingers, watching the clock and waiting for one o'clock so they could be served. From the outside, it was amusing—a roomful of people blue in the face for want of a drink, being denied by a blue law—but the participants were not amused. When the traditional Danish Marys finally arrived, made with aquavite instead of vodka, Roger's face lost some of its tension. Linda was occupied with dribbling her Shirley Temple back into the glass, and they were, at last, ready to talk.

"How was that party Friday night?" Roger asked innocently. Forest looked at him, surprised.

"How in the hell did you find out about that?"

"I know about every party I'm not invited

to, dear boy. I have a highly developed sense of paranoia." Forest knew it was true, and sad.

"It was just a party, and I wasn't party material. I stank up the joint. I was attacked by Selina and I seemed to take it out on my brother. Would you believe I poured a drink on his head and then went screaming out into the night, yelling 'Sunny days'? I was a regular, bona fide, you-know-what." Forest glanced at Linda and saw that his politeness was lost on her.

"Understandable, I'm sure," Roger said, finishing his drink. "How drunk were you?"

"Not drunk enough to justify it, even if I lie to myself. I wanted some advice on a weather thing and . . ." Forest paused and considered what he could tell Roger. "Actually, I'd like to ask you about it too." Roger diverted Forest urbanely. Roger was a master at keeping small talk small.

"Your obsession with the weather is going to make you a celibate and lonely old man, Forest. Tell me about the flesh instead. Did you at least fall in lust?" Forest buried the confidence he was about to share and sipped at his drink. Then, despite himself, a gleam came into his eye.

"There was one young lady, very pretty, very different, and very young. I think she was trying to save me from myself. She couldn't have been more than twenty." Roger smirked at Forest and leaned across the table.

"If you're going to rob the cradle, old friend, why not take my daughter. She had a positively wicked mind and I promise I'll look the other way. As a matter of fact, I see someone I must have a word with. Don't go away, I'll be right back." And he was gone, edging his way between tables, dodging waiters, and heading for the far corner of the room. Forest looked at Linda helplessly and signaled the waiter for another drink. Linda looked back at him innocently, but he didn't believe her for a moment. Some brunch. And they hadn't even served the food yet.

MONDAY

JULY 10

THE BRONX, NEW YORK

Susan Albright pushed the massive steel door aside with a couple of silent grunts, wheeled, and with equal difficulty closed and locked it behind her. She continued another 20 feet down the corridor to the next door. The six-inch key slid easily into the lock, but before she turned it she peeked through the thick, tiny window. There was no one on the other side. It was just one of those automatic things one does in maximum security. Susan's face was pretty by anybody's standards and usually carried an incredibly infectious smile, but now her lip twitched in anger. Why hadn't they told her that Sunny had been transferred up here? She berated the inefficiency of the institution for the thousandth time. She had gone to Ward B to see Sunny at his request. When she got there, a nurse told her that Sunny had bitten another inmate and been sent up to M.S. It had happened before. In spite of her job, Susan couldn't put aside the frustration. Sunny was retarded and psychotic. "Some combination," she thought. "You would think one would get used to the uselessness of the situation." Eighty percent of all the inmates released eventually came back. Was the 20 percent worth the hope? The question never went away.

Locking the third door from the inside, Susan turned to face the ward. Where was everybody? With the exception of an old man whom the orderly orderlies had named William Tell, because he kept balancing food on his head, and Madame LaFarge, quietly rocking away in her non-rocking chair by the window, the day room was noticeably empty.

A strong hand gripped Susan's arm from behind. Having learned to suppress her feelings when she was on the wards, Susan turned quietly to face a 6-foot, 4-inch black lady, affectionately known as "Big Bama."

Her eyes glazed and her grin slightly twisted, Big Bama said, "Hello, Miss Susan." Each word took an eternity, and Susan felt her long-developed patience and understanding falter a little.

"Where is everybody, Bama?" she asked.

"Hello, Miss Susan," Bama said again.

Susan started over again, slowly. "Hello, Big Bama. Where is everybody?"

"Outside," said Bama.

"You mean up on the roof?" Susan asked, trying desperately to make eye contact. "Is Sunny up there?"

Bama nodded affirmatively and raised her

hand in slow motion, pointing a long, slender index finger at the ceiling.

The master key opened the roof door the same way it opened all the others, and Susan mechanically closed and locked it behind her. She went through the same procedure at the top of the stairs. Once outside, she glanced up at the rapidly gathering clouds and wondered if she had been mistaken at seeing a perfectly sunny day only a few minutes ago. The rooftop, enclosed in wire fencing on three sides and a high brick wall on the fourth, was about 70 feet square and covered with gravel. Benny and Briggs, the two orderlies of the M.S. Ward, sat bullshitting in a little shelter next to the wall. They acknowledged Susan's presence with a nod. Nothing too friendly, mind you, since Susan's job didn't exactly promote friendship. She was hired by the state to look after patients' rights, and that put her in the wrong as far as the hospital staff was concerned. Aware of the situation, Susan was always friendly and tactful with the staff, but her relationships were clearly with the inmates. Whenever patients had a whim to leave the institution, they would put in a request and Susan would have to investigate the feasibility of arranging for a release. Michael "Sunny" Davies had made such a request. His fourth. Once, he was sent back to live with his mother and ended up biting a butcher on the Grand Concourse. Now he wanted out again and Susan would have to go through the motions.

Twenty inmates, transfixed as they walked,

stood, leaned, or rocked, were spread out over the rooftop landscape. Susan wondered if the general public knew just how accurate *Cuckoo's Nest* and *Rose Garden* actually were.

Sunny's vacuous expression changed to a smile as soon as he saw Susan standing in the doorway across the compound. He started toward her as quickly as his Thorazine-sedated body would allow. He was halfway across when the heavens opened up. No warning drops, no thunder, just a sudden, steady downpour—the kind you think can last for only a minute. The rocking and the walking stopped. The rooftop residents looked skyward as the water splattered off their faces and drenched their clothes in seconds. Not one of them made a move for the shelter.

Benny was up on his feet, waving his arms and screaming obscenities at them. "You stupid bastards, get in here." He couldn't believe they were just standing there in this downpour. "Get over here, Are you crazy or somethin', get over here."

The irony of Benny's last scream caused Briggs to double up with laughter, and the inmates, anxious to emulate anyone who wasn't one of them, also started laughing. Within seconds, the entire roof was giggling and experiencing the rain like the children they were. Benny ran out among them, turning them toward the doorway. A grinning Sunny reached out for Susan and tried to pull her out into the rain, but she resisted. "It's only water, Miss Susan," he said. "It won't kill ya."

CHAPTER FIVE

If the weekend had been uneventful, it had also given Forest's ego time to heal. He awoke Monday morning with new energy, his dream images still fresh in his eyes. He had been having a nightmare. He was lost in the desert and a giant vulture with Selina's face was circling over him waiting for him to drop. But suddenly, a lightning bolt flashed out of the empty sky, exploding the monster and burning it to ashes. Before the ashes could reach him, however, they turned into a gentle rain, bathing his face and burning body. He had closed his eyes, and when he opened them there was Jenny Wells, her golden hair an aura around her face, her blue eyes soft and calling as she extended her hand to him. Forest had pursued her and, to his growing joy, she didn't retreat. As he got closer, he felt a stirring inside him, a sexual excitement and desire he almost couldn't contain. He had awoken with physical proof of the intensity of his dream.

Forest reached out and turned on the weather radio and unconsciously his mind began absorbing the data. Today the routine was reassuring. Smiling to himself, Forest swung out of bed. The clue was Jenny, or at least she was symbolic of the answer to his problem. On his way to the shower he stopped and looked at himself in the mirror, staring into his own eyes. A lock clicked in his head. "You are a weatherman, Forest Hill," he said to himself. "Do what you do." "I know," he answered himself, "I will." Then he stepped into the shower and scrubbed the last three days off his body and down the drain.

Clean and determined, Forest wrapped a towel around his still-trim waist and padded down the hall to the living room. He sat down at his desk and stared at his briefcase for a moment. Then he picked up the phone, tucked it under his chin, and with his right hand played a tune on the touch-tone buttons. With his left hand, he worked the combination lock on the briefcase. By the time he had reached his office at the network, the case was open, his charts and documents exposed.

"Forest Hill's office. Micky Leary speaking."

"Hi, kiddo. It's me." She snorted.

"Whoopee, boss. What else is new? You coming to work today?"

"No, Micky, I'm not. But I want you to do something for me. Call General Harlan Wells at the Pentagon and set up an appointment for me to talk to him."

"For when, Forest?"

"For today, so you're going to have to step on it." There was a pause while Micky considered whether she could ask the question, but being who she was, she did.

"I'll try, boss. I honestly will. But what if the general is busy or something?" Somehow she managed to keep any trace of sarcasm out of her voice.

"He's not too busy for this. First tell him who I am. If that doesn't excite him, tell him it's a matter of great importance. You can use the phrase 'national security' if you have to. And if that doesn't work, mention his daughter's name, Jenny Wells. Call me back." Micky inhaled audibly.

"Say, what's going on here? You enlisting, or are you getting married?"

Forest smiled and murmured into the phone affectionately, "Don't be a schmuck. Call me back." He was only half dressed, still looking for a pair of clean socks when the phone rang.

"Yes, Micky."

She laughed proudly. "Well, well, well. You are famous. We didn't even have to declare a national emergency. The general will be thrilled to meet you." Forest's hand tightened on the phone. "He'll see you at two. You're booked on Eastern, Flight 941, leaving La Guardia at 12:30." Forest blinked and rapidly calculated his timetable.

"Listen, Mick. That was a nice piece of work. Do me another favor, will you. Work up the weather for me today and have it ready for the show."

"Sure, boss, I'd be delighted. But are you sure you trust me?" Forest looked out the window. The sun was blazing and the sky was cloudless. It was another day of heat wave.

"Of course I do, Micky. Of course I do."

CHAPTER SIX

Whatever romance flying had once possessed, it certainly no longer existed for the businessman. The shuttle flight to Washington was like an extended bus ride across town, except you were sure of getting a seat. You bought your ticket on the plane, choked down a drink and a half, and you were there, fully aware that it took longer to get to and from the airport than it did to fly. But for Forest, the trip was, as always, a wonderful adventure through a serene and magically shaped world of clouds.

Forest got out of his cab at the Pentagon and stopped and stared. No matter how often he visited Washington, it never failed to impress him. As his eyes swept the horizon, he could see the Lincoln Memorial, the White House, the Washington Monument, and the Jefferson Memorial. It was an enormous amount of historic marble. And looming in front of him was the world's largest office building. Suddenly he wondered what the hell

71

he was doing there. His precious briefcase felt flimsy now, and he shifted it from hand to hand. But he was here, and there was no point in quitting without even trying, so he squared his shoulders in an unconscious imitation of his brother, and marched in the front door.

An officer at the central information and admission desk took Forest's name and called to confirm his appointment with the general. Then he issued him a visitor's tag and told Forest to pin it to his lapel. He also gave him a small, printed floor plan and circled the location of the general's office. It looked simple but, of course, it wasn't.

The Pentagon is made up of five floors in five concentric rings, connected by ten spokelike corridors. The general's office was listed as 3-C-138. The code told him that the first digit was the floor, the letter the ring, the next digit the corridor and the last two digits the room. Forest looked around him. He was on the concourse level, which resembled a miniature indoor city—with everything from a bookstore, bank, and dental clinic to a florist and bakery.

Forest found a ramp and headed upward, passing models of planes and missiles and hundreds of paintings glorifying the past and present American military. There was something vaguely obscene about it, Forest thought, like a woman who was too rich wearing all of her jewels at once. On the third floor, he found the A ring and followed it to the first corridor, went down the corridor to the C ring, and turned left to search for room 38. By a miracle of blind luck, determination, and a willingness to ask questions, he was able to get to General Wells's office in less than fifteen minutes.

Pausing to collect himself before going in, Forest examined a large painting hanging on the wall outside the general's door. It was an oil that commemorated the beginning of the final Union triumph at Chattanooga, or so the legend read: "Union troops under General Hooker, clearing the Confederates from Lookout Mountain, Tennessee, on the 24th of November, 1863." It had been painted in 1863 by a H. Charles McBarron and was titled, "Battle of the Clouds." Forest chuckled to himself and opened the door. He knew he had come to the right place.

The general was apparently important; his office was more like a suite of offices. Forest found himself in a reception area—a large, carpeted room with several army-green, leather-covered couches and chairs. A blond, crew-cut, baby-faced soldier in uniform was sitting behind a large mahogany desk, typing, talking on the phone, and chewing gum all at the same time. His face was a perfect picture of innocent concentration, and Forest was amused to observe that secretaries and receptionists were all basically the same, male or female. It was, no doubt, a function of their job. After a moment, the soldier stopped typing and hung up the phone. He didn't stop chewing, however. Forest smiled at him brightly.

"Hi. I'm Forest Hill and I have an appointment with General Wells." The soldier looked down at an appointment calendar and then back at Forest.

"You certainly do have one, Mr. Hill. I had to do some juggling to fit you in, though. The general's busy like crazy."

"Thanks. That was good of you."

The soldier stood up and shrugged. "Don't thank me, buddy. It was the general. He has a thing for weathermen or something. I'll tell him you're here." The soldier walked to a door behind him, knocked twice, briskly, and went in, closing the door behind him. Forest wondered whether he had been kidding, but didn't care; his palms were beginning to sweat. The door opened and the soldier waved Forest in.

In the distance, over what seemed like a mile of carpet, Forest could see a heavy-set, balding man with a cigar in his mouth, sitting behind a huge U-shaped desk. He had rich, bushy eyebrows, a set of well-fed jowls, and he filled his uniform in a perfect caricature of capitalistic overindulgence. As Forest started the long walk across the room, he took in the American flag behind the general on his right and another flag behind him on the left. The windows looked out over lawn and a fountain, and the walls were lined with maps. The general didn't rise until Forest reached his desk, then he stuck out his hand and pumped Forest's once firmly.

"Pleased to meet you, Mr. Hill. Sit down, sit down." Forest sank into one of the two plush chairs in front of the desk and watched as the general slowly lowered his bulk into his own chair. The general puffed rapidly on the cigar

74

stuck in the side of his mouth, until his head was wreathed in smoke. His eyes were focused inward, remembering something, and he was chuckling to himself, but it wasn't a pleasant sound. After a moment, his attention returned to Forest and he took his cigar out of his mouth.

"You're funny, Mr. Hill. Yes, sir, you are a funny man. I catch your show whenever I get to New York. My goodness, what you do to a weather report is quite unique." His porcine face was crinkled into laugh lines and he pointed his cigar at Forest, gesturing with it as he talked. Forest noticed that he was not a neat smoker. Beside the ashes he was sprinkling on the desk, the general had managed to chew the end of his cigar into a wet, unappetizing mess.

"Thank you, General. I'm delighted you enjoy my show." Forest was about to continue when the general interrupted him.

"How's your brother, Arthur?" He didn't pause for an answer. "A hell of a fine fellow, your brother. And a damn good soldier, too. You know, he's taken my little daughter Jenny under his wing. She's at Harvard studying computer math or something, and old Arthur got her a summer job down here at Goddard. Damn good of him and Valerie to watch out for her . . . get her to take a job down here near her dad. It's about the only time I get to see her these days, now that she's at college. Harvard! A boy's school. Not even Radcliffe. Well, at least she didn't end up at West Point

75

like me." He laughed expansively at his joke, and Forest wondered whether he was ever going to stop talking and decided that it probably wouldn't be on a voluntary basis, so he jumped in.

"As a matter of fact, I met Jenny at a party just the other night, General. She was there with my brother and Valerie. Jenny's a lovely young lady, and she's got a sharp eye. She was smart enough not to be taken in by any of that crowd."

The general winked at Forest. "Including you, son?"

"Especially me, sir. She thought we were all a bunch of dull, old phonies, and she told me so. I liked her for it." Forest smiled at the memory. The general looked proud and puffed some more on his cigar.

"She certainly has a mind of her own, my daughter. And a mouth to match it." They sat silently for a moment and then the general sneaked a look at his watch and leaned forward to Forest. "Well, what can I do for you, Mr. Hill? I assume you didn't come all the way down here just to shoot the breeze with little Jenny's father." Forest swallowed. Now that the moment was here, he didn't know exactly how to start.

"Actually, it was your daughter who gave me the idea to talk to you. Not directly, but she made me remember that you're the man in charge of weather for the army . . . and there's something I thought you should know about."

76

The general leaned back expansively. "Well, that is part of my job, although there really isn't that much to it, but whatever I can do for you, I'll certainly try." Forest picked up his briefcase and put it on the general's shiny, empty desk. He worked the combination as he talked.

"It's like this, General. A lot of people think of my weather reports as comedy shows. And I admit that there is that aspect to them. But, at the same time, it happens that my forecasts are very accurate. In fact, they're the most accurate of any weatherman on the air." Forest wasn't boasting, he was just trying to lay the groundwork for his presentation, but the general wouldn't let it pass.

"If you do say so yourself, Mr. Hill?"

"Yes, General Wells. If I do have to say so myself. I'm telling you this because in order to achieve this high degree of accuracy I do more research, more specific investigation, than any of my colleagues. That means I don't rely on just satellite photographs and broad wind and temperature changes. I dig down further, to find out exactly what's happening in each specific area of the country. The general was trying hard not to look bored.

"I think that's real fine, Mr. Hill. I had assumed that you knew your job. I mean, they wouldn't be paying you all that money just to clown around, now would they?" Forest ignored the general's sarcasm and plunged on, taking papers and charts out of his briefcase and arranging them on the desk.

77

"In the course of doing this research, General, I began to notice something strange. At first I thought I was mistaken, or that I was getting inaccurate information. But when it comes to weather I'm a little compulsive, so I had all the figures checked and rechecked and what it comes to is this. Over the last two years I have found a number of weather . . ." Forest paused to chose the exact word, "occurrences in the United States that shouldn't have happened. They were not consistent with the laws of nature as we know them, and yet they happened. Each of them was a disaster." Forest stared at the general soberly. "A weather disaster!"

Under Forest's scrutiny, the general blinked slowly and his eyes became shrewd. Whatever joviality there had been in his face left it. "That's mighty interesting, Mr. Hill," he drawled. "Mighty interesting. But why tell me about it? I'm no scientist. I'm just a tired old soldier pushing a desk here for the army." He attempted a laugh that didn't work. Forest stood up and separated his papers into four piles and then leaned over the desk toward the general. The desk was so large, however, it did little to bring them closer together.

"I brought this to you, General, because I'm worried. I'm no super patriot and I'm not an alarmist, but there's something strange happening to our weather and I want to make sure that someone in authority knows about it. Do you know about it, General?" He peered intently at the fat man, but his gaze was met evenly.

"No, son, I'm not sure as I can say I do. Why don't you tell me all about it." Forest felt as if he were being patronized and began to bristle, but he grabbed hold of himself before he showed it. All that mattered was getting a hearing; the facts would speak for themselves.

"Let me tell you about four of these strange occurrences, just four, and then see what you think." General Wells nodded benignly and dropped his old cigar into a wastepaper basket. He took a fresh one from his breast pocket, bit off the end, and spit into the basket.

"I'm listening, Mr. Hill. I'm all ears. Let's hear what you've got." He tilted his body back in his chair, managed to get both his feet on his desk, and half closed his eyes as he puffed on his cigar. Forest's heart began to beat faster as he realized he was actually going to have a chance to tell his story.

"On June 9, 1972, the Canyon Lake Dam burst above Rapid City, South Dakota. Two hundred thirty-six bodies were recovered. One hundred twenty-four were missing. Property damage was in the hundreds of millions. It was the nation's worst flood since the great Mississippi Valley one in 1927." The general grunted in agreement.

Forest was trying to be factual, precise, and unemotional. He had an abundance of details. and if his presentation sounded rehearsed it was only because he had run over it so many times in his head. He opened a folder of documents: synoptic charts, satellite pictures, and news photos of the flood and its aftermath. There were pictures of cars leaning upright against telephone poles, beds perched in trees, and trees planted in houses.

Forest slid the folder across to the general. "The local weather report for that day had been variable cloudiness with a chance of scattered showers and thunderstorms. Perfectly accurate for the relatively weak warm front moving into the area." Forest waited for the general to look up from the folder. "That weak front dropped fourteen inches of rain into Rapid Creek in just six hours! And that, sir, given those atmospheric conditions, was impossible!"

Forest waited for a reaction, but all he got was a puff of unemotional cigar smoke. The general adjusted his genitals.

"First of all, son, it was possible, because it happened. Second, and I'm sure from your obvious attention to detail that you're aware of this, the Department of the Interior's pilot dropped over six hundred pounds of dry ice into a bank of 'scattered' clouds west of the city. Now that was a mistake, because the officer in charge of the project insists he told the pilot to seed the clouds south of the city. The flood victims, of course, claim that the government was negligent."

"I wasn't aware that cloud seeding could increase rainfall by more than ten percent," Forest said pointedly.

"Neither was I. But that one's still in the

courts, so I guess it's a moot point. What else you got?" Forest considered for a moment and decided not to press the point. He opened another folder and turned it to face the general. It read, "Johnstown Flood."

"On July 21, 1977, the city of Johnstown, Pennsylvania, was devastated by a flood. Sixty-seven died and four thousand were left homeless."

"Quite reasonable," the general interjected, "when you compare it to the flood of the same name that killed two thousand in 1889."

"Twenty-two hundred," Forest retorted. He realized that the game had begun in earnest. "This year's flood, General, was caused by a thunderstorm that hung over the city for almost nine hours and dropped approximately eight and a half inches of rain."

The general turned his palms up, as if to say, "What's your point?" Forest sank into his chair in frustration. The man was just refusing to see his point. Forest stood up again and pushed the file across the desk to the general. Reaching across the desk, he spread out the papers in front of him. When he found the synoptic chart he wanted, he tapped his finger on a little black dot with a flag sticking out of it. The flag had two long bars and a short one. The long bars indicated a wind speed of 10 knots each and the short bar a wind speed of 5 knots.

"The five flags show a south-southwest direction at a speed of twenty-five knots for the upper level winds," he said slowly and deliberately. Then he put a series of NOAA satellite photographs in front of the general. "But the storm is standing still, And that, sir," he said, mimicking the general's previous shrug with a larger theatrical gesture, "is physically impossible."

The general remained unfazed. "I repeat . . ."

"I know, I know it happened." Forest's annoyance was showing, but he didn't want to argue his point until he had presented all of his evidence. He opened the next folder.

"Let's look at another one, General. During the week of June 20, nine major blazes struck Arizona and New Mexico. The largest one broke out fifty miles southwest of Los Alamos. The fire covered eleven thousand acres and ended up causing ten million dollars' worth of damage."

"I believe that was more like thirteen million, Mr. Hill." Forest could see that the general was enjoying pecking away at him.

"Much of Los Alamos Scientific Laboratory was destroyed. That's one of your major nuclear research facilities, isn't it, General?" Forest got a noncommittal nod for an answer. "Well, theoretically, those fires were caused by lightning from heavy thunderclouds moving at about twelve knots from west to east."

The general stirred himself and leaned forward on his desk. "The fires were definitely caused by lightning, son. We have eyewitness verification of that. And it's not all surprising considering it happened during one of the worst droughts the West has ever seen. Ground moisture had been reduced to the lowest point in half a century. Now where's your . . . irregularity?"

"You're missing my point, General," Forest said sharply. "The lightning over Los Alamos came from thunderhead clouds of a size and cluster only found around the equator. What the hell was a tropical thunderstorm doing over New Mexico?" Forest didn't wait for what he knew would be an irritating answer. He plunged on.

"Finally, let me tell you about a disaster that happened just last Friday and about its set of . . ." he was about to say *impossible*, "improbable circumstances. A little town called Garnett, Kansas, was completely wiped out by a series of three tornadoes that seemed to have come from nowhere."

"They usually do," the general muttered, almost under his breath. Forest circled the desk, resisting an impulse to strangle this gross, exasperating man.

"The tornadoes moved east at about forty miles an hour. And the three vortexes, each about a hundred yards wide, strafed everything in front of them." Forest laid a grouping of six long-distance photographs on the desk. "Six hundred and eighty people were killed, the highest fatality ever recorded due to a tornado."

"Triple vortexes have occurred before," the general said peevishly.

"True, but not with so much speed or power.

83

Kansas has a very sophisticated tornado warning system, which usually gives people time to get into their storm cellars. The two extra funnels appeared almost instantaneously, and the town was leveled before half the people could get to safety. Also, the major damage usually would have been to wooden frame houses, but two factories built of cement were demolished. That means that the force of the winds at the outer wall of the tornadoes had to have been at least six hundred miles an hour." Forest stood looking down at the general. "Twice the strength of the average tornado!"

The fat man looked up at Forest, not at all uncomfortable at having him towering over him. "So?"

"So, there was no way for those tornadoes to form in the first place. Not then. Not there." Forest pulled the set of satellite photographs and synoptic charts out of the folder. He pointed to a set of numbers over Garnett, Kansas. "In order to have a tornado, you need plenty of heat, and we've got it. The temperature rose steadily over the two days. But look at this." Forest put the satellite photographs in front of the general. "The entire area was blanketed by cloud cover for three days. There was no way for the sun to heat that up. So what the hell made the temperature go up?"

General Wells looked at the weather map closely for a moment, tapped his fingers on the map, shrugged, and then said nothing. Forest went back around the desk and sat down. He was tired suddenly. He felt as if he had been

84

fighting an uphill battle and he hadn't even gotten to the hard part yet.

There is an axiom in the army that no one gets to be a general by accident. Certainly, in the case of Harlan Wells, it was more than true. Behind the facade of the home-spun slob who seemed permanently distracted, there was a sharp mind and a driving personality. Forest watched it emerge like a snake uncoiling, with fascination and a touch of horror.

The general shifted the dead cigar in his mouth and placed both hands flat on his desk. His face showed nothing. "You'll have to pardon me, Mr. Hill, if I'm just a little bit confused about what's got you so upset. I've heard your story and I can understand why you're mystified. Hell, so am I. Those are some mighty interesting events you got a hold of there, but what's getting your dander up so? You sure as hell ain't expecting logic from the weather, are you?" Forest sighed with exasperation.

"No, General, but I do expect the laws of nature to remain constant so some degree. When they aren't, again and again, I have to suspect that something's wrong. And that worries me." Forest looked at the General and saw that there was no other way but to blurt it out. "General, I think our weather has been thrown out of kilter. I think the whole system is in danger and these are just symptoms of what's to come." He looked the general straight in the eyes. "And I think that the military experiments on weather are the cause of it."

The general didn't blink. His face turned up

in genuine amusement, and he began to laugh. The sound was doubly grating on Forest's ears, because he knew it wasn't phony. The fat man stood up and came around the desk. He sat himself in the guest chair facing Forest and patted him on the knee.

"Look, son, I think you're getting a little excited about nothing. You can blame a lot of things on the military, but this isn't one of them. Sometimes, like with everything else in life, you have to say, 'Well, that's a freak,' and let it go at that." The general patted Forest's knee again, and Forest recoiled. He could feel his anger rising again.

"That's not good enough, General. It just doesn't wash. You can't explain away that much death and destruction—that many strange events—by calling them freaks and forgetting about them." The general could see that Forest was ready to pop and he tried to pacify him.

"Now take it easy there, son. Calling something a freak doesn't mean it's going to be forgotten. You can be sure that we keep track of these things. And it doesn't mean that there's no explanation. It just means that the explanation may be at the end of a long chain of events that goes back beyond our sight. Just because we don't have the answers now doesn't mean there are none, or that we won't get them." Forest shook his head vehemently.

"Someday won't do, General. This problem has to be dealt with now. I believe these disasters are the tip of the iceberg and that if the military doesn't stop experimenting with the weather, this whole planet is in danger of extinction. I've studied this carefully and I don't see any other cause or answer to the problem."

The general chuckled and threw his cigar in the direction of the wastebasket. "I don't want to insult you. Mr. Hill. I know you're a weatherman and that you learned all this, but maybe you've forgotten some of the basics. So forgive me, son, if I refresh your memory. When it comes to weather, you can never say never. There is no doubt that the world's weather patterns are changing and there are a lot of theories as to why.

"The most popular theory is that we're in the middle of a prolonged cooling that will eventually put us smack dab in another ice age. But of course not in our lifetimes, which makes it just a little more palatable. On the other hand, there's the opposite theory, which says we're in a warming trend. Both sides have a lot of logic and factual support to back up their positions." The general shrugged and got up to pace. Forest bowed his head and gritted his teeth as the general continued his lecture.

"Then there's the sunspot theory, which says the weather cycle changes every eleven years. Or you've got the earth axis wobble position, the build up of dust in the upper atmosphere theory, the Greenhouse effect, and the reverse Greenhouse effect." The general was making it sound humorous, but Forest wasn't laughing.

"You see what I mean?" the general continued. "Nobody knows. And if you think you have some weird events, how about the fact that in odd-numbered years we tend to have one kind of weather and even-numbered years another? Or that in the stratosphere over the equator the wind blows west one year and east the next? There are at least sixty theories floating around, any one of which theoretically explains illogical weather, so if you have one, Mr. Hill, feel free to add it to the list. Just don't blame it on the military. My job is tough enough."

The general had returned to his desk and he sat, impassively looking at Forest and drumming the fingers of one fat hand in front of him. The two men stared at each other in silence. Forest knew that the interview was over but, more than that, he knew that something bigger was also over for him. The general's bland, smug face confronted him like a stone wall. He had tried, truly tried. He had done his homework and he had done his private worrying. And, finally, he had put himself and his reputation out on a limb because he cared and because he was scared. But now, it was finished for him. If no one would listen, and if nobody believed him, why should he care?

Maybe he was wrong. And maybe it didn't matter either way. At least in this lifetime. It was their problem, let them handle it. Forest stood up and began collecting his papers. He looked at the general and smiled at him with his best TV-personality face. "Sorry, General, for wasting your time," he said, putting the papers in his case, "and, I guess, mine too." They both could feel the change of atmosphere in the room. The general smiled warmly back at Forest.

"Don't you worry about it, son. And don't be hard on yourself." He put both his palms on his desk and pushed himself erect. "You were trying your best and I can certainly see that your heart's in the right place. I wish there were more like you. The problem is," he said, winking at Forest, "we're *all* human."

As Forest snapped his briefcase shut, the door to the general's office opened. Forest turned to find Babyface standing there. The general must have signaled him in some way to come and show Forest out. Forest turned back to the general and reached out his hand over the desk.

"Thanks anyway, sir. And thanks for your time." They shook hands and Forest felt surprising strength in the fat man's grip.

"Think nothing of it. And do say hi to your brother, will you?"

Moments later, having retraced his steps through the maze of the Pentagon, Forest found himself standing in the warm Washington sun. He flagged a taxi to take him back to the airport, feeling angry and depressed and more than slightly ridiculous. But he also felt as if a weight had been lifted from his shoulders.

At the airport, on impulse, Forest decided to call Arthur. Listening to the phone ring in Arthur's office, Forest thought to himself that this was as good a place as any to start cleaning up his act. But when Arthur's secretary finally answered, Forest found out it was not to be, at least not for the moment. Arthur was out somewhere and she had no idea where.

Forest boarded the plane and found that he'd been stuck with a center seat. He buckled his seatbelt, tucked in his elbows, and tried to lean back. This certainly wasn't his day.

CHAPTER SEVEN

Forest rushed through the control room on the way to his office at a quarter to six, cursing rush-hour traffic, taxi drivers, his own stupidity, the army, General Harlan Wells, and the world in general. On one monitor he could see Roger Moss already in place on the set, practicing looking dour as he rehearsed his opening story. On another monitor he could see that his weather board was set up and ready to go. It was the first thing that had gone right that day. Good old Mick.

As Forest ran through the corridors wrestling with his tie and collar button, he realized that he hadn't given a moment's thought to what his gimmick of the day was going to be. He silently prayed that Micky had thought of that, too. He opened the door to his office and by the instant smile that appeared on her face he knew that she had everything covered. Micky, however, took one look at Forest and swallowed her elation, smile and all.

"Not a good day, boss?" she asked sympathetically. Forest threw his briefcase on his desk and started to untangle himself from his jacket, shirt, and tie, popping buttons as he went.

"Don't even ask, Mick. You wouldn't want to know. Just tell me who I am tonight and what I'm doing." Dropping clothes on the floor until he was naked to the waist, he turned and faced her. "I assume from that smirk you had on your face that you've come up with something highly original. Yes?" Micky's grin returned.

"Yes, sir, I have. Tonight you're going to do the first silent weather report." Forest frowned, not understanding. "You're going to do it in mime. You know, like Marcel Marceau. Act it out with your body. No words. A television first." Forest stared at her in disbelief, but Micky didn't budge. "And unless you have a better idea," she glanced at her watch, "that you can get ready in seventeen minutes, you better take off your pants, put on this leotard, and sit down so I can get you into white face. And while you're sitting, I'll run it through for you."

Micky stared impudently at him and held out a small black ball of cloth that Forest assumed was the leotard. He realized that she was enjoying the situation, enjoying having power over him. He also realized that he had no choice. He didn't have a better idea because he didn't have any other idea. And, come to think of it, it wasn't a bad piece of schtick; the first silent TV weather report. Forest graced her with a mock bow and began to unbuckle his pants.

"It seems," he said, "that I have no choice but to put myself entirely in your hands."

"You don't have to go that far, boss. Leave your underpants on." She threw the costume to Forest and watched him for a moment as he struggled into the unfamiliar garment. Then she turned away and walked to his dressing table. It bothered her that he could dress and undress in front of her as if she weren't there, as if she weren't a woman. She spread the sheets of weather data she had prepared on the table and opened a jar of white grease paint. When she looked up into the mirror, she saw that he was dressed. Forest was looking into the mirror also, but at himself. To Micky, he looked like a circus acrobat and very sexy, but by his expression she could see that he wasn't sure he liked it.

"Sit, sit, it looks fine," she said. "And you only have twelve minutes left, Forest sat. Micky began to smear makeup over his face while she told him the script. "The weather today was exactly like the weather yesterday, boss. I don't mean almost, I mean exactly. At ten different times in ten different cities, the temperatures were identical. And there's nothing moving around us from any direction to change it, so I figured you could do a 'What can I say?' routine. I left yesterday's map and numbers on the board and put up today's next to it. As far as the weather report goes, all you have to do is walk from one to the other and point." Micky paused to admire her work on his face and then began applying color to his lips and cheeks. "And as far as the show biz goes, you're on your own. But we don't have to worry about that, do we?"

"No, *we* don't," he answered. His mind was racing, trying to remember the bits and pieces of pantomime he had seen and trying to figure out how to fit them into a weather report. Forest wasn't worried; his specialty was improvisation, but he needed a few minutes of quiet to get ready. And Micky wasn't through talking.

"Your mail is on your desk. Nothing special. And the only important phone call was from your brother." Forest's body tightened. "He said he was flying in tonight on Delta, Flight 913, landing at LaGuardia at 6:17. He said that he wanted to see you right away—tonight— and that he would call you from the airport when he landed. Forest pushed Micky's hands away from his face and looked up at her.

"Goddamnit, Micky, why the hell didn't you tell me that right away?" She shrugged nonchalantly because Forest didn't seem angry.

"I don't know, boss. I just try to follow your priorities: business before everything, including family. Right?" Forest let the jibe pass.

"Damnit. I tried to reach him in Washington this afternoon and missed him." He stood up and put his arm around Micky. "I could have saved him a trip if I had only called in for messages. You seem to be the only one who's doing anything right today, kiddo." Forest smiled down at her and tightened his arm around her. The knot in his stomach had un- clenched and Forest realized that he had been carrying it around since Friday night.

Arthur had always been quite a man with a gesture, but this was really something. Forest felt warmth rising to the surface of his skin. He was glowing and he knew it. And he didn't mind if Micky knew it too. He wanted to share it with her.

Forest unwrapped his arm from around Micky and grasped her by the shoulders. He could see that she had no idea of what was go- ing on or why she was being subjected to this much affection. "It occurs to me, Miss Leary," he said deliberately, "that the reason you were wrong about my priorities was because I was wrong about my priorities. Business does not come before everything." He bent down and planted a wet, firm kiss on her forehead, smearing her with red and white grease paint. "Especially family!" Forest reached around her and gave her ass a gentle pat, and then he was gone in a mad dash to the studio, leaving Micky Leary awash in the wake of her confu- sion and emotion.

Forest slipped into the TV sound stage, clos- ing the big door silently behind him, and moved carefully across cables and around cameras to the weather section of the set. Sal Brenner was halfway through the sports and Forest just had time to take a quick look at the weather maps Micky had set up. She was right. It was like a duplicate day. Forest moved into position while Sal gave the out-of-town base-ball scores and waited.

There was a surge of energy and confidence in his body and he didn't bother thinking ahead. He knew he would be spectacular tonight, and that he would do it on instinct alone. He didn't need to think. Forest looked over at Roger and found him looking back, eyebrows up, apparently commenting on his costume. Forest made an ugly face and silently mouthed the words, "Fuck you." But as Roger's face prepared an equally silent insulting reply, a technician from the control room slipped a sheet of paper in front of Roger and disappeared.

Distracted, Roger looked down, started reading, and then looked back at Forest. He pointed down at the paper and then at Forest and held up both his hands and squeezed them together. The signal meant, "News Flash. Condense your segment." And before Roger could send a second signal indicating how big a story it was and how long it would take, the sportscast was over and Roger was on camera.

"I have just been handed this news bulletin. Only moments ago we learned that a plane has crashed into Flushing Bay, just short of the runway at La Guardia Airport." Roger looked up from the paper into the camera. "As I said, this tragedy has occurred just moments ago, so we are unable to tell you . . ." Roger paused and looked down at the new sheet of paper that had just been slipped in front of him.

"This just in. The plane has now been identified as Delta's Flight 913 from Miami to New York, via Washington. At this moment we are still unable to tell you the cause of the crash or how many fatalities are involved, but we do know that there are some survivors."

At that precise moment, Forest lost possession of his senses. His eyes were open, but he didn't know what he was looking at. His ears could hear Roger talking, but he couldn't understand a word because his mind was screaming, "That was Arthur's plane!"

"We will continue to bring you bulletins throughout the evening as we receive them," Roger continued grimly, "and we hope to be able to give you a full report on the eleven o'clock news. And now, quickly, the weather with Forest Hill."

Until that moment, Forest had been elsewhere—outside of his body, somewhere over Queens, over Flushing Bay, over La Guardia. Yet, when Roger intoned the words, ". . . the weather with Forest Hill," he snapped back into himself like a yo-yo into a palm. He arrived with a jolt and found himself staring at a red light and camera that were staring directly at him. By instinct, his eyes flicked to the floor director and he saw him holding one finger aloft. He had one minute.

Forest was standing between two large maps of the eastern United States. There were no cloud symbols on the maps, nor rain or wind directions. There were no indications of fronts moving in or out; there were only numbers and names of cities. Forest opened his mouth and leaned forward, ready to say something. Then, reconsidering, he let his mouth close again. He leaned backward slightly and let his arms rise from his sides, his hands hanging bent from his wrists, palms upwards, in a classic shrug.

Inside his brain, Forest heard nothing and wondered who was telling his body what to do. Suddenly his left arm shot out with a hand cocked at the end of it and a finger pointing. Forest's head turned slowly to see what he was pointing at. It was a map; he was pointing at the word *Yesterday*. Then his right arm shot out with an identical gesture, but Forest didn't turn to see where it was pointing. He stared directly into the lens of the camera, his face sliding, like clay melting until it became a picture of sadness caused by pain from the constant insults of life. Then his head turned slowly to find his finger pointing at another map and the word *Today*.

For a moment he stood frozen, arms outstretched, pointing at the two maps. Then part of his mind saw a man with a clipboard and stopwatch signaling thirty seconds and rolling his hand under his chin to say "Wind it up." Forest let his hands begin to descend slowly down the faces of the two maps. His outstretched fingers passed "Boston 87° —Boston 87°"; "New York 91°—New York 91°"; "Washington 93°—Washington 93°." As his hands reached Washington, the fingers began to open and Forest's body began to bend until by the time his hands had reached "Miami 98°—Miami 98°," he had performed a complete and deep bow to the camera. The camera zoomed in as Forest rose from his bow and, with five seconds to go, the camera was framed fully on his face. At that moment a tear appeared in the corner of Forest's left eye and rolled slowly down his cheek. The director in the control room pushed a button and cut to Roger for the wrap-up.

The instant the red light went out, Forest began to run. It appeared he would impale himself on the camera in front of him, or run over it, but his body turned and swerved and his feet moved between the cables with their own eyes until he was out the door and moving through the corridors at twice the speed he had come flying in, only a lifetime ago. He burst through the revolving front door and leapt down the twelve steps to the street. He saw a taxi with its roof light on, but there was a woman just opening the door. Forest came at her from the back, ready to brush her away when she turned, and he stopped. And he stopped. And he stopped. It was Micky's face that stopped his body, and he looked into her face until his head and heart stopped running.

Micky stood on the curb, holding the door of the checker cab open, not looking at Forest, just being there. But the taxi driver, who had been sitting stolidly in the isolation of his plastic-protected front compartment, suddenly felt his money-clock erupt and turned to see what the story was. What he saw was Forest in a black leotard and clown makeup, and although it is a traditional legend in New York that a cabbie will pass a black woman to pick up a man in a gorilla suit, it's not always necessarily so. The driver opened the money vent in the plastic partition and shouted, "Whatya say, huh? How about you hail another cab?"

Micky ignored the driver. She grabbed Forest and pulled him past her into the cab. "Your briefcase and clothes are on the seat. There's money in your pocket and there are tissues and cold cream in your case." She leaned into the cab a little, wanting to see Forest's face. "If you want, I'll go out there with you."

Forest's answer was a whisper. "No. No, thank you." He was quiet for a moment and then she heard, "Thank you anyway." He reached out and pulled the door shut and, before she was ready for it, the cab sped away into the anonymity of traffic. Micky stood in the gutter in front of the giant netword building, among workers entering and leaving, and finally let go her tears. She made no noise as she wasn't sobbing. It wasn't that kind of pain. It was just, she felt, that you don't say, "Thank you anyway," to family.

Inside the network, the switchboard had just become undermanned. But strangely enough, the calls weren't for information about the plane disaster. They were about Forest, about Forest Hill and his weather report. And on the twenty-seventh floor a vice-president, after checking on Forest's salary and length of his contract, invited some other vice-presidents in to watch a tape of the broadcast. Over their drinks they agreed that it would be a crime not to save the tape. There was no question, it was a classic.

CHAPTER EIGHT

Inside the cab on the way to the airport, Forest mechanically covered his face with cold cream and wiped off his makeup. A pile of tissues had formed at his feet, but Forest was unaware of them. He didn't notice that the traffic going out of the city was even worse than it had been coming in. All he could think about was that it was his fault that Arthur was on that plane. If only they hadn't fought . . . if only he had called Arthur over the weekend . . . if only he had called his office from Washington for messages . . . so many ifs. And there was still one more—if only Arthur survived the crash.

A flash of lightning and a clap of thunder startled Forest out of his reverie. He looked out the window in amazement and saw that it was pouring. They had just driven into a storm. Rain on the Grand Central Parkway always slows traffic, but the combination of the storm and the accident at the airport now

brought it almost to a standstill. Forest having
had ample time to clean his face and put on the
clothes Micky had provided for him, found
himself staring anxiously out the window,
hoping for the traffic to start moving and waiting to catch a glimpse of the airport. The rain
beat against the sealed windows of the cab,
and the heat inside fogged them over. The
driver, muttering taxi-ese, was trying to clear
his windshield with a piece of the *Daily News*.
Forest used his hand to make a porthole.

He had given up thinking about the situation
and had given up worrying. All he could focus
on was getting to the airport. Like a child, he
promised himself that if he could just get there
in time everything would be all right. All at
once, the traffic began to move as the rubber-
neckers ahead passed the airport and saw that
there was nothing to see and drove on. But it
was only a momentary spurt. As soon as they
had gotten up to speed and rounded the curve
leading to the entrance to La Guardia, the cabbie jammed on his brakes, avoided piling into a
line of cars, and they were crawling again. But
at least Forest could see the airport lights
ahead.

Deciding he couldn't wait any longer, he
leaned forward and peered through the plastic
partition, trying to read what was on the meter. What would have ordinarily been $7.50
read $11.75. Forest didn't care. He took $15
out of his pocket and rapped on the plastic.
"Listen," he shouted. "I'm getting out here.
Stop for a second." He shoved the bills into the

payhole. The driver shrugged and stepped on the brakes. He had long ago decided that Forest was a potentially dangerous loony and he was glad to be rid of him, even if it did leave him stranded in traffic. For a New York taxi driver, he philosophized, that's business. Any day you don't get killed is a good one.

The car stopped and Forest grabbed his briefcase and jumped out into the rain and traffic. He knew his umbrella was in his case but he ignored it. He began to run, first down the highway between lanes of cars, and then cutting in front of cars, crossing from lane to lane toward the embankment. He didn't hear the screeching tires as drivers stabbed at their brakes to avoid hitting him, or the angry blaring of horns. He didn't care about the cursing men screaming at their wives about that idiot who could have got them all killed. Forest just ran, rain streaming down his face, blurring his vision and soaking him. His shoes were filled with water and the rain that had soaked his clothing made him feel twenty pounds heavier.

After running and sliding up a grassy knoll, he could finally see the curved building that housed all the major airlines. He stood for a moment, panting, and realized that although he was only two or three hundred yards away from it, an acre of parking lot and an eight-foot fence still stood in his way. Forest punched the fence and, while the metal rattled, tried to find a way through or around it, but in the dark he could see practically nothing.

Forest threw his briefcase over the fence

and watched it hit the hood of a brand-new Chevy Impala with a satisfying thud. Then, sticking the toes of his shoes into the triangular wire holes, he climbed the fence. At the top he paused and then jumped, with some satisfaction, onto the same hood. But the hood was wet and the soles of his leather shoes were slippery and Forest lost his footing and bounced off the car landing on his coccyx. Sitting in the mud, Forest asked himself what the hell he was doing. Why was he taking out his frustration and anger on some poor slob's brand-new car? Forest wiped his face, trying to clear his eyes, felt in the wet dirt for his briefcase, and painfully stood up. He peered into the distance, looking for where Delta would have a sign announcing its presence, but the rain was relentless. All Forest could see was the general shape and light of the building.

No matter. Forest began to run again, weaving between empty cars, his body hurting and no longer working at full speed. And now he was forced to watch the dark shapes and treacherous terrain he was battling. Banging his way across the parking lot, he soon noticed he wasn't running anymore, and what had been a lope became a trot. By the time he got to the exit, just across the road from the terminal, he had to force himself to walk.

La Guardia is built on two levels: the upper for departures and the lower for arrivals. On the ground level, no cars are allowed to stop for more than a moment, except for the long line of taxis that edge the curb. When Forest

105

had passed through here just a few hours ago, there had been the normal, organized confusion of travelers and vehicles. Now there was chaos. Forest was five airlines away from Delta, but he could see that it was engulfed. The twirling rooflights of police cars, screaming horns, running people, and a log jam of passenger cars formed a barricade around the entrance. The overflow reached out in both directions and came close enough to touch him.

There was nothing to be learned on this level. He had to get upstairs to the gate or to wherever they had set up a control post to deal with the disaster. Forest crossed the road, weaving through cars and scurrying people, and went in through the American Airlines entrance. The long hall with its revolving baggage units was mobbed, and Forest could hear the sound of hysteria in the air. Panic had spread throughout the airport. Joining a mass of flowing bodies, Forest edged onto an up escalator and was wedged in from both sides. He had to wait for the moving stairs to reach the top before he could walk.

Forest was swept along in a tide that seemed to be aiming for a specific location. Letting himself be carried along, he observed the personality of the crowd. It was a true demographic sample, representing every age, race, and social stratum. Parents, husbands, wives, lovers, and children were united in fear and pain, and it was the unity of their emotion that was carrying the surge of humanity forward.

It was a strange sensation and not an uncomforting one. Forest let himself go with it.

"The plane crashed short of the runway."

"In the water . . ."

"No survivors . . ."

"I'm sure she wasn't on it. . . ." There was a babble of fragmented information, questions, and curses, but it was clear that no one had any real information.

The human organism of which Forest was now a part was relentlessly pushing its way down a circular feeding corridor, and he peered overhead at the signs and arrows, trying to find out if the crowd was at least heading in the right direction. By the time Forest was able to read the Delta sign in the distance, so could everyone else and the organism became an animal; Forest could smell the odor.

Having found their destination, there was a mass surge forward and then an unexpected push backward. It was as if they had run into a wall and were bouncing off it, and, because they were unable to see what was stopping them, every physical contact suddenly produced hostility. While they had been moving forward, pressing against bodies in front and being pushed forward by others from behind, the hostility had gone unnoticed. But, now, when the movement reversed, the crowd instantly became aware of personal space. Elbows extended themselves laterally, hands reached forward to prevent any more backward movement, and what had been a unified flow turned into individuals fighting for room.

Aside from isolated emotional outbursts, however, there was a strange quiet. It seemed that every person there wanted information and they were straining to hear anything, even though many of them had never been quiet enough to listen before in their lives. By standing on his toes and looking over the heads of the crowd, Forest could see that there was a barricade at the entrance to the concourse, manned by police and airline officials. It was obvious that they couldn't let this mass of emotion anywhere near the gate or near any access to the tarmac or airfield itself.

While the airline personnel were trying to calm and gently steer the crowd to another location, there was a constant stream of activity passing around the barrier. Firemen carrying oxygen, medics carrying stretchers, and men in airline coveralls appeared as if from nowhere, burst past the barrier, and disappeared down the empty hole of the tunnel. Forest could hear their feet pounding off into the distance and then their echo. And every now and then someone would emerge from the tunnel, looking stunned and exhausted, eyes not quite in focus. They would blink at the straining faces of the crowd and then turn and walk away, trying not to run.

Forest found it agonizing to stand trapped in the crowd, waiting, knowing he was just going to be directed to another location. And it was sweltering, as if the body of the crowd had developed a fever; wherever sweat broke out there was the rancid smell of fear, with no wind likely to blow it away. Forest saw how many people still stood between him and the gate and decided that he would find a way around them.

Movement forward or backward was impossible, but sideways seemed neutral and Forest was able to work himself to the inner wall of the corridor on politeness alone. Along the wall, there was enough body space to move, but only backward. Still, at this point, any movement, even backward, was progress. There were a tantalizing number of doors in the wall, some blank and others marked PRIVATE or AIR-LINE PERSONNEL ONLY. Forest tried each one and found them all locked, and then one wasn't and he slipped through and closed the door behind him.

He was in an inner hallway that ran parallel to the outer arc of the concourse. Forest could hear typewriters and teletype machines, phones ringing, and people shouting. He turned to his right and began to run. He was totally ignored by the people he passed; their minds were outside the terminal, at the crash, and if they had had somewhere to go they probably would have been running too. Forest tried to estimate the distance to the barricade and, when he thought he had reached it, he went on. He was running in the direction they had been sending the crowd, and if he stayed in the inner corridor, he might be able to beat some of them there.

Forest's ears first told him he was getting close; in the distance he could hear noise—the too-loud, unintelligible blur that comes from too many sounds being made at once. And with every step, the population of the corridor increased until Forest found himself dodging and weaving, slowing, and when he had finally been reduced to a walk, he was there.

All the doors between the inner and outer corridors had been opened, blending the hysteria outside with the frenzied attempt at efficiency inside. The people in the inner corridor were trying to deal with the logistics of the disaster and the people in the outer with the emotion of it. The intensity of each group was equal. For Forest, it was like stepping into the eye of a hurricane. The energy around him was so palpable and violent it rose even above his own. Strangely, it insulated him from his emotions and left him free to observe and function.

CHAPTER NINE

Forest knew he was backstage—behind the lines—and pressed himself against the wall and stood watching and listening. He was trying to separate the sounds and find someone in authority who would be his best source of information. He tried focusing on people with telephones, in an attempt to read their moving lips. When there was a shout, he looked for the source to see if anyone was directing this madness. And as he stood there straining, voices, words, questions and answers began to emerge, but they were disconnected and incomplete.

"Physicians Hospital and Elmhurst General have been alerted and are receiving . . ."

"No, we don't know yet. It could have been lightning and there was an explosion . . ."

"Goddamnit, where the fuck is the passenger manifest from Washington? We have people here. . . ."

111

"Yes, sir, there are survivors being brought in, but we still haven't found the crew."

Forest felt a hand on his arm, gripping him with conviction. He had been so absorbed that the touch startled him. Attached to the grip was a large man in uniform. The man was talking to him. ". . . to be here. If you are a relative there is . . ." Forest had made the mistake of standing still in a world where everyone else was moving; even the ones who were sitting down were twitching and jiggling. He was clearly an outsider and had to be removed. Forest accepted the logic. But until he looked down at the man's hand gripping his elbow, he had no idea what he looked like. When he looked up into the man's eyes, he saw, just before they were averted, what a sodden, disheveled, muddy, and mad figure he presented and he could understand why the man was doubly concerned.

But before Forest could form the words to explain himself, a shudder passed down the hall, its waves shaking everyone. The guard was an old man and he looked away, confused, as the volume increased and he released Forest's arm. Forest could see him reaching for something to attach himself to, to involve himself in, that was part of the life-and-death drama. He seemed to be looking for what would surely be his last opportunity to make a gesture, a sacrifice. But as they both watched, the palpitation passed and activity returned to a level of what now seemed normal hysteria. The news had penetrated, had been absorbed and dealt with, and Forest marveled at the tolerance level that seemed to be able to surmount pain and pity and devote all its energy to function. The two men had been drawn into the experience, but now that it was over they were back to where they had begun. They had shared something without learning anything. Forest took the guard's arm.

"My brother was on this plane," he said slowly and distinctly, as if he were talking to a child. "He is a major in army intelligence and I am a newsman. How can I find out what's happened to him?" The guard's head was bobbing on his neck like an antenna, a tentacle searching for something to touch, but he seemed to hear Forest talking to him. After a few seconds he began to speak, like a doll with a drawstring recording inside, while his face still searched elsewhere for a function.

"The airline is doing its best to deal with the disaster. As information is received, it is relayed immediately. If you are a friend or relative of someone on the flight, you can help most by going to the Cosmosphere Lounge, where all the passenger information is being channeled. It does no good for you to be here. You won't get information any faster and you're just in the way. If there's anything we can do to help you, please let us know. Otherwise, let me direct you to the lounge." The old man half-raised his right arm and flapped his hand at the end of it, indicating the direction Forest should follow. Forest headed for the lounge; he realized that in this situation he was a civilian.

The Cosmosphere Lounge was a VIP room that had been hurriedly converted into an operations center for dealing with friends and relatives of the passengers. If the mood behind the lines had been frantic, in the lounge it was hysterical. When Forest entered, an airline official was repeating an announcement he had obviously made many times before.

"We are terribly sorry to confirm that Delta's Flight 913, from Miami via Washington, has been forced down just short of the runway. We still don't know the cause, but there are survivors. They are being brought out by rescue teams right now. There was no fire, so the chances for everyone are very much better.

"Please let me advise you that if you are a friend or relative of a passenger, this is the best place for you to remain. All information is being announced immediately. When we know a passenger has arrived at a hospital, we'll let you know and make arrangements to get you there as quickly as possible. I repeat, please remain here in the lounge and we'll try to do anything in our power to help you. Thank you."

The announcement did little to induce calm. The room was filled with sobbing and screaming, and more distraught people were arriving all the time, not only relatives but friends of relatives as well, some still clutching the late edition of the evening paper with its one word headline: "Crash." Old people and young, parents dragging children who were crying for other reasons, all were filling the room with the unbearable sound of pain.

Forest was jostled aside by a newly arriving group and edged his way to a wall, trying to get his bearings. The airline had set up three desks, each with people in contact with the hospitals. As soon as they were informed that a passenger had arrived and been identified at a hospital, they would call out a name and number, "O'Brian, a party of two," and a group of people would surge at the desk as if to swallow it. One of the problems seemed to be that several families of the same name but of no relation to one another had been notified by the airline or had arrived on their own. All were in an emotional state, but once they were sorted out both groups exploded with joy and relief. The wrong families were freed from tragedy and could go home. The right families rejoiced because they had survivors. They were still announcing only the survivors.

Forest looked around, wondering what to do. The airline had brought in coffee and was installing telephones everywhere; the coffee was going slowly, but they couldn't keep up with the telephones. There were several doctors moving through the room and Forest watched one inject a woman with a hypodermic needle. She had gone rigid and her body was twitching, her mouth open in a silent scream. She was obviously in shock. It seemed to

Forest that a great many of the people needed, or were asking for, sedation.

A Puerto Rican group in one corner had now grown to an enclave of more than twenty-five and were wailing and rocking in unison as they clustered around someone in their middle. As Forest stood with his back against a wall, trying to absorb this nightmare scene, it looked to him like a Hieronymus Bosch painting of the damned in hell, except that he was in it.

Gradually the level of the noise began to subside, but without any loss of its intensity. The passenger manifest from Washington had finally arrived and was being read aloud. The names were being checked against information lists they already had; if the person was at a hospital, it was mentioned.

"Jones, Helen. Physicians Hospital."

"Jones, Arnold. Elmhurst General."

"Katz, Morris. Missing."

"Klieger, Herbert. Booth Memorial." Everybody assumed that missing meant dead. Forest heard Arthur's name read from the list. It was followed by the word *missing*.

The reading of the list sent some of the people scurrying from the room, pushing past and stepping over those who were forced to remain, immobile in their agony. It sent others rushing to the desks, where they seemed to take out their anger and frustration on the airline personnel. It was unbearable. Forest knew he had to leave or he would lose not only his ability to function, but also his sanity.

116

CHAPTER TEN

Not knowing where he was heading, Forest made his way out of the lounge and into the corridor. By comparison, it was silent. He looked down the long corridor at the barricade to the concourse. The mob that had surrounded it earlier had been dispersed and now only some reporters with mobile cameras stood waiting.

Irresistibly, Forest was drawn to the tunnel. He could see that there were still people entering the concourse, but they weren't running. He felt a terrible pain as he realized that the urgency was over and that the clean-up had begun. The few people who emerged from the tunnel seemed to be in shock and brushed past the reporters, unable to speak even if they had wanted to.

Forest stood at the head of the concourse, staring past the barricade, down the long hall. He was just standing. He was unwilling to accept that since Arthur was still missing, he was therefore dead. But he was numb, too. He couldn't seem to think. It was as if there was no place to go and nothing to do except stand and watch, not even really observing the emergency workers coming and going. So it wasn't until he found himself staring at someone that Forest became aware he was looking at a face he knew. There were three soldiers coming up the tunnel and one of them was Babyface, the receptionist in General Wells's office. It didn't make any sense, and at first Forest thought he was hallucinating, but the wad of gum was there and Babyface was working it, and that was a reality.

Forest thought that they were coming out of the tunnel and decided to wait for them, but when he saw them turn and head for a flight of stairs, he began to run toward the barricade. "Hey, soldier. Wait a second!" he yelled. As his voice rolled off the empty walls, the three heads turned toward his. Forest reached the barricade and stopped. Two policemen had edged toward him to make sure he didn't try to cross, but Forest wasn't trying to, he just wanted to make sure that Babyface could see him.

"You work for General Wells," he yelled. "I saw you this afternoon in his office. Remember me?" The soldiers had stopped. Babyface turned to face Forest and squinted at him, wrinkling his forehead. "My name is Forest Hill," he shouted, and waited for the echo to recede. The soldier took a couple of steps toward Forest and the wrinkle left his brow. His jaw started

118

to chew again and Forest could tell that he had been recognized. "I need to talk to you for a minute. Please . . ." he called, waiting while the soldier slowly decided to walk the rest of the way up the hall. There was a small commotion going on behind Forest as the other reporters put his name together with his face, but Forest ignored it and kept his focus on the soldier, trying to will him closer.

Sensing that Babyface was approaching him reluctantly, Forest was puzzled, until it dawned on him that he was surrounded by reporters and cameras. The soldier had to be thinking that Forest wanted to use him in some way to get an exclusive over the rest of the mob. Forest smiled at the oncoming face and held out his hand long before the soldier was close enough to shake it. The ritual worked. Instinctively, Babyface reached out his hand and Forest grabbed it, and then, immediately, Forest's left hand gripped the soldier's elbow and pulled him closer.

"Listen," he said, leaning forward, trying to get nearer to the man's ear. "I don't know why you're here or what you're doing out there, but my brother was on that plane. His name is Arthur Anspacher and he's a major in military intelligence. I can't find out what's happened to him—whether he's dead or alive." Forest could feel the resistance leave the other man's body and he released his grip on him. Babyface leaned back on his heels and looked into Forest's eyes. His own eyes widened for a moment, but that was his only reaction. Then the soldier turned to one of the policemen.

"Let this man through," he said. "He's with me." Forest ducked down and slid under the barrier, before the cop had a chance to react. He could hear the outcry this produced from the press on the other side and he started walking, not waiting for the soldier or the cop to change their minds. But Babyface had moved as quickly as Forest and was now walking at his side. When they were halfway between the barricade and the two waiting soldiers, Forest felt the man grip his arm, stopping him.

"I didn't know who you were," he said softly. "I mean, your names are different. I'm sorry."

"That's okay. It happens all the time, but usually the other way round." Forest was making conversation, waiting for the soldier to say something. Babyface had let go of him but said nothing. "I appreciate your helping me," he said. The soldier coughed, clearing his throat.

"Oh, that's no problem, sir . . . except, well, I don't think I'm going to be much help." Forest turned to look at the man's face, but the soldier had lowered his head. "I . . . I have some bad news for you, sir," he mumbled. "I'm afraid your brother is dead." Forest felt as if a well had just been tapped inside him and in its pressure to escape, it was driving water out of his eyes. He started to turn away, but the man gripped Forest's arm and started them walking again.

Letting the arm propel him, Forest tried to take stock of the situation. To his surprise, he felt no shock. It seemed that his mind had accepted the reality long ago. He began blinking his eyes rapidly, and gradually they cleared until he could see. Then he reached out to the extremities of his body and began to take repossession of his faculties, his feet and his hands, and finally his breathing. Now all he had to do was silence the deafening voices crying in his head.

Just before they reached the two soldiers waiting at the stairs, Forest caught a small blur of motion out of the corner of his eye. The soldiers turned and started down the stairs; Babyface had sent them on ahead with a flick of his wrist. They walked in silence, only the clacking of their shoes punctuating their passage. Finally Forest could stand it no longer; he needed external sound to balance the discord inside him.

"Do you . . . ah . . ." Forest fought to control his voice, "know what caused the crash?" The soldier began to talk, his voice soft and unemotional, but it was soothing to Forest because it was neutral. He could listen or not; it really didn't seem to matter. Forest concentrated on walking and let the words flow over him.

"The accident seems to have been caused by a sudden thunderstorm. No pilot in his right mind will fly into one, but this one did, or was caught by it, or they were hit by lightning. If it was just the storm, a sudden downdraft could have forced the plane into the ground before the engines had time to react. If it had been a prop plane, they would have been all right, but it takes a jet engine five or six seconds to respond to a pilot and at a couple of hundred feet off the ground that wouldn't have been enough time. If it was lightning, something could have exploded, but that's highly unlikely. Or maybe it was a bomb. We won't know until they put all the pieces together."

They were walking at an abnormally slow pace, as if their steps were being measured, and Forest allowed the arm and voice to guide him. The soldier didn't stop talking. "The plane was only about half full and the passengers were scattered around the cabin. When the plane hit the water, it skipped across it like a stone and then impacted onto the shore, breaking into pieces. The debris is widely spread in the water, and some of it is almost 500 feet up the shoreline." They had almost reached a door leading to the airfield. Through the upper half, Forest could see pockets of light and blurs of movement in the distance.

"Are you sure," Forest said, not looking at the soldier but staring out into the night, "that you found my brother?"

"We're pretty sure, Mr. Hill. But we'd like you to make a positive identification. It's pretty gruesome out there and you'd have to walk through some tough stuff." Babyface paused, his hand on the metal pushbar that would open the door, and he looked at Forest to see if he was willing to experience the ordeal.

Forest was willing enough. At that moment he could have walked through fire without noticing it. But something else was bothering him. The last time he had seen Babyface he had been a receptionist for General Wells. Now he was asking Forest to identify his brother's body. Why? Forest continued to stare out the window. He asked his question gently.

"Why do you want me to identify Arthur? I mean, why are you here in the first place?" The soldier's answer came quickly and smoothly and without rancor.

"We're here because it's part of our job. Whenever military personnel are involved in a disaster, we investigate, especially if they have rank or are in intelligence." He paused. "Okay?"

Forest pushed the door open and they stepped out into the cacophony of the disaster itself. Every emergency vehicle in New York City has its own siren, its own pulsating wail. Together, the combination of police, fire, ambulance and other assorted official frequencies produced a chord that chilled the blood. The vista looked to Forest like a painting of the aftermath of one of the great ancient battles where the living were picking through the dead.

Forest followed the soldiers across the tarmac and out into the night, feeling like he was in an obstacle course at a horror house; much of what he had to avoid stepping on was human. Although he felt no curiosity about what they were doing, and had avoided observing

123

groups of men working, eventually he couldn't help but see what they were doing. Flood lamps were trained across the runway and out into the water, where even more powerful beams were aiding frogmen in their search for bodies. Teams of men were assigned to recover bodies, and each team scoured a separate area. Everyone was dressed in coveralls, but some men carried cameras and others had iridescent orange flags, rolls of tape, tags, markers and heavy plastic bags.

A sudden flash from a camera blinded Forest and when his pupils refocused he found himself staring at a group bending over a body ... or a piece of one.

The equipment suddenly made sense. One of the men attached a tag to the body. Then they placed the body in the bag with its belongings, zipped up the bag, and taped a tag to that, too. Another man marked a number on the flag and stuck it in the ground next to the head of the bag. Then they all rose slowly and walked toward the next pile on the ground, only ten feet away.

There seemed to be no pattern as to who had survived and who not, or to where they had been found. People sitting next to one another had been blown in different directions, one breaking only a rib while the other was decapitated. Forest, tip-toeing through the devastation, suddenly found himself looking down at a lovely teenage girl clad only in tennis sneakers. She lay sprawled in what would have been an inviting pose except for the fact that she was dead. Many of the victims had been ex-pelled from the plane at such velocity, or pulled with such enormous suction, that clothes, un-derwear, even jewelry had been stripped away from them, leaving them not only naked and dead, but also extremely difficult to identify.

Forest followed the soldiers blindly, unable to comprehend the reality of the situation. They had been walking a long way and there was a smell in the air of something burning, even though there hadn't been a fire. Ahead, the two soldiers stopped and Forest felt Ba-byface take his arm again and bring him to a halt. There was a pool of light in the distance and in it a flag and a black plastic, zippered bag.

"This is where we found your brother," Forest heard a voice saying into his ear. "And he'll have to stay here for just a little longer. But if you can identify him now, you can save your family a lot of trouble and grief at the . . . later." Beyond the bright circle of light, Forest could see a group of men in white cov-eralls and baseball caps systematically combing the ground. On their caps were the letters FBI.

And then, what had been so agonizingly slow until now, became too fast. Before he knew it, the soldiers were moving, he was moving, and then he was staring at the dead face of his brother Arthur. He heard voices asking, hands touching him, but he could only lean down the long tunnel of his vision to try and get closer to the face that had been his friend.

It was Arthur. It is Arthur. How could there

be any doubt about it? I mean, look at him. Look at his face. There's the scar where I once bit him in a fight. . . . Too quickly, the zipper closed, leaving Forest staring into black plastic, and then the world twirled and Forest was moving again. It seemed he had identified his brother.

CHAPTER ELEVEN

Forest stood blinking in the unfailingly impersonal neon of the terminal and tried to understand what had just happened. He had no idea how long he had been out on the field, what papers he had signed, or how he had gotten back here. But it wasn't a dream, and Forest knew that something was over that could never be taken back.

When emotion is unbearable, people often reach for function. Forest chose responsibility as his life line and decided that he should call Valerie. The simplest chore he could handle was to look for a phone but, as his eyes swept the corridor and encountered the lounge of the cursed, he knew he had to go elsewhere. There was poison in the air here and Forest had already breathed enough to die.

The corridor led to a passageway and to an escalator and eventually to a section of the airport that was untainted by the cringe of death. Finally, there were bustling and bumping bodies, stranded passengers waiting for flights, irritated normal people whose lives were being disrupted by something that was happening elsewhere and were treating it like a pain in the ass. It was the other side of the thin membrane that separated chaos from reality, but everything in Forest clung to it, breathed it in, and as it dulled his senses, he let it lull him.

Airport payphones are standup affairs that give even less illusion of privacy than the famous pissoirs that used to dot the streets of Paris. Here one tries to turn one's back, but is forced to shout; the need for volume denies the concept of intimacy. Perhaps that's why they're called public phones.

Forest dialed Valerie's number in Washington, no longer Arthur and Valerie's number, and waited for the operator to intercept so he could charge the call. On one side of him he could hear a man explaining to his wife why he was going to be late getting into Pittsburg that night. On the other side, a man with a young blonde wrapped around him was explaining to his wife why he wouldn't be home at all. Fascinating, Forest thought, how different people use tragedy. The line was busy.

Forest hung up and tried again and again and again, each time having to go through the operator to bill the call. On each side of him, the procession of human drama continued to be played out on the phones, but Forest had lost interest. He was trying to figure out how to explain to Valerie, while part of him was praying that she already knew.

When the connection was made, Valerie answered before the first ring had finished, and from the tension and expectation in her "Hello," Forest could hear that he was going to have to tell her.

"This is Forest, Val. I'm at the airport in New York." Before he could continue, there was an explosion of relief on the other end.

"Oh, thank God, Forest. Thank God it's you. I've been calling and calling ever since they announced it and I haven't been able to find out anything. I've called both airports and the airlines and your office and your home and I still don't know what's happened to Arthur. Tell me, Forest. Tell me that Arthur is all right." There was no hysteria in her voice, but Forest could hear how hard she was fighting for control. There was silence on the line as Forest searched to find the right words—any words—that would let him utter the inexpressible.

"Are you there, Forest?" she asked.

"I'm here, Val," he answered, the pain and misery naked in his voice. And then it was over. She knew.

"Oh dear God. Dear, dear mother of God." He could hear the strength seeping out of her spirit. "He's dead, isn't he, Forest? My Arthur is dead?" Forest would have given anything to be there at that moment, to be able to reach out and hold her rather than say words. He sighed and leaned his head against the cold metal of the phone booth.

"Yes, Val. He's gone." She began to sob, but

very gently, as if she couldn't control the pain but was damn well going to control her tears. "Are you all right down there?" he finally asked. "Do you want me to fly down now?" He heard Valerie blow her nose and the sounds of her tears stopped.

"I'm fine, Forest. There are people here with me. Plenty of good, kind, gentle people. All of our friends. We could have a party except that Arthur . . ."

"There are some military guys here, Val, and I think they'll be flying him down to Washington." He had to change the subject.

"Ah yes, the military. They'll take care of everything all right. They always do, don't they?" Forest chose to ignore the sarcasm in her voice, but he certainly didn't blame her for it.

"Yeah, they sure seem to, don't they? Listen, I'll try to get things straightened out here as fast as I can and then I'll be down. Are you sure you're all right?"

"I'm fine, Forest," she answered steadily. "I'm as fine as can be expected.

"Valerie . . ." Forest hesitated. "I wish I knew what to say. I wish there were something . . ." Valerie interrupted him.

"Don't bother, Forest. There isn't anything, and he was your brother, too. Ironic, isn't it? He was on his way to see you." Forest listened for bitterness in her voice, but there was none there. She was just making an observation. Still, he couldn't help feeling that she must have held him responsible in some way, to some degree. God knows, he blamed himself entirely.

"I know he was coming up to see me. He left a message. But he didn't say why." Forest paused. "Did he tell you why, Val?"

"No. No, he didn't. Maybe he just wanted to be friends again. What does it matter?" Forest could tell she was having trouble hanging on now. "I have to get off the phone, Forest. There are things to be done and calls to make and . . ." Her voiced just trailed off. "Good-bye, Forest. Take care of yourself. I'll see you soon."

"Good-bye, Val," he said, and then he heard her hang up. Forest held the dead phone in his hand for a moment and then carefully put the receiver back in place. He saw that his hand was shaking and he felt enormously tired. He stood there knowing he had to go somewhere and do something but, for the life of him, he couldn't figure out what.

A chill ran down Forest's spine and he felt as if someone were staring at him. He turned to find Jenny Wells standing there, tears running down her face. They stood motionless for a moment, acknowledging their mutual misery, and then Jenny stepped toward him.

"I don't know if you remember me, Mr. Hill, from the party the other night?" She took a swipe at her eyes with the back of her hand, in an attempt to dry her tears.

"Of course I do, Jenny. You were there with my brother and Valerie." This produced another rush of wetness, and she bowed her head.

Forest stood there helplessly, not knowing what to do, but envying her ability to cry. Suddenly she looked up, blinking rapidly, and reached out her hand. Forest took it. It was small and soft and it was pulling him.

"I think we both need a drink, Mr. Hill. Would you mind?"

"My name is Forest, and I think you're right," he said, and he let her lead him down the corridor, farther away from the disaster area. He was glad, he realized, that he had her hand to hold.

The cocktail lounge was crowded and noisy, but somehow they managed to get a table and order drinks. Jenny sat across from him, quietly watching him, and Forest was grateful for her silence. When the waitress brought their drinks, Forest immediately ordered another round and almost dove into his. He was half finished before Jenny had taken two sips. Finally she spoke, softly, as if trying to justify why she was there infringing on his pain.

"I was on my way home, back to Washington, when I heard the news. I went to that terrible lounge and then they just announced . . ." Forest looked up at her from his drink and she stopped.

"I'm sure you must have cared for him very much," he said mechanically. Then he went back to his drink. Before Jenny could answer, the waitress appeared with more drinks. Forest handed her his empty glass and ordered another round. Jenny now had two glasses lined up in front of her. But the waitress didn't leave. She was staring at Forest.

"Say," she said, recognition in her voice, "aren't you Forest Hill, the weather guy? I watch you all the time. Could you give me an autograph for my daughter?" She pushed a cocktail napkin and a pencil in front of Forest. "Make it to Sally, please." Forest picked up the pencil and wrote, "To Sally, Sunny Days. Forest Hill," and handed it back. He had done it completely automatically. The waitress was beaming. "Thanks a load, Forest. I'll be right back with your drinks." She rushed off and Forest attacked his glass.

"I cared for your brother more than you can know, Forest. He and Valerie were like parents to me. I feel like they're the only family I have. Arthur was very good to me." Jenny could see that Forest was in trouble and she was trying to get him to talk. Forest didn't want to.

"Yeah, he was good to everybody," he mumbled. "Especially to me." He was staring into his glass, twirling the ice absently.

"You two had some fight the other night, though. What was that all about?" It seemed that Jenny was determined not to let him sit there and brood.

"It was about nothing, Jenny. Just some stupid thing that didn't matter then and certainly doesn't matter now." He looked up at her concerned face. Then suddenly he blurted. "We didn't even have a chance to make up. I never talked to him again . . . and he was on his way

133

here to see me and . . ." He raised his glass and tried to choke back his emotion.

"Hey, Forest! Sunny days this ain't. How 'bout some sun?" A drunk two tables away had recognized Forest and was shouting over to him and waving. By reflex, Forest looked over at the man, smiled, and waved back. Jenny leaned across the table to Forest.

"Look, this is insane. Why don't we get out of here and go someplace more private. I'd really like to talk to you some more." He could feel that she was trying to help, but Forest felt that nothing was going to help him at this moment except being alone.

"I'd really like to go home, Jenny. And there really isn't much more to say, is there?"

"Have you eaten dinner?"

"No, but . . ."

"I know, you're not hungry. Well, you have to eat. And if there's no one else at your place . . ." Forest let the question hang for a moment.

"No, there's no one else." She smiled.

"Then I'm going to cook you dinner. Come on." She stood up, and Forest remembered the stubborn streak he had seen in her at the party. Miss Jenny Wells, daughter of the general of the same name. What the hell, maybe it would be better not to be alone. Forest sighed, finished his drink, and threw some money on the table. Then he followed her out of the lounge. She was holding his hand again.

CHAPTER TWELVE

Jenny had led Forest through the terminal, onto the taxi line, into the taxi, and it wasn't until he had given the driver his address and they were on their way that she released her hold on him. She seemed to have evaluated their relative degrees of shock and pain and decided that she had more strength at the moment. They sat without having to talk, grateful, for once, for the famous New York cabbie's unstoppable monologue.

"You hear about the crash? They say the storm forced it down. What a tragedy. But if God had wanted us to fly, huh? Some rain. Who can figure it? You just can't figure the weather. It was a beautiful day and I was just driving along, and whoosh, down comes this flood from the sky. Right outta the blue. Listen, the Grand Central's all flooded and no traffic's gonna move through there tonight. You want I should go over to Queen's Boulevard? It's longer, but it'll probably be quicker. This goddamn storm is costing me a fortune."

Gradually, the driver wound down and concentrated on weaving his way through the snarled Queens traffic. As they neared the city, the storm seemed to be abating also. Finally Jenny turned to Forest and asked him the inevitable question.

"Why did the pilot try to land the plane in a storm like that? Why didn't he avoid it, fly around it? I mean, isn't that insane?" Forest stared straight ahead for a long time and then answered without turning to Jenny, as if the words were being wrenched out of him.

"As of six o'clock tonight, there was no storm on the radar scope. I don't think the pilot knew what hit him." They said nothing more until they reached Forest's apartment house on Riverside Drive. The rain had stopped. In fact, the streets were bone dry. It hadn't even rained in Manhattan.

CHAPTER THIRTEEN

Forest felt like a stranger when he entered his apartment. He felt as if he had been gone for a year. Everything seemed completely different to him, but it was only that he had changed since he left this morning. He was just seeing the world through new eyes.

He left Jenny sitting in the living room while he wandered around turning on lights, getting ice from the kitchen, and then mixing them both drinks. Jenny accepted hers without a word; she still needed it and she was still working on her first.

"I hope I'm not being too personal," she said with a smile, after taking a sip, "but your clothes look like they're soaking wet. Maybe you should change into something drier than a martini." Despite himself, Forest smiled too. Then he looked at himself in the mirror and frowned. He looked bedraggled, like a wet dog.

"By God, you're right. Be back in a minute." Forest went into the bathroom, stripped off his clothes, and threw them into a pile on the floor. He put his drink on the edge of the sink and stepped into the shower. The rush of hot water began to take away the chill in his bones, and now he could feel how tired his body was and where he ached.

Jenny leaned back and smiled when she heard the shower running. She didn't know when it had started, but she had begun to care about what happened to Forest Hill. She had seen his pain and had become concerned about him. There was something defenseless and vulnerable about the man, even if he was twice her age. And there was something else, something that attracted her in quite a different way.

Looking around the living room, it was clear to Jenny that there was no woman in his life, at least no one, permanent woman. The furniture was a melange of castoffs and utilitarian pieces; a modern steel and glass coffee table stood in front of an antique sofa that needed reupholstering. But what fascinated her were all the weather paraphernalia in the room. If his wife had taken all the furniture, she had certainly left him all his toys. At the end of the room, next to his desk, was an impressive array of what looked like very sophisticated equipment. There was an instrument panel surrounded by several strange-looking machines, and on the wall, a multifaced clock showing different time zones. But also scattered around the room was a wonderful collection of antiques. There were polished brass and dark wood thermometers and barometers and several beautiful but bizarre instruments for which Jenny couldn't imagine any use.

The walls were covered with maps and charts, aerial views of the earth, ancient maps of the world, and pictures showing weather. Jenny got up and went to look at them more closely. There were prints, lithographs, and a few oils, each depicting the effect of a storm on the sea, land, and on people by every kind of storm one could imagine. Jenny felt there was something gruesome and scary about this collection of destruction.

Over Forest's desk she found the only pictures in the room not related to weather. These were photographs of what must have been his parents, of him as a small boy, of him on his college swim team, and of him and Arthur. Jenny was peering closely at the picture of the two brothers when Forest returned. He was wearing a full-length, blue terrycloth robe, and with the hood over his head he looked like a monk. Jenny moved quickly toward him and away from the picture and its associations.

"I promised you dinner and dinner you shall have. Point me at the kitchen." She saw his eyes flick over to the picture and then back to her. Then he pointed over his shoulder and started walking toward his desk. He was standing looking at the picture when he heard Jenny call.

"Forest, this is outrageous. There is nothing in your refrigerator. How do you stay alive?"

"Like every other bachelor in the world. I

139

eat out. But there's a steak in the freezer. Take it out and let it defrost. I'm in no hurry to eat, if you aren't" Forest was sitting at one end of the long sofa, his hood pulled back, nursing his drink, by the time Jenny returned. She sat down at the other end and looked at him. There was a moment of awkwardness between them, of tension.

"I don't know if I should feel safe sitting here with a partially dressed stranger, Mr. Hill," Jenny said demurely.

"I would be glad to put my hood back up if you wish, Miss Wells," he answered seriously. Then they both laughed. Jenny smiled at him. She liked the way he looked with his hair tousled from the shower, and she could see in his eyes that he liked the way she looked. And he did. Suddenly they were comfortable with each other again.

"I was looking at your collection, Forest. You have a lot of beautiful things. But everything seems to be involved with the weather." Forest leaned back and put his arms on the back of the sofa. He looked around the room. What she had observed was true.

"First, let me say in my defense that I am a meteorologist and that some of the equipment here I use in my work. That panel over there is connected to instruments on the roof and lets me measure temperature, humidity, wind speed and direction, barometric pressure and rainfall. Those other two things are thermofax machines, which receive weather maps. The little one gives me satellite pictures every twenty minutes from twenty-two thousand miles up. And that one over there is a teletype machine. As for the rest of it, I have to admit that weather is also my hobby. It always has been. And I suppose when a man's business is also his hobby, you could call it an obsession." He smiled ruefully, admitting this character flaw.

"Never had any desire to do jigsaw puzzles? Or model airplanes?" Jenny was teasing him gently.

"Nope."

"How about sports? Golf? Bowling? I saw a picture of you on a swim team."

"Swimming was and is exercise for my body, so I still swim three or four times a week. Unfortunately, it doesn't do much for the mind, except waterlog it." Forest shook his head, sending droplets flying off his hair.

"How about women, Forest? Doesn't sex qualify?" Jenny was pursuing the banter relentlessly, yet there was an openness and sense of humor about the way she asked such personal questions that Forest found disarming. He found himself answering honestly.

"Women seem to be an area in which I haven't been too successful, judging by my marriage. And sex, well, I don't have anything against it, but it just couldn't ever be hobby material for me. I have a friend who uses it like that and I think he finds it very unsatisfying." Jenny smiled candidly.

"Well, it's nice to know you have nothing against it, anyway. So why weather? What's so

141

fascinating about it for you? Why do you care so much if it rains or not?" Now she was being perfectly serious. Forest could see that she really wanted to know and he was forced to formulate an answer because he wanted her to understand. He realized that he wanted her to understand him.

"I grew up on a farm in Iowa, Jenny. It wasn't big and my parents were always fighting to keep it going. The weather meant everything . . . how big the crop would be . . . or whether there would be any crop at all. A sudden frost could destroy us before we ever got started. A hail storm could wipe us out before we harvested. Believe me, we took the weather very seriously.

"And as I grew up and learned some history at school, I began to see that what was true for our little farm was also true for the whole world and all of mankind. I understand in my bones why the ancients worshipped weather gods . . . rain gods, lightning gods, thunder gods."

Forest looked at Jenny and saw that she understood. He went on, his enthusiasm growing. "Weather is the pond we live in. And what happens to the pond changes us, or makes us change ourselves. Of course they don't teach history like that, but that's how I saw it, and it made a deep impression on me." Forest stood up and looked back at Jenny to see if he was boring her. "Should I go on? I tend to get excited about this stuff and run off at the mouth." Jenny was watching him raptly. She

142

had taken off her shoes and had pulled her feet up under her on the couch.

"Please, I'd really like to hear this," she said. She meant it. A grin flashed across Forest's face, not his TV smile, but the real Forest; the excited, alive, caring combination of boy and man that Jenny had been catching glimpses of ever since she'd met him. Forest perched himself on the arm of a big leather chair, arranged his robe, and tried to organize the ideas and information that were surging through his mind.

"Basically," he began, sorting as he talked, "you can look at history and weather in two ways. There are major changes, like ice ages, that alter the face of the planet. Those are easy to see. But even little changes influence history." Jenny was nodding intelligently at Forest, her eyes sparkling, and he remembered that she was a student at Harvard. Maybe she would really understand. He went on.

"Take Louis the Sixteenth and Marie Antoinette for example. Everyone talks about the social unrest that had been brewing to form the revolution. But nobody explains that it was a drought that hurt the grain crops that caused the bread riots in Paris. It was the weather that did them in. And that's just one." He chuckled.

"Look at the American Revolution. You could say weather helped ignite that, too. Britain in the 1770s was going through a severe cold period. This hurt their crops and they were forced to import food. So when old Georgie needed more money to pay for it, the taxes in the Colonies went up and up and up until we rebelled." Forest looked as proud as if he had just written the Declaration of Independence, and Jenny wasn't about to do anything to burst his bubble.

Forest got up and started to walk as he talked, pointing to pictures on the wall as he made his points, and now Jenny began to see that what Forest had collected wasn't random, but rather a visual history of the effects of weather. He stopped in front of a daguerreotype of an old battle ship and stared at it for a moment.

"Our Civil War," he said turning back to Jenny, "might have been very different if not for the weather. The same cold period that helped start the Revolution was still plaguing England, and they were still dependent on imports. They got their cotton from us, or from the South to be specific. Well, about ten years before the Civil War the South began to show signs of unrest and the English got worried. So they started to develop an alternate source for cotton in Egypt. If the South had rebelled in 1850, which they almost did, they might have won. England would have intervened to save its cotton supply since the Egyptian cotton wasn't ready yet. When the South finally got around to declaring its independence in 1860, the cotton crisis was over. England had a supply from Egypt and that's why my name is not Beauregard."

Jenny laughed and then jumped right in. "I

notice that's the second American that was directly influenced by weather in Europe." Forest beamed at her in appreciation. She was quick and she was listening.

"And, of course, there's more." Forest went on. "The Allies were able to invade Normandy only because of a good break in the weather, while Hitler's invasion of Russia was thwarted by snow and cold that crippled his armies."

"And that's just what happened to Napoleon, isn't it?" Jenny added. Forest nodded.

"Twice. The weather got him twice. Once with snow in Russia, and then with rain at Waterloo." Forest peered at an inscription printed below an oil painting of rain-sodden French soldiers. "As Victor Hugo described it, 'A few drops of water . . . an unseasonable cloud crossing the sky, sufficed for the overthrow of a world.'" He looked at Jenny and she smiled back. Forest came and sat on the couch near her, not next to her, but not all the way at the other end.

"Do you hate me yet?" he asked.

"Hell, no," she snapped back. "At least you're intelligent and have some information to back up your case. And I do assume you have some other theories you haven't even told me yet." Forest looked at her sharply, suddenly sobered.

"Theories? Yeah, I sure do, or did until recently. But it doesn't really matter much now, does it?" He saw that his glass was empty and that Jenny had finally finished her drink, and he got up to get refills. But Jenny stopped his hand on her glass.

"I'll tell you what," she said. "You have another drink and I'll have a joint to keep you company." Her hand was still resting lightly on the back of his. "To tell you the truth, I don't usually drink that much." Forest turned his hand over and clasped her gently.

"I'll tell *you* what," he said smiling. "You have another drink with me and I'll share your joint, just to keep you company." Jenny nodded, and while Forest made the drinks she took a small vial of grass and a packet of rolling paper out of her purse and quickly and expertly rolled a thin cigarette.

Forest came back, set the drinks on the coffee table in front of them, and sat down close to her. He lit the joint for her with a lighter from the coffee table and watched her inhale the smoke. She passed him the cigarette and watched while he inhaled deeply. As he held the smoke down in his lungs, Forest gazed at her face, enjoying seeing her from so close. Her skin was clear and soft and looked eminently touchable.

They smoked slowly, passing the joint between them, and occasionally took sips of their drinks as their mouths got dry from the drug. When the cigarette got too small to hold without burning their fingers, Jenny dropped it in the ashtray. Irrationally, it pleased Forest that she hadn't taken a roach clip out of her purse like some hippy chick. It made him feel warm toward her, and he knew the marijuana was taking effect.

Forest leaned back and put his feet up on the

coffee table, letting the gentle waves rise and fall inside his body. Outside the window he could see the Hudson flowing and on it the moving lights of barges and tugs moving up and down the river. Across the Hudson he could see the lights of Jersey, twinkling brightly, night masking the ugliness and leaving only the comforting spots of brightness. It was a sight that always gave him pleasure and sometimes even gave him peace.

A tune floated into Forest's head and he began to whistle it under his breath. After a moment, Jenny started to giggle. It was an infectious sound but Forest, in an attack of paranoia, quickly turned to see if she was laughing at him. Her face crinkled merrily and the giggles rose in pitch, as if she couldn't stop herself. She seemed to be trying to purse her lips to whistle back at him.

"I'm sorry," he said, "I seem to do that sometimes. A tune comes into my head and I whistle." Jenny shook her head as the rush subsided.

"It's not that you were whistling, Forest. It's *what* you were whistling. Tell me, can you name that tune?" Forest thought for a moment.

"Of course I can." He half sang the words to her. "Don't know why . . . there's no sun up in the sky . . . stormy weather." Jenny started to giggle again.

"Don't you see, Forest? That's a song about the weather." Forest saw, and also saw that

147

she wasn't laughing at him. He felt a little giddy and high and decided that she was right, it was funny. He decided to go with it.

"Perhaps it would surprise you to know," he said with mock seriousness, "how many songs there are about the weather." Extending one arm, he struck a pose, and in a totally off-key but happy voice sang:

> *I'm singin' in the rain,*
> *just singin' in the rain.*
> *What a glorious feeling,*
> *I'm happy again.*

Forest stopped and looked at Jenny, and then another song popped into his head and he sang:

> *A foggy day in London Town*
> *had me low, had me down. . . .*

Jenny could contain herself no longer. "You're right," she said gleefully. "You can't sing and you have a lousy voice, but you are right. How about," and she sang in a clear, sweet voice:

> *Rainy days and Mondays*
> *always get me down. . . .*

Forest felt a surge of happiness. If talking about the weather was fun, singing about it was heaven. He stood up and did a small softshoe as he sang:

Grab your coat and get your hat.
Leave your troubles on the doorstep.
Just direct your feet
to the sunny side of the street.

Jenny could hardly wait for him to finish. Before the last word was out of his mouth, she was singing:

Little darling,
it's been a long cold lonely winter . . .
Here comes the sun.
Here comes the sun.
And I say it's all right.

The excitement was infectious and the challenge of the game was making them higher. Forest sank to one knee, clasped both hands to his heart, and, in a terrible imitation of Al Jolson, warbled:

The sun shines east,
the sun shines west,
but who knows where
the sun shines best?

They both burst out laughing simultaneously, and when it subsided Forest waited for Jenny to answer. He realized that they were talking to each other in code. Jenny understood it too, and it was she who changed the tone. She sang softly now, and with emotion.

Sunshine on my shoulders makes me happy.
Sunshine in my eyes can make me cry ...

Forest got off his knees and sat on the couch next to Jenny. He looked into her eyes and half whispered:

I'm as restless as a willow in a windstorm. ...

and she whispered back:

The answer, my friend, is blowin' in the wind.
The answer is blowin' in the wind.

They looked at each other, so close to one another, and then Forest looked down.

I'm always chasing rainbows,
watching clouds drifting by. ...

It was a question and they both knew it. As Jenny's voice answered him, he felt a tingle of expectation unlike anything he had ever experienced before.

Don't let the sun go down on me.
Although I search myself,
it's always someone else I see. ...

As she sang, Forest's head rose until he was looking again into her deep-blue eyes. They never wavered for a moment. Forest's heart was pounding, but it was the reeling in his

150

mind that surprised him. This beautiful twenty-year-old girl-woman had managed to reach out to him, touch him, and make him want to touch her. She saw him, knew him, and liked him for who he was.

Forest felt something open in him that he hadn't known still existed. He reached out with both hands, and Jenny put both of her hands in his. There was no shock of electricity, but rather it was as if they were old friends, so exactly did their hands fit. Forest spoke now to Jenny, slowly and softly:

> *I'm gonna love you*
> *like nobody's loved you,*
> *come rain or come shine.*

And Jenny responded, also speaking slowly and softly:

> *You are the sunshine of my life.*
> *That's why I'll always be around.*

Then, together, they leaned forward and kissed, gently at first, their lips just touching, still holding hands, and then pressing closer toward one another, deeper and deeper, as they let their arms circle each other and hold. There was no urgency, only an exquisite sensation of completeness and an anticipation of what was to come that they both seemed willing to prolong.

Their lips parted reluctantly and Forest took Jenny's face in his hands, looking at her, dev-

151

ouring her, and then nibbling at her eyes and ears, drinking in her scent, rubbing his face against her softness.

Jenny's hand stole into Forest's robe and rubbed his chest, stroking, making his nipples hard. And then her other hand went under the cloth and explored the warm flesh. She opened the top of his robe and buried her face against his chest, drawing him to her by linking her arms around him. Forest breathed Indiana sun in her hair and closed his arm around her again. It was time, and they had time, and the world was spinning gently in a slow and perfect waltz.

Forest reached down and slid his arm under Jenny's legs and lifted her and himself into the air. She was so tiny. He could hear her cooing as she nuzzled his neck and he carried her to the bedroom. He put her down on the bed softly, almost afraid to break the contact, but Jenny wanted him now as much as he knew he wanted her. She unbuttoned her blouse, watching him watch her with delight, and by the glow of the river lights he saw that she wasn't wearing a bra. Her breasts were large and rounded curves that arced into his reaching hands. Her nipples rose under his fingers and he heard her suck in her breath.

Then, in a scramble, she had torn off her skirt and panties and Forest was free of his robe and they lay side by side kissing and touching, rubbing each other's precious flesh, warming themselves with each other, exploring and teasing, until every inch that separated them was too much.

Forest slid slowly and easily into her living warmth and waited while the ripple of ecstasy at their joining passed through their bodies, and then, as if they were one, as if they had always known each other's tempo, they danced, entwined, matching and opposing, until the music, the pounding of their hearts, the coursing blood, crashed with them into an explosion of release. And even after it was over for him, Forest could feel wave after wave still moving through her, and he held her as they subsided.

Jenny began to laugh and it was a sound that Forest had never heard before. It was pure joy and contentment, abandon and release, and pleasure at the perfection of being alive. And Forest laughed, too, because he couldn't help himself, and because it felt so good. And then, to his surprise and delight, he discovered that he was still hard and wanting, and still inside her, and he could feel her wanting him, reaching from the inside to hold and caress him. So they made love again. And then, once more, again.

Finally, they lay quietly next to each other, only their fingers touching, the tips slowly circling. For Forest the experience had been cataclysmic because it had been more than sexual. A whole emotional side of his nature that he had shut down and hidden had suddenly exploded into life. The aches caused by Selina hadn't disappeared, but now there was a positive flow to balance them. As much as it frightened him, Forest knew he was fully alive again.

And as he lay there, another song rose to the surface, until he could hear the words in his head.

> *Gone with the wind,*
> *just like a leaf that has blown away.*
> *Gone with the wind.*

He tried to put it out of his mind, but it wouldn't go. Goddamn Arthur, he thought to himself, getting himself killed like that. And then, the dam broke and Forest began to sob. Jenny lay there watching him, letting her own tears run down her face.

TUESDAY

JULY 11

PORT CLINTON, OHIO

Eliot Giroux raced his wife Margaret and his twin daughters Elise and Marielle down to the end of the dock. Somehow they all arrived in a tie, out of breath and full of enthusiasm for the day they would sail their new 21-foot cruiser-racer. A spring of sailing rented boats along the shores of Lake Erie was enough to make Eliot realize the need for a boat of their very own.

Elliot took the christening step aboard. She was a compact little craft: dinette, galley, toilet, tip-up rudder, retractable swing keel, and it would sleep all four of them. A damn good buy for $1,630, he thought.

The brisk but pleasant wind left Margaret's cheeks tinged with color as the two fourteen-year-olds lowered the picnic basket, filled down to their dad.
mostly with lemonade and hard-boiled eggs,
Soon they were busy preparing for some sort of Junior Americas Cup as Eliot untied ropes

and pointed and shouted instructions to everyone. The girls giggled with excitement as they hoisted the jib. Eliot raised the mainsail and both boat and crew jumped to attention. With as much enthusiasm as a family of four can muster, they were under way. Margaret, a natural romatic, couldn't help wish they were this happy all the time. After all, hadn't she and Eliot always worked out their problems?

They were too lost in their own thoughts and the spice of the day to notice the low line of billowing clouds hugging the horizon over Toledo. Nor did they notice the gradual heightening of the swells and the steady spray from the tops of the climbing waves.

The squall line did not give them any clue that the weather had changed, but then the mainsheet tore out of Eliot's hands with such fury that he would have sworn that a large hand had wrenched it away. They all ducked successfully as the boat heeled downwind and the boom jibed, making its attack on the entire family. Eliot regained control of the mainsheet, but there was suddenly a sense of panic among them.

The winds, gusting irrationally with cross sheers of about 50 miles per hour, brought no rain but shoved the boat through the water with such a force that its wake looked like that of a high-speed power boat. All four leaned far out over the upwind rail for counter balast. The tips of the waves leaped up like angry tongues trying to pull the boom down into the foaming mouth of the lake turned ocean.

The boiling, twisting, almost reachable gray-black clouds were now directly overhead, climbing in and out of one another with such ferocious unreality that the Giroux family froze with fear just when they should have been trimming the sheets. Suddenly the mast rose to its full vertical height, and the boat shifted back on an even keel. Eliot breathed a sigh of relief as the boat plunged forward into the trough between two waves. In what looked like slow motion to the Girouxs, but was actually only a half second, the 21-foot cruiser-racer buried its bow under a wave while the strength of the following wind ripped the stern out of the water. The mast, and of course the entire boat, pitchpoled forward over the bow, flipping completely upside down.

Fortunately they were all wearing life preservers, so their bodies were eventually washed ashore near Ashtabula, to be identified by next of kin.

It was reported in the papers the following day that the north-northeast winds tilted Lake Erie's surface so much that the difference in the water level at Toledo, on the west end, and Buffalo, on the east end, was 16 feet.

CHAPTER FOURTEEN

Forest was awake, but afraid to open his eyes. He was afraid that it had all been a dream, a hallucination caused by the drinks and pot and misery. He didn't want to open his eyes and find Jenny gone.

She wasn't. Her face was laying on the pillow next to him and her blue eyes were looking directly into his. She was smiling at him and Forest warmed as if someone had just turned on the sun.

"Hello," she said. "I was watching you sleep. You take a long time to wake up." For some reason, Forest decided to tell her the truth.

"I was afraid you wouldn't be here." Jenny crinkled her nose.

"Fat chance, buddy. I'm not finished with you yet." Jenny snuggled closer to him and kissed him sweetly on his lips. Forest closed his eyes and reached out for her, but she was already gone, burrowing down under the covers.

"Hey, where are you? What are you doing?"

he asked, lifting the covers and looking for her. She hadn't gotten there yet.

"Just looking around," came her muffled reply. "I lost something last night and I know it's here somewhere." And then she had gotten there. Forest could feel her warm breath on him and then her fingers softly stroking what didn't need to be urged into readiness, and then her wet lips and curling tongue around him. He started to move, to reach down for her, but she reached up and pushed him back flat. Forest let his body relax and closed his eyes. He gave himself to the pleasure she was giving him and it was glorious. He only hoped that it would never end, at least not for a long time. And Jenny seemed to feel the same way. She was drawing on him slowly, caressing carefully, not accelerating the pace or intensity, just enjoying hearing him begin to moan.

At that moment the doorbell rang. Jenny didn't stop. The bell rang again.

"Oh, goddamnit," Forest half yelled and half moaned. Jenny stopped for a second.

"If that's the phone, ignore it," she said, and then she started on him again.

"If it was the phone I would, Jenny. It's the goddamn fucking door." The bell rang again and Jenny's head popped up from under the covers. Her hair was tousled, her eyes were sparkling, her breasts were inviting, and Forest was throbbing.

"Well, answer the door then and get rid of whoever it is. I'm not going anywhere 'till you get back." Forest got out of bed and

159

wrapped his robe around him, trying to mask his erection. He wasn't very successful and Jenny laughed at the sight of his pole pushing against the robe.

"You will hurry, won't you?" she teased. Forest hurried. The bell was ringing again when he opened the door to face an irritated mailman.

"The doorman says you're in, so you're in. Whatya do, sleep all day? I mean, some of us gotta work, you know." Forest didn't want to discuss his sleeping habits and he didn't want an argument. He tried to be polite.

"Sorry, didn't hear the door. What can I do for you?" The man held out a letter and a form to sign.

"I got a registered letter here. Just sign this. Right here on this line." Forest took the pen and signed, took the letter, and shut the door. He looked at the return address and suddenly the paper was on fire, burning his hands.

Forest didn't know what to do. He held the letter gingerly, staring at it as he walked back into the bedroom. Half of him was afraid to open it, the other half afraid not to. Jenny hadn't moved, but she could see at once that something was wrong. Not only had Forest's excitement visibly disappeared but he also seemed to be in a trance. Forest sat down on the bed next to her, now not even seeing her breasts or remembering what had been happening when they were interrupted. He was just grateful that she was there, that he wasn't alone.

He carefully placed the letter on the bed between them. "It's from Arthur," he said slowly. "He mailed it yesterday." Now Jenny understood. Her mouth rounded into an 'oh', but she didn't say it. They sat in silence, staring at the letter.

"Well?" Jenny finally said.

"Well, I'm not sure I want to open it."

"Do you want me to do it?" Forest looked up at her sharply, but he could see that she was really trying to help. He shook his head.

"No, it's my mess. I should be able to handle it." He picked up the letter and sat holding it for a moment. Jenny reached out and put a hand on the back of his neck and squeezed gently, massaging the tension. Forest didn't shake her off. It felt good.

Forest tore open the end of the envelope and pulled out the folded paper inside. Jenny had slid closer to look over his shoulder, and the warmth of her body against the goose bumps on his skin made him feel hot and cold at the same time. He unfolded the paper carefully and they both stared in amazement at the contents.

It was a photostat of a blueprint, with a note attached to it. The note said:

Dear Hothead,

After having cocktails with you on Friday night, I did some checking and I think I've stumbled onto something. There is a weather program, code-named "Thursday Group," going on to the tune of $120 million. What's bizarre is that I've never heard of it and neither has anyone else I've been able to talk to. At those prices there ought to be an explanation, so I'm digging a little deeper. Be in touch if I come up with anything more.

Meanwhile, maybe you can decipher this blueprint—it was the only thing in the file.

Love,

Arthur

P.S. You may not be as stupid as you look.

They were the most exciting words Forest had ever read. Leave it to Arthur to reach out his helping hand, even from beyond death. He folded back the note and they stared at the copy of the blueprint.

"What is it?" Jenny whispered in his ear.

"I'll be damned if I know. It looks like some kind of weather chamber, maybe a cloud chamber, but not like anything I've ever seen before."

"And," Jenny added, "if I'm not mistaken, those handwritten notes look like they're in Russian." Forest nodded in agreement and continued to stare at the paper. Finally Jenny broke his concentration. "Forest, how come Arthur mailed this to you when he was coming to see you the same day?"

It was a good question. Forest picked up the envelope and looked at the postmark again. The time registered on it was 9:27 A.M. "He must have mailed this in the morning and I guess he didn't decide to come to New York until later in the day. The message he left with Mickey came in around three o'clock. Maybe he found something else." Forest's temples were pulsing with excitement, but Jenny was plainly confused.

"What does it all mean, Forest?"

"It means," he said vehemently, "that I'm not crazy." He stood up, waving the paper in his hand, and looked down at Jenny. "It means that my brother did believe in me. It means that my theory isn't as crazy as people kept telling me it was. And it means that I'm not finished with this thing, not by a long shot." There was life in Forest's eyes again and his body seemed to fill with energy. Jenny didn't know why it excited her, but it did.

"Well, are you going to let me in on the secret? Are you finally going to tell me your theory?" Forest looked at her nude body and intelligent face for a moment, considering, and then decided.

"Sure I am. Why not? Maybe I can get one Wells on the home team. Do you have a lipstick?"

"Of course I do. In my purse in the living room." Forest reached down and grabbed her hand and pulled her to her feet. Then he led her, still naked, into the living room, and while Jenny rummaged through her purse, he went to the stereo and put on a record. Jenny was mystified, but also willing to let Forest do it his way. So far his way had always been more interesting.

163

"What I'm going to demonstrate to you," he said, taking the lipstick and unscrewing its red tip, "is one of the basic principles of weather on our planet. It's called the Coriolis Effect, and what it shows is the wind deflection caused by the earth's rotation."

Forest pointed at the hole in the center of the record. "This is the North Pole, and this," he said, pointing at the rim of the record, "is the equator." He began to turn the record slowly, counterclockwise. "And this is the direction in which the earth spins in the Northern Hemisphere." He put the lipstick at the hole. "Now, if a wind blows straight south from here, watch what happens." Forest drew a straight line from the north pole to the equator, but by the time the lipstick had reached the edge of the record, Jenny could plainly see that it had become a curved arc, bending to the right.

"The direction of the drift is reversed in the Southern Hemisphere, of course, but the principle is the same. The earth's spin always causes a drift in wind." Forest gave her back the lipstick. Jenny looked at it sadly; it was ruined. "Do you understand this so far?"

"I understand the idea," she said, heading for the couch. "But I don't get the theory yet." Forest smiled at her impatient intelligence.

"The first part of my theory isn't theory, it's fact. I've collected data on a large number of incidents where winds and clouds didn't follow the laws of the Coriolis Effect. They moved in

164

straight lines, moved in the wrong direction, or didn't move at all"

To Forest's surprise, Jenny didn't bat an eyelash. "Why do you think this is happening?" she asked. She was sitting curled on the couch, like a kitten, and the sun made her skin glow pink. Forest went and sat beside her.

"I think it's happening because the military has been doing weather experiments and has unbalanced our system. There's no other rational explanation. I told Arthur my theory Friday night and that's what caused the fight. And then yesterday afternoon I went down to Washington and saw your father, with all my charts and data." Jenny looked shocked.

"You saw my dad? Why didn't you tell me? What did he say?"

"Your father said to forget it and chalk it up to coincidence. He said he loved you and to send his regards to Arthur. And I didn't tell you because it didn't come up until now. But don't you understand, that's why this letter from Arthur is so important. It means that there is something going on that's bigger than anything I had imagined. And if he thought it was worth pursuing, then it's worth pursuing." Forest reflected for a moment. "I was going to drop it and give up, you know?"

Jenny took his hand. "I got that feeling last night. But what are you going to do? If Daddy says there's nothing . . . and he is Weather at the Pentagon." Forest wasn't listening, he was thinking. Then he made up his mind.

"I'll tell you what I'm going to do. There's a

man, a Professor Karapov, who was an old friend of Arthur's and mine. In fact, he was my advisor in graduate school. The university's only an hour outside Washington. After the funeral I'm going to look him up and get him to translate this diagram for me." He looked at Jenny. "At least it's a start."

"Yes," she agreed, "at least it's a start." She grinned wickedly at him. "But you're not leaving right now, are you?"

"No," Forest answered, not sure what she had in mind.

"Good. It's nice and warm on the couch and I think you're slightly overdressed for the occasion." Jenny leaned forward and reached for the belt of Forest's robe. "Let me see," she said seriously, "where was I?"

WEDNESDAY

JULY 12

PINE BLUFFS, NEBRASKA

Brightwater sat cross-legged on a flange of rock overlooking the entire valley. Snow-white hair trailed gracefully over his shoulders, framing the wrinkled proud profile of a Pawnee elder. His six-year-old grandson William, as he was now called, sat beside him, and they both glowed as the sun licked the top of the surrounding landscape before it's customary dissappearance.

They had been sitting for the better part of a half hour, the old man absorbing all there was to nature, the boy trying to understand.

"Can we go fishing tomorrow, Grandfather?"

The old Indian did not change his gaze but answered after apparent thought. "It will rain tomorrow."

The boy glanced up at the single star just barely visible in the darkening blue sky and then squinted over at his grandfather. Wrinkling his nose, he said. "The weather report on the radio didn't say anything about rain."

The white head turned slowly and even before their eyes met, the boy knew he had trespassed on a generation. He steadied himself for the rebuke, but then, in an effort to ward it off, asked, "How can you tell it's going to rain tomorrow, Grandfather?"

"Because I know," and even as he said it, he knew it was not enough. "Have I not told you about the Great Spirit who lives on top of the roof of the sky?"

"Yes, Grandfather, his voice is the thunder we hear in the clouds."

Brightwater knew his grandson loved the old stories and he was proud William remembered them. "And the great Thunderbird is always followed by a flock of many smaller birds."

William smiled and interrupted. "The beating of their wings causes the rumbling we hear after every thunderclap."

Brightwater smiled inwardly. "Have I not told you about the powers that the Great Chief Tirawa gave to all his other gods? That he sent Shakuru, the sun, to the east to yield light and warmth?"

William interrupted again. "And Pah, the moon, to the west to light the night." Indeed, he had told him many times. Each time, however, the stories had a different purpose. And William sensed that, if not the purpose.

Dusk had settled quickly on this summer's eve and the stars turned on their lights in rapid succession. Brightwater pointed to the evening star shining in the west and looked at his grandson, who responded accordingly.

"The Bright Star," William said, beaming, "mother and creator of all beings."

"And the Big Star in the morning?" Brightwater asked.

"He is the warrior who stays in the east and guards over his people to make sure no one is left behind in their journey to the west."

"Good, and the first star of the evening is in the north, the Pole Star."

William looked up and nodded. "And in the south," he pointed over his shoulder without turning, "is the Star of the Spirits. Tirawa then placed another star in between each of the four Bright Stars and it was their job to support the sky. When all this was done, Tirawa spoke to the evening star. Brightwater closed his eyes and somehow changed his inflection. "I will send you winds and clouds and lightning and thunder, and you will plant them in the heavenly garden, where they shall become human beings, and I shall cover them in buffalo robes and they shall wear moccasins on their feet." William never ceased to be mesmerized by the haunting, knowing quality of his grandfather's voice. "So you see," Brightwater opened his eyes and looked directly at William, "the Great Spirit is in all of us. We are the wind and the rocks and the fishes. We may look different, but we are all Tirawa's family, and if you listen very, very carefully, you can understand their language." Brightwater turned back to the moonlit valley. "You can hear the

169

wind whispering to the trees and the trees talking to the rocks. The rocks then speak to the streams and the streams babble to the grass, who gives the message to the birds, who fly up and sing the story to the clouds."

"But what do they say, Grandfather?"

The old man's wrinkles parted to form the first smile of the day, as he raised himself into a standing position. "They say it will rain tomorrow."

And it did.

CHAPTER FIFTEEN

It was a large throng that stood sweltering at Arlington National Cemetery that Wednesday afternoon, a tribute to Arthur's popularity. Forest, standing between Valerie and Jenny, listened as the chaplain mouthed platitudes about loss, dust to dust, and strangely, felt nothing. For him, Arthur wasn't in that flag-draped box. He was long since gone, and now he was everywhere. And certainly part of him was now in Forest and in the mission to which he had dedicated himself.

The mourners, by some instinctive protocol, had split themselves into two groups on either side of the grave, the military on one side and the civilians on the other. Every now and then, Forest caught General Wells's eye and was struck by the amount of hostility the man was generating. Could it be that he resented Forest's being there with Jenny? Forest was also surprised to see Babyface there, but he could never quite catch his eye. The biggest surprise, however, was that Professor Karapov had come to the funeral. Forest had spotted him earlier, several rows back, and was shocked by his appearance. The man had become a shadow of the vital personality Forest had known, and looked haggard and drawn.

Forest once again darted a sideways glance at Valerie to see how she was holding up, but her strength was amazing. Her back was straight, her face impassive, and she seemed, like Forest, to be waiting for the ritual to be over and to get on with it, whatever *it* would be for her. He at least had a purpose—an involvement to dull his pain—and he felt he was in a partnership with his brother. But Forest wondered what emotional legacy Arthur had left Valerie to sustain her now. She had no children, and Arthur's career had been her life. What would she do now? And what, except Arthur's spirit, was holding her up like this now?

Finally it was over; the chaplain had finished and closed his black book, the guns had been fired, the box had been lowered into the ground, and the sod had been sprinkled. How quickly a man's long life had been packed away. Now the exodus began, orderly and polite, but certainly as quickly as possible; graveside was nowhere to linger and nowhere to chat. Forest let Valerie be led in the direction of her limousine and, keeping Jenny by his side, he searched out Dr. Karapov.

The old man—and this was the first time Forest had thought of him in this way—seemed distant at first. His greeting was awkward and formal and there was no bear hug from him, as there had been the last time they'd met. Forest attributed it to the funeral, and introduced Jenny.

"Dr. Karapov, I'd like you to meet Jenny Wells." Karapov smiled at Jenny, his eye for a pretty girl seeming to overcome whatever other strain he was feeling.

"I am, of course, pleased to meet you, my dear, despite the . . . circumstances. Any friend of Forest—and so attractive—is always a pleasure." He bowed slightly, but didn't kiss her hand. The flow of the crowd was moving toward the long line of automobiles and they let themselves move with it. All around him, Forest saw friends of Arthur and Valerie, people who recognized him and nodded sympathetically, but none of them approached him to offer condolences. It was as if Arthur's death was Valerie's loss alone, and he was just part of the supporting cast. Very strange, he thought to himself, is a brother less than a wife?

The crowd began to thin as they neared the cars, and Forest could see General Wells and Babyface coming toward them purposefully. At the moment, the general looked like an anxious parent wanting to reclaim his little girl. Sorry, old buddy, Forest thought maliciously, the damage is already done; I've already penetrated the lines and infiltrated the troops.

"Mr. Hill," the general was puffing slightly, "allow me to offer my condolences." Forest nodded. "I see you've met my daughter again," the general went on, "and apparently you didn't repel her quite as much as you thought." Jenny shot him a look of pure venom, but Forest ignored the barb.

"General, I'd like you to meet Professor Karapov, an old friend of the family."

"We're acquainted," the general growled. "How are you, Karapov?" The two men shook hands stiffly.

"Good, General," Karapov answered somewhat nervously, "but very sad. Such a sad occasion." The general squinted at him.

"Sad? It's a fucking tragedy, that's what it is. Sorry, Jenny." The general reached out his arm and wrapped it around Jenny's shoulders. "Let me give you a ride back into town, okay, baby?" From the strength of his grip on her, Forest thought she really didn't have much choice. She looked up at Forest with anger burning in her eyes and Forest could see her jaws moving from clenching her teeth. He winked at her.

"Good idea. Why don't you go with your dad. I wanted to have a word with Professor Karapov anyway. I'll call you later." Jenny winked back, leaving the general bristling at their intimacy. He nodded curtly at Karapov and Forest and turned away, almost carrying Jenny along with him. Babyface turned and followed them. He hadn't even blinked at Forest.

Forest watched them go for a moment and then took Karapov's arm. "Let me walk you to your car, Professor. It's been such a long time since we've seen each other." Forest wasn't letting go of Karapov, nor was he giving him a chance to talk. He knew what he wanted. "How are things at the university? So much must have changed since I was there."

"Yes, Forest," Karapov answered wearily. "There is so much that is different, you wouldn't recognize it. You must come and visit me one day and I'll show you around. We can have a nice long chat." They had reached the professor's ancient car. Forest knew he was being crude, but he bulled ahead.

"You know, Professor, I'd like to do that. I don't have a car here and I've really nothing else to do, so how about now?"

"Now?" Karapov seemed stunned.

"Sure," Forest answered smoothly. "It's a nice afternoon. I'll drive down with you and then take a bus back. You don't mind, do you?"

"Of course not, Forest, my boy." The professor suddenly became jovial. "I'd be delighted by your company and Irena will be overjoyed to see you. You know how much she always doted on you, like you were one of her children."

Forest helped Karapov into the car, on the passenger side. "I'll drive, Professor. Just wait a minute while I tell Valerie where I'm going, and we'll be on our way." Karapov blinked his agreement, but seemed to be a little overwhelmed by the speed at which all this was happening. In the distance there was a faint rumble of thunder. They both looked up at the cloudless sky.

"Strange weather we've been having," Forest said evenly, "don't you think, Professor?"

CHAPTER SIXTEEN

They had been driving almost an hour, and although it had been ten years since Forest had last visited the university, he was still able to drive by reflex. The single rumble of thunder they had heard at the funeral had grown into a symphony of bass drums and seemingly out of nowhere storm clouds had formed. They were driving directly into them.

The conversation had been desultory at first, but Forest had kept at it and finally the old man began to chatter happily, reminiscing about the old days, complaining about the changes at the university, and anticipating his wife's delight at seeing Forest. But there was a nervousness to Karapov's manner. His hands wouldn't stay still in his lap and kept leaping about, picking at the lint on his suit, clasping the other hand, and then leaping out again. Forest watched him out of the corner of his eye as he drove and wondered what had aged him so and what kind of worry had given him that haggard, tired look.

By the time they reached towering Hamilton Dam and could see the once tiny but now sprawling university town, it was pouring. Rain, rain, go away, Forest thought to himself, get out of my life for a while.

"Forest, if you don't mind, stop in front of Calder Hall." Forest hadn't been listening. "Stop just over there, by that big building. There's something I have to do. It will only take a minute." Forest pulled the car over in front of the steps and watched the professor hurry through the rain, his slight limp slowing him down. And then he noticed that there was a sentry box outside the building and that there were two armed soldiers guarding the entrance. That, Forest thought to himself, is very strange. Forest sat drumming his fingers on the steering wheel and wondered what the hell they had in that building that warranted armed guards.

But before Forest had much time to ponder the mystery, he saw the professor hurrying out of the building. True to his word, he had been brief. Forest noticed that he was now clad in an unstylish black raincoat. Karapov pried open the door and slid into the car, seemingly oblivious to the fact that the water streaming off his head had turned his sparse gray hair into a tangled mop.

"Just the thing, Forest," he exclaimed happily. "I remembered that I had left my raincoat in my office and," he winked
178

conspiratorily at Forest, "you know how women can be. Irena would have been so worried about my health that she would have bored you to death tonight with her concern." Forest didn't bother to point out that the professor had soaked himself needlessly getting the coat, or that his head was now, indeed, sopping wet. His eyes filled with affection as he gazed at one of the truly eccentric scientists he had ever known, and yet a man who had maintained his warmth, concern, and friendship for those he loved.

"Home then, is it, Professor?" Forest turned the key and started the car.

"Ah yes, my dear boy," Karapov sighed. "Home."

CHAPTER SEVENTEEN

The Karapovs lived in a beautifully restored eighteenth-century house on a quiet, tree-lined street. As Forest pulled into the driveway, a wave of nostalgia came over him. How many times he had visited here as a student, working out problems on his thesis with the professor and being comforted and mothered by Irena when he was troubled. There was a warmth coming from the house that shone out into the night, and even the heavy rain couldn't obscure it.

As she always did, using some kind of sixth sense, Irena greeted them at the door. She was a plump woman with bright rosy cheeks, and she looked like a caricature of a Russian peasant. But her darting eyes missed nothing; she knew her husband and had been protecting him from the world for many years. She was, of course, dressed in a crisp white apron, and Forest wondered, absurdly, whether she wore it to bed.

Irena's face lit up with genuine delight when she saw Forest and she held his face tenderly in her hands before kissing him on both cheeks. She murmured condolences into his ear as she held him tightly for a moment. Then she saw the professor and began clucking like a mother hen. She quickly took his raincoat and hung it on the wooden rack behind the door. Karapov accepted her fussing without complaining, but he barely had time to put his keys down on the Philadelphia high-style stand before she hurried him off to dry his head. Forest stared at the professor's key ring and smiled seeing that he still carried the talisman of the ivory white chess knight. Then Forest inhaled the familiar odor of the house and felt himself relax.

As he walked into the living room he could hear Irena upstairs, scolding the professor for getting his head wet, and he smiled. Forest looked around the room and saw that nothing had changed. When the Karapovs had emigrated from Russia in the 1950s they had embraced Americana with gusto. Maybe it was their excitement and delight at this beautiful, different furniture, or maybe it was a way then to combat the wave of McCarthyism that was sweeping the country, but they had acquired a wonderful collection of antiques. And because they had started collecting before it became fashionable, what they had was probably now worth a fortune. Forest was pleased to know that his old professor would never starve. He walked slowly across the hooked rugs covering the wide plank floors and ran his fingers over the scrollboard on the Chippendale highboy.

"Forgive me for leaving you alone, dear boy, but Irena . . ." Karapov burst into the room and gave Forest a little shrug of helplessness. "What would you like to drink? A little vodka, eh?" The professor rubbed his hands together and chortled, as if this was their little secret.

"A little vodka, Professor, and a lot of ice," Forest answered, completing the ritual. Karapov scurried into the kitchen and Forest wandered over to an oil painting by Albert Bierstadt. It was titled "Beach Scene," but it mostly showed clouds. It was eerie how they seemed to be moving.

"Always the meteorologist, Forest. You see, it is inevitable how we are attracted to it." Karapov had prepared a tray with ice, two glasses, and a bottle of Stolnychya, still frosted from having been stored in the freezer. He set the tray on a low table between two soft chairs, sank into the cushions of one of them, and gestured to Forest to take the other. Then he began making the drinks, concentrating as carefully as if he were performing a laboratory experiment. Forest leaned back and watched him with affection. Remembering the past, Forest knew that if they weren't careful they would kill the bottle before dinner was served. Irena had disappeared as usual, and wouldn't intrude until she had created a mound of succulent food.

Karapov handed Forest a crystal glass and

then clinked his own against it. They drank, and then the professor passed a hand over his face as if to wipe away some sadness. "To Arthur," he said finally. They clinked again and drank, stillness filling the room. Forest saw that it was up to him to change the mood. He wanted to ask the professor some questions and show him the blueprint, but he didn't want it to appear obvious why he had come. So he decided to edge into the subject of weather slowly, knowing full well that Karapov's passion would carry the momentum until the right moment.

"I know you must think I'm out of touch, Professor, doing a TV show instead of pure research, but I'm not. I still keep up with the journals. In fact, I just read a fascinating article by Bryson and Kutzbach on the cooling theory."

"Ah yes," Karapov nodded, delighted to talk about his favorite subject, "from Wisconsin. They've done a sixteen-hundred-year analysis of the weather that is, in my opinion, unfortunately accurate. The fourteen cases of cooling they cite show a remarkable consistency in pattern—a maximum temperature drop within forty years of inception and the variation for return between seventy and a hundred and eighty years." Karapov swirled the ice in his glass and stared at the cubes. "There seems to be little doubt that we are on the verge of a little ice age." He looked at Forest with a challenge in his eyes.

"Forest, if history still intrigues you, as

much as it did when you were my most brilliant student, you will remember the last little ice age we had and its devastating effects." The text flashed in front of Forest's eyes.

"Sixteen hundred to 1850." He smiled as he remembered trying to explain the little ice age to Jenny, and where that discussion had led. "Northern Europe had winter weather for most of the year. The Russian steppes were covered with snow year round. Crop failures everywhere. And plague. And the absense of monsoons almost devastated China, India, and the Phillipines." Karapov acknowledged his accuracy with a silent toast and a healthy slug of vodka. He looked at Forest sternly, tilting his head and wagging his finger for emphasis.

"But you must remember that in 1850 the total population of the world was only a billion people. We are now four billion." Karapov paused and poured them each another full tumbler of vodka. "There is no way our present agriculture can support these four billion people under the climatic conditions you have just described. So we are cooked, eh? Or rather, frozen." He broke into a laugh that would have sounded ghoulish had Forest not understood how ferociously Karapov cared about the problem.

"But what about all the advances we've made in the food sciences?" Forest asked, realizing that he was genuinely interested in what the professor was saying. "We're working on hybrid animals, fish farming, and there are all

184

those new miracle grains. And we're learning to store for emergencies. I remember reading somewhere that our grain reserves are up to six hundred million tons." Karapov was enjoying himself. He leaned back in his chair and snorted at Forest. Taking another sip of his drink, Karapov peered owlishly at Forest.

"First of all, they are nowhere near that. But even if they were, how long do you think the world could hold out if there was an emergency?" Forest ventured an underestimated guess.

"Six months?"

"Thirty days!" was Karapov's reply. Their eyebrows rose together, Forest's in surprise, the professor's in acknowledgment. "But that's not even the worst of it. Not by a long shot." Karapov leaned forward, relishing the bomb he was about to drop. "Assuming the cooling theory to be correct, do you have any idea what will happen to this planet if our average temperature drops by only one degree?" Forest could imagine, but the professor was already explaining. "India will have a major drought every four years and will be able to support only three-quarters of her population. Russia will lose all of the territory of Kazakstan to permanent winter. Northern Europe will lose about thirty percent of its food production capacity and Canada will lose half."

Forest tried to calculate what those numbers meant, but the professor was now rolling. He refilled his drink and let Forest decline another, then stood and began to talk the way he did in the old days in halls jam-packed with students.

"The problem is easier to understand in terms of people. Europe now supports three people for every two and a half acres of tillable land. A one-degree drop in temperature would mean that only two people could be fed. Twenty percent of the population would need to be fed by the grain reserves.

"India will need between thirty to fifty million tons of grain to keep a hundred and fifty million of their people from dying. And China, believe it or not, faces the worst problem. The land that now supports seven people will only feed four. And after all the grain reserve is handed out . . ." he paused ominously, "we will still lose ten percent of the population of the world." Karapov walked to the window and stared out at the rain.

"Ten percent is such an abstract mathematical term that it's almost impossible to conceive of the scope of the catastrophe." Forest could see that the professor wasn't lecturing now, but seeing in his own head the devastation that lay ahead. "Ten percent of four billion people," he muttered into the glass, "is four hundred million people. Four hundred million people! More than we've been able to kill in all our wars put together. And that," he said, turning to face Forest, "is only the first year."

Forest joined Karapov at the window and peered out at the rain. It showed no sign of abating. "Surely," Forest said, trying to comprehend the idea of that much death, "four hundred million people don't just keel over and starve to death."

Karapov sighed. "No, of course not. Only one out of ten actually 'keels over' from an empty stomach. About that, you are correct. The other nine are killed by epidemic diseases. But the root cause for all of the deaths is chronic malnutrition. Bodies weak from hunger are particularly vulnerable to cholera or small-pox." Karapov went to the small table and added ice and vodka to his glass. This time Forest accepted his offer of a refill. The professor went on.

"Chronic malnutrition! It sounds like a pimple next to cancer. Such a passive disease. A semantic platitude for an unbelievable hor-ror. But Jon Tinker, the British writer, described it quite accurately. He said that chronic malnutrition makes people go blind from a lack of Vitamin A or get diseases like pellagra, scurvy, beriberi or rickets. It makes people die from malaria, cholera, or even a cold. Children are physically and mentally stunted. It is the end of hope. People become like animals, fighting over a scrap of food, doomed to an unending fate of birth and death."

There was silence as Karapov let the scope of the impending disaster sink in. Forest was about to speak when Irena came bustling in, with an array of incredible odors. "Come, come," she said, "enough drinking and talking. It's time for eating and talking." She picked up the tray and both men followed her into the dining room.

The table was set with white linen and her good silver, and there were candles burning in silver candlesticks. The setting was warm and inviting, but not as inviting as the food she had prepared. There was borscht with dollops of sour cream floating on top; blinis, crepes filled with caviar and sour cream; rice pilaf; and, if that weren't rich enough, a beef stroganoff. Irena was a marvelous cook, and Forest hadn't eaten homecooking in a long time, so at first there was silence at the table as everyone savored the food. After the first rush of enjoyment had passed, Forest returned to the conversation with the professor. He didn't want them to lose their train of thought.

"But surely you've only been presenting one side of the coin, Professor. Isn't our agricultural technology producing weather-resistant strains of grain to withstand just this kind of change? And isn't the chemical industry bringing out new miracle fertilizers every day?"

Karapov finished chewing and regarded Forest with some amazement. "Of course they are, my boy. They have to bring out new fertilizers almost every day because they fail so quickly. Everything blooms wonderfully for a couple of years but then becomes worse off than before. The harvest diminishes rapidly and it's impossible to add any more fertilizer to the land because it would poison everything."

Karapov poured some wine into Irena's glass from a carafe on the table and then did the same for himself and Forest. "As for the new grains they're developing," he continued, "all they've produced so far is a constant comedy of failure. The last three super rices they planted, in turn, were destroyed by disease, eaten by insects, and blown right out of the fields by the wind. It seems we can't yet create overnight in laboratories what it took nature millions of years to develop. And even if we could, the expense to make them grow would be out of the question."

As they continued eating, Forest suggested one possible solution after another. Each of them the professor dismissed. Over babka and coffee, they began discussing experiments in genetic manipulation to produce high-yield protein. Karapov again scoffed at Forest.

"Ah yes, hydroponics, or fish-farming as it's called. While it's true that fish can produce more protein from grains and meal than animals do, we're a long way from the first fish ranch. And the cloning experts tell me they're working on a chicken that never sees an egg but grows in a totally artificial environment, a bubbling embryo of chemicals. How would you like yours, on white or rye?"

Karapov rose from the table and kissed his wife tenderly. "Thank you, chutchkaleh, for a wonderful dinner," he said, beaming. She glowed at his praise and hurried into the kitchen. The professor put his arm around Forest. "Come, we will have brandy in the living room." As they walked, Karapov continued to talk.

"You see, Forest, what these near-sighted scientists have failed to see is that the hunger problem is a far more complex matter than merely providing food for people who are starving. The cause must be attacked, not just the symptom. And the cause . . ." he leaned close to Forest as if he were imparting a secret. Forest smelled the wine on his breath and realized that Karapov was already a little drunk. "The cause," he whispered, "is, of course, the weather! We must find some way to modify the weather, before it modifies us." Karapov chuckled humorlessly. "But that, my young friend, would be something like learning to be God."

While Forest smiled and watched the old man going about the business of getting brandy and glasses, his mind was racing. This was the moment he had been waiting for all evening. The professor had finally opened the door.

"But there are proposals being made for weather modification, aren't there, Professor?" he asked innocently.

"Proposals? They are idiots' delights. They want to dam up the Mediterranean and the Bering Strait. And reroute the Congo river. They actually want to spread ashes over the Arctic, blacktop the Sahara, and detonate H-Bombs over the North Pole. And the Arabs are trying to tow in icebergs for drinking water." Karapov laughed and Forest laughed with him. He noticed that Karapov's words were becoming slightly slurred. "The answer," the old man

190

mused, "if there is one, has to be so much more basic than that."

Forest began to probe further. "But there are people working in other areas of weather modification, aren't there? Like the World Meteorological Organization and the military, and there are probably others. Hurricane control, cloud-seeding, things like that, right?" Forest saw a spark of new interest come into Karapov's eyes. The professor leaned forward in his chair.

"Why do you ask, Forest? Surely you know as much about it as I do."

"No, I don't think so, Professor, and that's one of the reasons I'm here. I need your advice on something I don't understand." Forest had adopted the tone of student to teacher, and Karapov fell into it naturally as well.

"Of course I am always happy to help you in any way I can. You've always known that. What is troubling you?" Forest had already decided that he would take Karapov into his confidence, so he took a deep breath and began. The professor sipped at his brandy and listened carefully.

"I've been getting more and more worried, Professor, about the repercussions of weather modification experiments. I talked to Arthur about it and he poo-pooed it. I talked to General Wells about it and he did the same, and I was ready to let the whole thing go. But then I got a note from Arthur that he mailed just before he died. He had done some poking around and had come up with a name—Project Thursday—and this." Forest took the blueprint out of his pocket. "He couldn't understand it and neither can I." He handed the paper to Karapov. "The notes on it seem to be written in Russian, and I hoped you'd be able to translate them for me."

Karapov's hands seemed to tremble slightly as he unfolded the paper slowly, or maybe they had been trembling all day. He held the document up, nearer to the lamp at the side of his chair, and examined it. "And what," he said finally, with more than a touch of irony in his voice, "did you interpret this to be?"

Forest fidgeted in his chair. He picked up his brandy and then put it down, untouched. "It looks like a highly sophisticated cloud chamber of some sort, but certainly more advanced and complicated than anything I've ever seen or heard of. And since Russia must be as interested in weather modification as we are . . . I thought this might be a key to the strange weather we're having." Forest watched Karapov's face carefully and saw a wave of emotions pass over it; surprise, incredulity, and, finally, he saw him erupt into laughter. The professor shook the paper in his hand at Forest.

"This blueprint is the key to nothing, Forest. I'm sorry to have to destroy the mystery and intrigue for you, but the writing on this paper is mine. I don't know how Arthur got hold of it, and I guess we never will, but this is a plan for a chamber that was never built. It was a silly idea I had years ago, which turned out to

192

be totally impractical." Karapov folded the paper and threw it onto the little table. "So much for secret documents." He picked up his brandy glass and took a long drink. There were beads of perspiration forming on his forehead, but Forest was beginning to sweat too.

Karapov put his glass down and rubbed his hands together. He seemed to be enjoying the role of debunker. "So you thought that because it was in Russian . . ." he chuckled. But Forest didn't laugh along; he couldn't even force a smile. He just stared at the professor as he talked. "As for the weather experiments, I told you they have been mostly follies, including mine. The weather is strange because we have entered a period of extreme instability in our climate, as we discussed. The seemingly unexplainable happens and we try to find the cause, because we are scientists. But also, because we are men of science, we must deal with reality. And Mother Nature is still a far more powerful force than we poor mortals."

Karapov observed the expression on Forest's face and smiled at him as if he were a little boy. "You came to ask your old professor some questions, and you pout because you don't like the answers? Come, come, there are many disappointments in life and many frustrations in science. We will live through it, eh?" The professor was finished with the discussion and looked tired and a little drunk. He was ready for Forest to say his good-nights. But Forest wasn't quite finished yet. There was one more thing he had to ask about now. He drained the last drops of his brandy, trying to form the question in his mind, and then suddenly decided against it. He knew the answer.

Forest put his glass down and stood up. "I must go now, Professor. I have to be in New York tonight. But I'd like to say good-bye to Irena and thank her for such a marvelous dinner." Karapov pulled himself to his feet.

"Irena," he bellowed, "come here. Forest is leaving us."

"Does the bus still leave for Washington every hour?" Forest asked, waiting for the obedient Irena to appear.

"Of course it does," Karapov chuckled. Some of the strain seemed to have oozed out of him. "There are things that do not change, eh?" Karapov gently elbowed him in the ribs. "It has been too long, my friend, between visits. But I'll drive you to the bus station if you promise to visit us again soon."

Forest glanced out the window. It was dark and the rain seemed to have let up a little. "I think I'll walk over, Professor. The bus stop is only five minutes away. I'll just walk across the campus."

Irena bustled into the room, drying her hands on her apron. "Forest," she complained, "not so soon? We haven't even talked. All night you and he are discussing, and we haven't even talked yet." Forest's heart went out to this dear, sweet woman who so truly cared. He took her into his arms, towering above her graying head, and held her warmly.

"Soon," he murmured to her, feeling

194

strangely protective. "Soon I'll come and visit again. And the next time for a long time." He held her away from him and looked into her eyes. Then he kissed her cheek. Karapov was waiting for the farewell to end and was circling nervously when suddenly he was struck with an idea and started to leave the room.

"Stay there a moment, Forest," he called over his shoulder. "I'll get you my extra raincoat." He stopped at the door. "And then I will have to come to New York to get it back and we will see each other soon." He disappeared upstairs. Forest and Irena looked into each other's eyes easily and with a lifetime of past affection. They needed no words to talk.

"Irena!" Karapov called from somewhere upstairs. "I can't find the blue raincoat."

"Ach," she said smiling, "he is useless sometimes." She disengaged herself from Forest's embrace. "I'm coming, I'm coming," she called, and she went to help the professor.

Forest looked around the room once again and then glanced down at the folded piece of paper lying on the low table. Then he turned, shook his head, and left the living room. He walked down the hall and found his briefcase next to the Philadelphia high-style stand. The professor and Irena came hurrying down the stairs after him and together managed to get him into the too-small coat. Forest had opened his briefcase and taken out his umbrella, ready for the onslaught outside.

He kissed Irena again, embraced Karapov, and opened the door. The raindrops were fat and heavy and falling with a vengeance. Forest snapped open the carbon-steel umbrella and stepped out into the rain. When he had walked down the driveway and reached the street, the door to the house closed behind him and he was alone in the dark and rainy night.

CHAPTER EIGHTEEN

The old oaks and maples lining the street afforded Forest some protection from the real force of the rain, along with his trusty umbrella, but it was sure going to get a test tonight. He looked into the darkness for the dam, which had always been visible from anywhere on campus, and was surprised that it was obscured. He quickened his pace and headed up the gentle slope of Central Lane, heading toward the main campus buildings.

The University, and the town that was part of it, had been built in the center of a perfectly symmetrical little valley that sloped away evenly from Hamilton Dam. A good many of the original eighteenth-century houses still stood on the south side of the valley. The university, on the north slope, had been built after the dam had gone up in 1934, but the founder of the college had been so in love with the old town that he had built all the campus buildings in the same eighteenth-century style. The effect was one of great warmth, Forest mused, if you weren't being drenched.

The rain, draining down the hillsides, rushed in streams past Forest like miniature rivers, and the blackness of the night and the arms of the trees being beaten by the rain gave a sinister cast to the scene. Occasionally a car would materialize out of the darkness and illuminate the wind-twisted trees. Invariably they slowed, questioning what anyone was doing walking on a night like this, and then they would rush on, sending up showers of spray, relieved they hadn't hit Forest.

By the time he had reached the Calder Building, his feet were wet to the ankles. He hadn't met another pedestrian and wasn't surprised. Forest stood under the trees across the street from the illuminated building and listened to the miniature Mississippi rush past in front of him. He knew he was far enough in the shadows to be invisible and, in fact, even at this distance it was difficult for Forest to make out the sentries huddling in their shelter.

Forest reached into his suit pocket and pulled out a ring of keys. He held the keys tightly in his hand, feeling the distinctive charm—the white chess knight—biting into his palm. Forgive me, Professor, he said inside his head. Forgive me for not trusting or believing you blindly, like I used to, but you lied to me. You can't dismiss Project Thursday that easily, not a hundred and twenty million dollars of it. And you admitted it was your chamber. So forgive me for what I'm about to do because you're not who you used to be and neither am I. And I have to see what you've got inside that building across the street, with soldiers guarding it. I have to know before I can put my brother's spirit to rest.

Forest felt something click inside him. His growing sense of purpose had finally gelled into determination. He had drawn a shade on his doubts and fears and put away his ifs and maybes. He was alone in the rain and he was going to get into that goddamned building and that was all he was willing to think about. He peered through the rain at the spotlighted steps and the soldiers.

A little voice murmured inside him, "That's great, Forest. Great resolve. Now, let's see you do it. How the hell are you going to get in?"

CHAPTER NINETEEN

As Forest stared at the building, an idea began to form. Calder was a large rectangle with columns all around it. The building itself was set back and there was a porch or promenade between it and the columns. Squinting through the driving rain, Forest could see that there were gutters running the length of the roof on all sides. Maybe he could use the weather to his advantage; after all, he was a weatherman, and it would be about time.

Forest walked down the street until he was out of the light shed by Calder, and crossed the street. Then he began to walk back, looking for a break in the hedges that lined the street. He found one 100 yards from the illumination and reluctantly closed his umbrella, grateful now for Karapov's raincoat. He slipped through to the other side and worked his way through the underbrush until he reached the building. And then he circled it, around the back, and then around the other side, until he had found out what he wanted to know. There was no entrance besides the front door, and there were two drainpipes instead of one. And that presented a problem; the entrance he was interested in was in the front of the building and completely visible to the guards in their sentry box.

Forest visualized the problem. As you faced the building, the guards were on the right side of the path leading to the big double door, their shelter just at the edge of the steps. There was a drainpipe at the right rear corner of the building and another at the front left corner. Forest made his way back to the drainpipe at the right rear corner. He needed to create a diversion. He took off Karapov's raincoat and tore it in half, struggling to separate the collar as he became drenched to the skin. Then he made half the coat into a ball and jammed it up the pipe, ignoring the water it was pumping up his sleeve. Using the tip of his umbrella, Forest jammed the cloth up the pipe until it wedged. Then he ran around to the back of the building to the left wall and edged his way as far toward the front as he could without being seen. He waited.

It took only minutes for the gutters to fill, as Forest had expected, but even he wasn't prepared for the explosive noise the water made when it came cascading directly down off the roof. Forest forced himself to wait for the guards to activate themselves, and prayed; they both had to go or it was useless. Forest let the seconds tick and then, impulsively crouched

201

and crawled forward so he could see the sentry box. It was empty.

Forest dove at the drainpipe, jamming the raincoat up the pipe frantically, and then began jabbing at it with his umbrella. He knew he had only a moment before they would return. The fucking coat wouldn't stay up there. Forest stabbed at it again and again, feeling like he was disemboweling some enormous creature. The raincoat held, and Forest threw himself back out of the line of vision. Panting from exertion and with excitement, he crouched, waiting for the wall of water to fall.

It seemed like an eternity. Nothing happened. Forest searched the ground in front of the drainpipe, looking to see if the cloth had been expectorated. He could see nothing. And then he was hit with a wall of water. It had worked. Forest rose and stepped inside the liquid curtain. He was invisible.

Because the building was lit from across the street, it was dim inside the columns now that it was veiled, and the roar of the falling water would cover his movements, he hoped. Walking along the promenade toward the large door, Forest felt like he was inside a waterfall, protected and safe, although the soldiers were only a few feet away from him. Then he heard them arguing and his illusion of invisibility disappeared.

Forest reached the door and stopped. The lock was a large one, and it was obvious which key on Karapov's ring would fit it, but now he was worried about the noise. Would the soldiers hear the lock click? Maybe there was an alarm system? And if not, would they hear the door snap shut? He could hear them clearly now, arguing about who would check the left side of the building and who would get the dry job, inside the wall of water. Forest had no more time to deliberate. He put the key in the lock and turned. The door swung open. Forest slid through the opening and eased the door closed, hearing it click and lock.

Inside, Forest leaned his back against the massive door and waited for his heart to stop pounding. He was in! He would figure out how to escape later. He could hear the guard cursing to himself outside the door and he held his breath as the guard tried the door handle. The door stayed locked and Forest exhaled.

A dim light filtered from a corridor on his left and allowed him to get his bearings. He was standing in an entrance hall that rose to the full height of the building, and he was facing a solid wall about 25 feet away from him. To his right was another solid, unmarked wall with two desks in front of it. Forest assumed they were daytime security checkpoints. To his left was an entrance to the corridor. There was nothing else to see: no windows, doors, or ornaments.

His wet, squishing shoes echoed as he crossed the marble floor and made him stop to make sure he was alone. But there was no one else there, at least not behind him. Forest turned the corner into the corridor and found himself in a long hallway which ran the entire length of the building. The outer wall was blank but the right, inner wall was lined with a series of numbered doors.

He tried the first one, hoping it would be open so he wouldn't have to work his way through Karapov's keys. Forest cursed to himself. It was locked. But after trying two of the keys, the third one opened the door. The light from the hallway showed an ordinary office, about 20 feet square, with two desks, chairs, and some filing cabinets. It wasn't what Forest was looking for.

The same key opened the second door, which made things easier; obviously he had found the master key. But the second room was a carbon copy of the first. The third door, however, opened into a full-fledged laboratory about 15 feet deep by 25 feet wide. Forest quietly made his way around the room, noting the usual test tubes in racks over a central counter, tape recorders and oscilloscopes mounted on the wall, and storage shelves and chemical sinks. He stood at the door before leaving, surveying the lab, trying to find something different about it, something unusual. But there was nothing. On the other hand, he wished he knew what he was looking for.

The fourth door opened into a men's room and, although he suddenly had to pee, there were other things more important. The fifth door was marked "Storage," and the sixth opened into a small conference room. There was an eight foot oval table and six chairs. Small meetings, he mused. A cork bulletin board ran along the inside wall and there was a video tape recorder at the end of the room. There was also a tape rack under the machine, but the rack was empty. Nothing.

Forest shut the door and looked down the hall. He was running out of time and doors. There were only two left. He hurried to the seventh door and unlocked it. It was another laboratory, twice as wide as the first one but not any deeper. But here, at least, he saw equipment that he recognized: radarscopes, a small computer bank, and rows of tapes for the computer. Since the tapes weren't locked, Forest figured they couldn't be too important and left them. And that was it. Bare. Sterile. Nothing out of the ordinary.

Forest stood in front of the last door and realized his palms were sweating. There had better be something special in this room, he told himself, or I'm in real trouble with the professor. He looked at the keys in his hand and tried to imagine how he would explain having taken them. He inserted the key in the lock and turned it. Forest opened the door slowly, almost afraid to look. What he saw was a small reference library. Shit! He closed the door quietly, resisting the impulse to slam it, and locked it again.

Forest stood at the end of the corridor, frustrated and perplexed. There was something wrong here. There was nothing to guard, no reason to post soldiers to protect what he had seen, and certainly not on a twenty-four-hour-a-day basis; some offices and labs, just a bunch of wide, shallow rooms.

But there was something else wrong. He slumped against the wall and tried to pin down what was bothering him by starting from the beginning. Mentally, he retraced his steps until he was standing outside, across the street in the rain, staring at Calder. And then it popped! The building was about 80 feet wide. But this corridor was only 10 and the rooms he had seen only about 25. That left close to 50 feet of spaced unaccounted for. But where was it? He hadn't seen any other entrance from the outside, nor had there been any in the rooms. There were no stairs or doors that he hadn't tried. Except one!

Forest leaped to his feet and ran back to the storage closet. Of course. Just because it said "Storage" didn't mean it was storage. The master key didn't fit and Forest's spirits rose. That was a good sign. He worked his way through Karapov's keys until finally the third from the last turned the lock. The door swung open toward him and Forest was faced with the disappointment of a vista of mops, pails, broom, and toilet paper.

Well, that was it. It had been his last hope. Maybe they were guarding a giant generator or something, Forest thought bitterly as he locked the door, but there sure as hell wasn't anything he wanted in the building. This had been nothing but a fucking wild goose chase and he was right back at the beginning. Forest's disappointment made him feel exhausted, but as he slipped the keys into his pocket, he realized that he was suffering from guilt and embarrassment that was even more debilitating. He had distrusted his old friend and professor and now he had to face him with some lame excuse. It had been a long day.

Forest looked at his watch. It was almost midnight and he still had to pee. He pushed open the door to the men's room and flicked on the fluorescent lights. At least that wasn't locked, he thought acidly. As he stood at the urinal, he experienced the first wave of relief. Then, by reflex, he catalogued the room: two urinals, two sinks, two stalls to his right, and one stall against the other wall. Add some white tile and a mirror and you have the average institutional john. Very exciting. Forest pulled the handle to flush the urinal and then wished he hadn't. The noise sounded like a waterfall in the empty room. On the other hand, there was little chance of his being heard over the storm outside. He washed his hands and studied his face in the mirror. He looked tired and grim, and combing his hair only made him look neater, not better.

"Ah well," he said aloud, "time to face the music." On his way out of the room he pushed open the doors to the two stalls and looked in. Clutching at straws? Just to make sure? Why not? Forest had reached the exit and was about to turn out the lights when he saw the other stall against the wall, staring at him. It was the only door he hadn't opened. His hand reached for the light switch, then stopped, and feeling stupid he crossed the room and pushed open the stall.

It was empty. Forest's pulse began to beat at a brand new rhythm. There was no toilet. And against the wall there was a door. At last, a door. There was a noise and Forest turned quickly, but it was only the plumbing gurgling. He reached forward and tried the handle slowly, praying that it would be locked. He smiled in satisfaction as the door resisted him. Then he fumbled in his pocket for Karapov's key ring. The lock was an odd shape and Karapov had an odd key; they married each other perfectly.

Forest pushed the door forward, his heart pounding. The light from the lavatory revealed a light switch to his left. Trying to control his excitement, he stepped forward through the door and pressed the switch and found himself standing in what appeared to be a control room. Two large rotating chairs were centered in front of a large console facing a glass wall that enclosed some sort of booth. Behind the glass, it was pitch black.

"At last," he said, thrilling at the sight. "At last!" Forest went to the console, searching among the mass of switches, knobs, dials, and buttons that festooned it. And then he saw a green square that said ON, and without thinking pressed it.

A huge chamber instantly appeared on the other side of the glass. Forest could do nothing but stand and stare at it, his mouth open. Arthur's blueprint—the blueprint he had left on Professor Karapov's little table—had just come to life.

CHAPTER TWENTY

Forest sank into one of the chairs and stared into the chamber. He didn't understand it any more than he had the blueprint, but now, at least he knew it existed. He felt as if a thick fog had suddenly lifted and he could finally see where he was.

Forest didn't know how long he had been staring at the machine, marveling at its complexity, when he heard the door of the men's room open behind him. The pneumatic whoosh sounded like a rifle shot in his ears, but he kept himself from moving. When he heard the scuffling limp crossing the tile floor, he knew that Karapov had come to find him.

He turned the swivel chair slowly to confront his former friend and teacher and was horrified by what he saw. Karapov stood in the doorway panting, one hand over his heart, the other clutching a revolver. He was soaking wet and the water was still running off his body, already making a puddle where he stood. And he was trembling. Forest could see Karapov's body shaking, causing the gun to jerk and waver in his hand. But it was the professor's eyes that scared Forest most. One eye looked glazed and the other was staring; one looking inward and the other out. Karapov was one step away from a dangerous edge and Forest was watching him teeter. And he knew that for the moment, there was nothing he could do about it but remain still and wait.

It took Karapov a long time to catch his breath. He leaned against the door jamb, breathing loudly, the in-and-out rasping filling the room, and at the same time his staring eye wandered and darted around the control room, into the chamber, and then back to Forest again. Forest held onto his nerves by holding onto the arms of the chair, and he tried to show no expression on his face.

"How did you know?" The low growl of Karapov's voice crawled across the room at Forest. The professor had turned his head so only the staring eye transfixed him. Forest measured his words carefully.

"Arthur told me. In the letter with the blueprint. It seems that Project Thursday has a budget of a hundred and twenty million dollars." Karapov shook his head distractedly, as if he were trying to negate the information. Forest could see a myriad of emotions agitating the old man as he tried to decide what to do next.

"Give me back my keys."

Karapov's demand was so unexpected and

pathetic that at first Forest didn't know how to react. But the professor's one vigilant eye confronted Forest with a fevered intensity. Forest reached carefully into his pocket and slowly extracted the key ring. He held it up so that they both could see it. The miniature horse dangled on the ring and Forest shook his hand to make it swing back and forth.

"Ah yes " he said evenly, "the white knight. An interesting symbol, Professor." Forest was talking to gain time now, time to let Karapov calm down and time to let Forest figure out how to get the gun away from him. "But symbols can be so misleading, can't they?"

Karapov's gaze faltered and he looked away. For a moment, Forest thought of throwing the keys at the old man and then jumping him while he was distracted, but Karapov seemed so on edge Forest was afraid the gun might go off if he made any sudden move.

"Here are your keys, Professor." There was scorn in Forest's voice as he said the title. "And here's your white knight . . . on the floor where it belongs." Forest bent forward slowly and put the keys on the floor. Then he pushed them with his foot so they slid over to Karapov.

The old man stooped tiredly to pick up the keys, never taking his eye off Forest. But when he stood, holding the keys in his palm, something seemed to go out of him. He stared at the white horse in his hand for a long moment and then looked up sadly at Forest. Karapov sighed deeply as he put the keys into his pocket.

"Ach, Forest," he said quietly, the anger now gone from his voice, "why did you have to do this? I didn't want you to get involved in this mess. That's why I lied about the blueprint." His eyes sought Forest's to confirm the truth of his statement. "That's why I lied. You don't understand what's going on . . . and what the consequences are." He waved the gun vaguely, but it was clear to Forest that he didn't intend to use it, at least not for the moment.

Forest turned his chair slowly until he was facing the giant chamber. He stared at it for a moment, thinking. "I was right, wasn't I, Professor?" There was no answer. Forest went on talking without looking at Karapov. "But why all the secrecy? Why the lies, especially to me?" He swiveled back around and faced Karapov, confronting him with his conviction. "And what the hell is scaring you like this? Your hands are shaking. You look sick. And now, all of a sudden, you're carrying a gun." The old man averted his eyes and passed a tired hand over his face.

Forest went on, pressing him harder. "Los Alamos, Garnett, Johnstown—all the disasters I've been yelling about—I was right, wasn't I? You've been doing major weather experiments and you've finally fucked up the whole system." Karapov refused to even look at Forest. "Answer me!"

The professor seemed to have shrunk since he had entered the room. He stood, huddled in the doorway and shook his head again and

213

again. "No, Forest, you're wrong." He was muttering so softly that Forest had to strain to hear him. "You don't understand. It's bigger than that. So much bigger . . ." His voice trailed off in a whine of self-pity.

Forest gripped the arms of the chair to prevent himself from flying at the professor and shaking an answer out of him. "Tell me, goddamnit!" He shouted. "Tell me what the hell is going on!" The professor didn't look up. He didn't flinch at the intensity of Forest's demand. His head shook a rhythmic no as if he were a mechanical doll, and he seemed to be hiding somewhere deep inside himself. Finally Forest heard him whisper.

"I can't tell you."

"What?" Forest spat.

"I can't tell you." Karapov's voice was louder. He looked up slowly. "You know too much already. It's too dangerous. I'm sorry, Forest I can't. Please, let it go." His eyes were begging.

Forest got up deliberately and walked over to Karapov. He stood inches away, looking down at the old man, waiting until he could control his voice. "You have a gun, Professor," Forest said, almost whispering, "use it! It's too late for me to let it go. I'm here, I've seen the chamber, and I'm not leaving until I know what's going on. So shoot me." Forest's voice bored into the professor like an ice pick. "I was your student. I was welcome in your home. We ate and drank together. Well, today you went

214

to my brother's funeral, tomorrow you can go to mine. There is no other way."

Forest stood over the professor, letting his message sink in. The physical force of his energy made it clear that there was no alternative. As he watched, he saw a shudder pass through Karapov's body. Then the old man began to shake spasmodically. At first Forest was afraid that Karapov was having an attack of some sort or a nervous breakdown, but then he heard him sob and realized that Karapov was crying.

Forest reached down and took the gun from the professor's limp fingers. Then Forest wrapped his arm around the old man's shoulders and held him close as he wept. Wetness came to Forest's eyes as he listened to the anguish and pain finally spilling out, and he looked down at the tangled, gray locks and wondered how they had ever come to this. Gradually the spasms subsided and Forest led his professor to one of the chairs and sat him down.

Forest sat in the other chair and waited, embarrassed at having to witness this private agony, yet having no other place to go. Finally Karapov gathered himself together and raised his tear-stained face.

"Ach, Forest, " he said at last, "what a terrible waste." His words were tentative and faltering, as if he were begging for understanding. "It began many years ago when my work was still in the theoretical stage. Somehow the military got wind of it and the next thing I knew I was working on a classified project. Money came pouring in for experiments and equipment and I began to make progress." Forest winced inside as he heard Karapov wrench up each word as he recalled his past.

"I was happy and they were happy and the years passed. At the time, I thought nothing of the implications, only of my work and the gift that I might be able to give mankind. It wasn't until we started to move from the theoretical into the practical that I realized how secret a project I was working on."

"How secret a project is it, Professor?" Forest asked this evenly, trying not to alarm Karapov with the importance of the question.

The professor leaned forward and whispered, as if afraid of being overheard. "Very, very secret, Forest. Practically nobody knew about it, until, of course, Arthur stumbled onto the file and the blueprint."

"Project Thursday?"

Karapov nodded and swiveled around to face the console. He pressed a series of glowing buttons and instantly the room began to hum. The chamber was coming to life. Forest peered at it, fascinated. It was a large, oval room about 50 feet wide and 80 feet long. The walls were covered with a black material that simulated outer space. From the domed ceiling hung a large globe that was beginning to glow. Forest assumed that it was meant to be the sun.

Karapov pointed to the floor and flicked a switch, revealing a globe 30 feet in diameter, which had been sunk into the floor so that only a third of it was visible. The surface of the globe was covered with a grid and with liquids and solids, forming a perfect topographical model of the earth's surface. Completely surrounding it were four layers of pipes, their open ends pointed at the globe.

"How far have you gotten, Professor, with your weather modification experiments?" Karapov moved a slide switch up two notches on the console and the hum grew louder. He glanced at Forest, a glint in his eye.

"You don't understand yet, do you, my friend?" The globe began to rotate slowly. The earth was moving on its axis. "We are beyond experiments. We can control the weather!"

CHAPTER TWENTY-ONE

Forest's mind struggled to accept the concept. He had just been told that man could control the weather, that the dream of mankind since the beginning of time was now a reality. It was too much. He stared at the professor and then turned to face the chamber. The blood was racing in his veins and he felt lightheaded.

"You must remember," Karapov said, looking over at Forest, "that this is only a model. But it is a perfect model, accurate to scale and completely capable of reproducing the earth's natural weather conditions." He paused for a moment, staring morosely at the console. "And, also understand, that anything I can do in this chamber can actually be done to the earth." Karapov's hands moved over the console, pressing buttons, turning dials, making minute adjustments, and he began to explain the mechanism to Forest.

"The four rings you see surrounding the

globe each have 360 pipes. With this we control the geostrophic balance of the earth. Each ring represents a zone of the atmosphere: troposphere, tropopause, stratosphere, and stratopause. Each pipe has its own temperature and pressure, and through them I can duplicate the equilibrium between the forces of wind and the rotation of the earth and the interchange of potential and kinetic energy between the atmosphere and the oceans."

Forest spoke, his voice dry and cracking. "It's certainly a long way from Wilson's first cloud chamber, methyl alcohol cooled with dry ice." Karapov chuckled as if he were beginning to enjoy himself.

"We are twenty years and many millions of dollars later, my boy. We know now that everything in the atmosphere—temperature, rainfall, wind velocity—is directly related to a constant gain and loss of energy, and that they are all composed of electrical impulses. What I've discovered is how to activate those electrical impulses. Everything in the atmosphere can now be controlled electronically."

Forest turned to Karapov with wonder on his face. "But that's incredible. It's marvelous." His mind was running wild with the potential for this enormous gift. "So what's the matter? Why did you call it a terrible waste? With this knowledge you could grow bananas in Brooklyn. And if you can do it, you can do it. Right?" Karapov shook his head sadly.

"Wrong, my friend. I was naive, an innocent among vultures. You see, we live in a world of predators. And weather, Mr. Weatherman, is power. He who controls the weather controls food. And he who controls food controls the world. It's that simple. And it turns out that being able to grow bananas in Brooklyn, or being able to feed the world, is not necessarily a good thing."

Forest was astounded. "What do you mean not a good thing? Have you gone crazy? Why the hell not?" Karapov smiled tolerantly at Forest and nodded his head vigorously.

"You see! You too are naive. Let me explain the facts of life to you, Forest, as they exist in the real world. As they were explained to me. Food has always been used to apply pressure for economic and political gains, especially by this country, which has always had so much surplus. The United States has always traded food for military bases, and when a foreign country refuses to knuckle under our ideological demands we refuse to sell them food and help topple the government. Like we did to Allende in Chile," Karapov snorted derisively.

"But that's the kind of blackmail that people will never stand for. Especially in a democracy."

"You may think so, my boy, but you'd be surprised at how little people care which government is feeding them as long as it prevents them from starving to death. That moment is coming for most of the world, and already exists for the rest."

Karapov wagged a finger at Forest. "And if you had been listening to me at the house," he chided gently, "you would have already understood how difficult the problem really is. You cannot solve the problem of hunger by simply feeding the hungry. Feeding all the starving people in the world today would merely compound the problem, because fewer people would die and more people would have more babies. Soon the population growth would so far outrun our capacity to produce food that famine would sweep the entire world."

Forest was incredulous. "My God, I can't believe it. This is like having a cure for cancer and being told you can't let people have it. I just can't accept the premise, but I sure would like to hear where this line of thinking takes you. Okay, you can't afford to feed the people. So what do you do?"

"You refuse to give them food unless they agree to drastic birth-control measures."

"Like what?" Forest asked angrily. "Mandatory sterilization?"

"Yes," the professor admitted.

"That's lovely. What a pretty solution." There was scorn in Forest's voice.

"It's a prettier answer than mass starvation, Forest. But unfortunately, it's a solution that doesn't work either. The policy can't be enforced. Mrs. Ghandi's son tried it in India and failed so miserably the government was thrown out of office."

Leaving Forest to ponder the problem, Karapov returned to his machine. His fingers once again played over the console and Forest turned to watch as two huge silver tracks rose

221

out of the floor and arched up over the globe, reaching from one end of the room to the other. One ran north to south. The other, a little smaller, ran east to west, following the curve of the earth more exactly. The professor waited for the arches to lock into place and then reached to his left and pressed three more buttons. They began to blink, their green lights throbbing on the console.

Karapov's hand was hovering over one more switch when he turned to Forest, a twinkle in his eye "Well, my very fine student, have you guessed how it's done yet?" He waited while Forest stared into the chamber. The two arches loomed before his eyes. It seemed so simple. So obvious. So frightening.

"Satellites?" Forest turned to the professor for affirmation and saw him beaming. Karapov reached down and punched a button with enthusiasm.

"Of course, Forest. Satellites. Like the gods, when it comes to manipulating the weather, it helps to have perspective. You have to work from the outside." A shiny replica of a satellite appeared from the hole around the base of one of the tracks. It rose slowly, as if it were blasting off from Cape Kennedy, and glided into a smooth orbit over the rotating globe.

As they watched, another satellite appeared out of the same hole and followed along the same track, 20 feet behind the first. Then, rising on the other arch, another satellite climbed into the sky above the earth. Finally they came to rest, hanging luminously against the black space of the chamber.

"The two on the higher track," Karapov explained, "are ThorStar geosynchronous satellites. That is, they simulate an orbit of twenty-two thousand and three hundred miles and move at the exact rate of the earth's rotation. The other one is a ThorStar II. It moves in an elliptical orbit, sixty-six and eighty-three one hundredth degrees below the other. Vectors from all three can be coordinated to any point on earth."

Forest was mesmerized. He watched Karapov playing the controls on the console like Rubenstein giving a concert.

"Now the machine is primed and ready to go into action," Karapov exclaimed.

"But to do what? What do you use it for if not to grow food? What happens next in your scenario?" he asked apprehensively.

"What happens," Karapov answered somberly, "is that you develop a dangerously explosive world situation where there are a great number of underdeveloped countries that have been backed into a corner. They are faced with strangling overpopulation and imminent famine, and they have nowhere to turn. So, like any animal backed into a corner, they fight. They attack. They have to expand to feed themselves and survive.

"There are now only twenty countries capable of delivering a nuclear bomb. But, as that young genius at Princeton has just demonstrated, given access to the materials it's possible to build an atomic bomb for less than two thousand dollars. The technology is available to everyone—in our public libraries. So tomorrow, those twenty countries may be forty, and the day after, sixty. So, you see, we are sitting on a powder keg, and the fuse is burning faster than anyone thinks."

Forest whistled quietly. The coldness of the logic was chilling, and he was beginning to get an inkling of where it was leading. It frightened him. He sneaked a look at the satellites hanging in the chamber, almost afraid to ask the next question, but more afraid not to.

"So what do we do, Professor?"

Karapov peered at Forest from under his bushy gray eyebrows for a moment. "Do you know what triage is, Forest?" he asked in a curiously calm voice.

"It's some kind of military term, isn't it?"

"Yes," Karapov chuckled mirthlessly, "it is some kind of military term indeed. It comes from battlefield hospitals where the influx of wounded is greater than they can handle. So they divide the wounded into three catagories. There are those who will die, even if they are treated. There are those who will live, even if they aren't treated. And there are those who will live only if they are treated. When triage is applied, only the last group receives treatment." Karapov paused to let his point sink home. "You understand, of course, how the analogy applies to the world situation?"

Forest stared at him in disbelief. "Are you trying to tell me that this is going on now?

That someone has divided up the world into countries that will survive and countries that won't? I never heard anything so barbaric in my life." He was truly shocked.

"The world has always been a barbaric place," Karapov said gently.

CHAPTER TWENTY-TWO

Karapov had turned back to his machine, as if he didn't want to discuss the matter any longer, and Forest was afraid to push him for the moment. He stared at the professor's bent head for a long moment.

"Would you show me how it works, Professor?" he asked quietly.

Karapov looked up. "Ah yes, of course, how it works." His fingers reached out to the instrument panel, as if by their own volition. "Now, to influence weather you have to find what I call 'soft spots,' instabilities where a small input of energy will produce a large reaction. Watch!" For a moment nothing seemed to happen, but then, over the Mediterranean, Forest noticed that a cluster of cumulus clouds was forming. He couldn't believe his eyes. They weren't smoke or mist, they were actual cumulo-nimbus clouds in miniature. Forest gaped as they gradually drifted together.

"We now have a small bank of clouds, yes?"

Karapov was now energetically involved in making magic. "By heating the surface of the earth beneath them, I can induce convection and make them grow." His hands danced over the board. "James Espy, the American meteorologist, discovered this principal in 1880. Now observe, when they reach the right level of moisture and temperature . . . *voilà!*" Actual rain started falling from the clouds and was absorbed into the grid covering the globe.

Forest had seen the clouds grow and the rain fall, but he had seen nothing emerge from the satellites. He couldn't figure out how the professor was doing it. But before he could question him, the clouds began to grow again, vertically.

"A separation of electrical charges is now taking place at a very rapid rate," he heard Karapov say. "The positive charges are accumulating at the top of the clouds and the negative charges at the bottom." The professor's hands were wandering over the controls again. "They are insulated by air at the moment, but I can break that down by overloading the negative electrons at the bottom, so that the electrical potential is so great between the cloud base and the ground that a gigantic spark forms to close the electrical circuit."

Karapov flicked a switch and Forest jumped. Bolts of lightning came hurtling straight down out of the cloud and struck Israel with a crackling intensity that overrode the hum of the machinery. Forest could contain himself no longer.

He shouted over the noise. "Are you using lasers?" Karapov touched another dial and the storm abated.

"No, no, dear boy" he answered, a steady hum returning to the room. "The satellites are powered by nuclear reactors that convert energy into electromagnetic waves and beam them down on frequencies that are virtually undetectable. Lasers are too easily spotted and don't have the variations I need for all the different kinds of weather modification. These are even smaller than microwaves, less than a centimeter, and incredibly accurate."

Forest was amazed, but he was getting used to the condition. "How accurate?" he asked.

"Enough to hit a tennis ball from twenty-two thousand miles away. Is that accurate enough?" Forest was satisfied, but he had a head full of other questions he wanted to ask. Karapov, however, seemed determined to answer them without his asking. "The problem at first was that one beam wasn't powerful enough to do the job. But now, when all three are intersected, there is enough energy to power New York City for a week."

Forest contemplated the chamber for a moment, brooding. And for a moment Karapov was also still. Finally, Forest allowed himself to ask the question.

"Do you mean, Professor, that the United states can now control the weather . . . and has decided to let a third of the world starve to death by denying them food and the weather to grow it?"

Forest was startled by the speed at which Karapov swung around to face him. "You still don't get it, do you, my boy?" he said, shaking his head sadly. "Starvation, bah! That's not the policy. That's much too slow, and we Americans are nothing if not activists. So we are speeding the process."

"But how, Professor?"

"With this." Karapov bowed his head in shame as he pointed to his machine. "With the weather! It is the curse of the inventor, Forest. The nightmare of the scientist. Alfred Nobel invented dynamite for peaceful purposes. And when he saw what man did with it he was so disturbed he donated all income from it to the Nobel Prizes, for the advancement of mankind. But it somehow hasn't balanced out, has it?"

Forest could hear the rage and frustration in Karapov's voice as he went on. "Do you think that men like Einstein and the others working in pure science to harness the atom intended to produce the atomic bomb? Of course not. But the military has a way of taking everything and turning it into a weapon. And that's what they've done with my discovery. From the ultimate gift to mankind, they have changed it into the ultimate weapon." Karapov couldn't raise his head to look at Forest.

"But how, Professor?" Forest asked, not wanting to accept the reality.

"Like this!" Karapov leaned forward over the console. The pair of ThorStar I's hovered over India, and ThorStar II, which had disappeared into the floor of the chamber, rose and began to track diagonally across the North Sea. Karapov's fingers raced across the keyboard, pushing buttons, and depressing levers. Suddenly a series of TV monitors lit up on the console.

The storm, which had dissipated its energy and spread out over the Indian Ocean, now began to gather together again, as if some magic hands were kneading a pile of dough. As the clouds joined, they formed an almost straight line, billowing upward as they crossed the coastline of China.

Karapov's eyes swept back and forth between meters and gauges and then leaped to the TV monitors which scanned the miniature storm from a lower angle. Forest watched with fascination and horror as the storm grew. The raw power of the turbulence was awesome.

Karapov had risen to his feet. His hand, palm open, fingers extended, was poised over a large button that pulsated with an amber light. Suddenly his hand swept down violently, as if he were swatting a fly. Forest saw a funnel of spinning air drop out of the clouds and smash the earth. Karapov slammed the button again and again in a frenzy, each time ejecting a whirling dervish of destruction from the clouds.

"Enough! I got it." Forest was on his feet, staring at the professor in horror. "You're murdering millions of people!"

Karapov flicked his hand and Forest forced himself to look back into the chamber. It was like watching a flower wilt at high speed. The storm began to lose its shape and substance and was gradually becoming invisible. The satellites floated smoothly down into their holes, and Forest watched the silver arches follow. Slowly, the lights dimmed and finally the chamber stood empty and lifeless, as if nothing had ever happened there. Forest threw himself back into his chair and closed his eyes.

CHAPTER TWENTY-THREE

The silence in the room was eerie. Forest could hear only Karapov's labored breathing and a whistling of wind in his head that sounded like 10,000 angels sighing, or a million children crying, far, far away. Behind his closed eyelids, he fought to black out the images of death and destruction that were flashing like a silent newsreel describing hell, and tried to gain control. There was so little time now.

He had started pursuing this so innocently, so naively, and so long ago. God, it seemed like years. And now he was faced with a discovery he didn't want to know about, a secret too big to handle. Forest had stepped through a door in a men's room and had found himself in another world, another reality, and now he knew why Karapov had brought the gun.

What was he going to do now? What could he do? Someone out there had the ability to control the weather. Control the weather! The implications were staggering. With that power you could do anything. You could control food, the economy, the emotional stability of any country in the world. You could make it rain on voting day, make it rain on weekends, and make it rain death.

Karapov was right. It was the ultimate weapon. Because it was invisible. There was no one to blame, it was just the weather. As long as it remained a secret.

Forest opened his eyes. Karapov sat slumped in his chair, looking tired and broken. "Professor?" he said softly. Karapov only grunted to himself, experiencing his own private pain. "Professor," Forest continued, "you said your machine was taken over by the military, but that the project was so secret that practically no one knew anything about it." Forest fought to keep the excitement out of his voice. "Does that mean that the way it's being used doesn't necessarily represent our government's official policy?"

Karapov's head came up slowly. His eyes were dull. "I don't know . . . I don't know. And what difference does it make? It's too late. There's nothing anyone can do about it. It's already being done."

Forest sat up a little in his chair. "Oh, I don't know about that," he said casually. He could feel waves of desperation rolling off Karapov, and he knew he had to fight it, without frightening him. "It might make a lot of difference. I mean, for example, who exactly does know about this?" The question hung in the silent air.

233

Karapov shook his head. "I don't know," he said miserably. "I don't know anything, Forest. The ones who know are the ones who know— the group who have been funding and developing it." Karapov glanced over his shoulder in fear, but they were still alone.

"Do you know who they are, Professor?" Forest was using his voice to caress the old man.

Karapov laughed morbidly. It sounded like a death rattle. "Don't be stupid. Of course not." His head swiveled toward Forest and he peered at him gauntly. "Do you think that if I knew who they were I would still be alive?" His fingers began to twitch in his lap. "As it is, they no longer need me . . . at least not for the moment . . . so even I represent a liability. They have the machine and they know how to run it." His hands shrugged helplessly.

"But you know that there is a group? That's something."

"It's nothing. A group like this is invisible. They are only tied together by an idea. A philosophy." Karapov let his eyes meet Forest's for a fleeting second. "I would have to say that their philosophy lies somewhat to the right, if that helps you." He looked away. "But it won't. They're not just in the military. They're in government and business as well. The project couldn't have succeeded otherwise."

Forest needed more. The old man was so fragile now he was becoming brittle, yet Forest needed a few more pieces of information. He had seen a glimmer of light at the end

234

of this nightmare and, although it was a dim light, it was all he had.

"Surely you must know something more, Professor," Forest coaxed. "After so many years, you must have learned something. Something." He could see that Karapov was terrified to speak, as if merely uttering a name would bring an instant reprisal. "Please, Professor. Please." Forest let an edge of urgency show in his voice. "Just tell me what you know." Karapov clasped his twitching hands together.

"The name of the group is Thursday, as Arthur told you," he said in a muted voice. "And they have named my discovery the Thursday Machine. Very ironic," he continued bitterly. "You see, Jupiter was the Latin god of all celestial happenings: wind, rain, thunder, lightning, even tempests. The Romans dedicated one of the days of the week—Thursday, 'Jovis Deis'—to him. It became Jeudi in French. In German, Thursday is Donnerstag, named after Donnar, their god of thunder and war. The Scandinavian god was Thor, and thus in English we have the name Thursday."

"Project Thursday and the Thursday Machine," Forest muttered to himself. "They sure make their intentions clear, don't they?" He reached out his hand and grasped Karapov's arm, trying to give him strength. "Who was your contact, Professor?" Forest was insistent now. "Can you tell me just one name?"

Karapov sat with his lips pursed as if he couldn't bear to spit out the words. But as he watched, Forest could see the anger rising in him until he was flushed with hatred. "The only name I know," Karapov's voice hissed with venom, "is General Harlan Wells."

CHAPTER TWENTY-FOUR

Forest should have been stunned, but he wasn't. General Wells. Of course. It made too much sense. Now that everything started to fit together, Forest realized what a dangerous game he'd been playing in his ignorance. Of all the people in the world to tell his theory to, he had chosen the one wrong one. No wonder the general had denied everything.

And he'd told him that he had told Arthur! Forest looked miserably into the now-empty chamber. Now he understood why there was no storm on the radar that night. Forest felt like he had put a gun to his brother's head and pulled the trigger. And then there was Babyface showing up so conveniently at the airport. And then Jenny! He had picked a great person to have an affair with. But who had picked whom? And who had infiltrated whose ranks?

"You are surprised, Forest?" Karapov

seemed to be taking macabre pleasure in the impact of his revelation.

"It's not so much that I'm surprised, Professor. I'm terrified." Forest was telling the truth. He knew now that once he left this room his life was worth next to nothing. The general had seen him with Karapov. Forest had signed his own death warrant.

"So now you understand why I tried to prevent you from getting involved," Karapov said sadly. "This is such an ugly business, and they are so ruthless." Forest's mind was racing like a frenzied rat through the corridor of a maze, looking for escape. There had to be a way out of it but he needed time to think, and time was just about out. One thing he knew was that he needed the professor's help. He needed all the information Karapov had, and more.

Forest knew he had to break the tension in the room before the professor would be of any use to him. The old man was so terrified that he couldn't see any alternatives. Forest searched for a solution and, as always, reverted to what came easiest to him, his TV personality. His face broke into a wide grin, taking Karapov completely by surprise. Forest had just undergone a total physical and psychological change. He went into a perfect impersonation of Laurel and Hardy, playing both parts.

"Well, well, Stanley. This is another fine mess you've gotten us into," he said, becoming the fat man. Then he shrank his body and became Laurel as he scratched the top of his head

238

in confusion and whimpered, "I'm sorry, Ollie . . . I was just trying to help." Despite himself, Karapov began to laugh, and Forest laughed with him. The anxiety that had been gripping them both for so long was suddenly gone and they let themselves go, roaring until it hurt, until they were bent over holding their sides, with tears in their eyes.

Gradually the spasms subsided. Karapov gazed at Forest with deep affection, the corners of his mouth still twitching in amusement. "What a talent you have, my boy. How you could always make us laugh . . . and how many classes you disrupted. But what could I say? I was always laughing the hardest."

"But I was also one of your best students, Professor. Don't forget that. You knew that I was a passionate weatherman, even then." Karapov nodded in agreement, remembering the old days fondly. "Well, I still am, Professor. And I am still your most devoted admirer. What you have achieved is the ultimate dream of every meteorologist. You, my own teacher, have joined the ranks of the immortals—Newton, Edison, Einstein, and now . . . Karapov." Forest swiveled to face the machine. He ran his hands over the metal of the console. "It's very beautiful, Professor. And awesome. You should be very proud."

Karapov shook his head tiredly. "No, Forest. I am ashamed. I have given birth to a Frankenstein."

"But that's not true. The machine is neutral. It has no will of its own. In your hands it could be a life-giving instrument for mankind. You could turn deserts into gardens and feed the earth. In Thursday's hands, it's a weapon of destruction."

"But unfortunately," Karapov pointed out, "it is in their hands."

Forest slapped his hand down on the console and stood up. "Then we'll just have to take it away from them!" He was excited now because he finally saw a way out. There was one way to fight this group and liberate the machine from the group's control that they couldn't stop. No matter how powerful they were.

Karapov began to protest, but Forest stopped him. "Look, Professor, let me ask you a question. You don't really believe that bullshit scenario you were telling me, do you? That was Thursday's logic, wasn't it? Not yours. Tell me the truth, Professor, because that's all we have left between us."

Karapov looked up into Forest's eyes and then down at his hands. His fingers were wrestling in his lap again. Finally he looked up. "No, Forest, you're right. I don't believe it. Where there is one answer, there is always another. And to take such violent and cataclysmic action before the possibilities have been explored is always a mistake. It is not scientific. And," he smiled bleakly, "it leaves no room for humanity . . . or God."

Forest's grin of relief was contagious. "Thank you, Professor. I thought I was going crazy. I thought I didn't know you after all these years."

240

"People change, Forest. They get tired. They become afraid."

"Not about the fundamentals, they don't. I don't care whether Thursday is the whole fucking U.S. military, or just that fat, cigar-smoking man in the Pentagon. Nobody has the right to play God. The people of the world have a right to have a voice in their own destiny, and they're not getting it. What's going on here is genocide. People from Attila to Hitler have tried to twist the rationale for mass murder into a saleable form, but it doesn't work. The world always fights back. And we have to fight them, or we're as guilty as they are."

Karapov smiled at Forest ruefully. "You are very young and passionate, my friend. And of course what you say is true. In principle. But I am afraid that there may be no way out of this one." Forest reached down and took the old man's arm, squeezing it gently.

"Listen to me, Arkady." Karapov looked up. It was the first time Forest had ever used his first name. "What were you going to do with the gun? Shoot me?"

Karapov nodded his head miserably. "And then, myself."

"But why?" Forest asked incredulously.

"Because of Irena. They threatened her life. I am useless now, and you know too much. But she knows nothing. She could live." Forest grabbed Karapov's other arm and shook him gently.

"So we're both dead men then. Ghosts. What have we got to lose? Please, Arkady, give us—

241

give those millions of people a chance. Just listen to my plan." Forest held onto Karapov until he nodded agreement, but Forest could see that there was no commitment. Still, one inch at a time.

"Arkady, try to understand something. Thursday's power isn't that they have your machine. Their power isn't even in their ability to control the weather. Their only power is in keeping it a secret. If we expose the secret, their power is gone. And none of us is in danger anymore." Karapov was listening at least, but Forest could see the doubt in his face.

"Look. I have access to a television network. In two minutes I can talk to thirty million people. I can expose Thursday fast, and diffuse them before they have a chance to kill you or Irena or me. If only you'll help me, Arkady."

Karapov was still resisting. "They'll discount everything, deny it as ridiculous science fiction. We'll be discredited as lunatics. And, dear Forest, forgive me for what I am about to say, but your image is not exactly . . . well, you are better known as an entertainer and comic than as a scientist."

Despite himself, Forest was stung by Karapov's observation. How long would he be haunted by the clown? "I can change my image in ten seconds, Arkady, if I can present facts. If I can show up with proof."

"But there is no proof!" Karapov shouted in frustration. "That's what I keep telling you. That's what makes it so insidious. There is no proof."

"There has to be," Forest shouted back. "There has to be something. Tell me what disasters Thursday has been responsible for."

"I can't, Forest."

"Why not, Arkady? Because you're still afraid?"

"No, damn you. Because I don't know!" Karapov looked away. "Once the program became functional I was excluded. So I'm in the same boat you are, I can only guess." He looked back at Forest helplessly. "Oh yes, I know that Nixon made it rain on a demonstration once. But what good does that do? And as for your documented disasters—Garnett, Johnstown and the others—who knows? I can't see what purpose they would serve, so I doubt that Thursday produced them."

Karapov sat down dejectedly. "Don't you see that the new, erratic tendencies of the weather play perfectly into their hands? It is virtually impossible to distinguish between a manmade disaster and a natural one. That's why it's the perfect weapon. It is invisible, and there can be no retaliation because there is no one to blame."

Forest slammed his fist down on the console. There had to be something! His mind was bouncing around in his head like a ping-pong ball, desperately searching for an answer. There was no way to get proof from the disasters themselves. Okay. Then maybe there was a way . . .

"What about the satellites?" he asked Karapov.

"What about them?"

"I don't know!" Forest didn't bother to hide his impatience. "You tell me. You invented them. Tell me about them."

Karapov pondered for a moment and then, for a brief moment, a light appeared in his eyes. "Well, there is one thing ... it isn't much, and I'm not sure how you could do it ... but ..."

"For God's sake, Arkady. What is it? Tell me anything. We're clutching at straws here."

"You see," Karapov began illustrating with his hands, "for the satellites to function they must be in a certain relationship to each other. They must triangulate the area they are affecting in very precise coordinates: eighty-three degrees, fifty-eight degrees, and thirty-nine degrees respectively."

Forest immediately understood. "And if we match up the dates and places the satellites were in functional position with the dates and places of disasters, we've got a lock! That's not bad proof, Arkady."

"But, Forest, it's not that easy. As of two years ago there were over three thousand five hundred satellites in orbit. And you'd have to go back a good number of years. It's like looking for a needle in a haystack."

Forest came alive. "At least we know what the needle looks like, Arkady. We have a chance. There's a place that tracks all those satellites—Goddard."

"Yes, Goddard Space Center. That's right. But they keep it all in computers, Forest. And it's a government installation." Forest smiled at the professor's objections.

"Let me take care of that, Professor. You've already done your part." He beamed at Karapov, determination and enthusiasm shining in his eyes. "It's worth a try, isn't it, Arkady? It's worth a try for two dead men." Karapov smiled back at Forest and nodded.

"Yes, Forest. It is worth a try." They embraced each other in a bear hug. At that moment, the lights went out.

CHAPTER TWENTY-FIVE

The blackness in the room was so complete that the two men held onto each other for a moment just for a point of reference. Then they separated and were alone in a sea of dark. Fear touched them simultaneously.

"The soldiers . . ."

"The general must have . . ." They stood frozen, listening for the sounds of pursuit over the too-loud reality of their own breathing. Then Forest heard Karapov patting himself— rabbit's feet moving over a wet lawn.

"Ah yes, here it is." There was a rasp and the professor managed to get his lighter working. They became conspirators over the flickering flame. Forest picked the gun up off the console.

"Let's go. We're getting out of here." Karapov looked at Forest, his face haggard and exhausted in the darkness, and smiled bitterly.

"You see, my boy, how they make us play their game. Now you have the pistol in your hand." He shook his head sadly and went out the door. Forest found his umbrella and briefcase and followed Karapov out of the control room, through the lavatory, and into the empty, echoing chamber. They groped their way through the cavernous space toward the door, pausing to listen for sounds and pushing each other on ahead.

They reached the large, wooden front door and the professor extinguished their light. Forest remembered worrying about how he was going to escape from this place and almost laughed out loud. He grabbed the handle of the door and turned the knob, crouching to the side of the door so that the bright spotlights wouldn't hit him. But there were no spotlights, and nothing could have prepared him for the darkness that lay outside. It was as if the whole town had disappeared. The waterfall Forest had created was no more, and the soldiers had left their post. There was nothing except for the brutal, pelting rain and a strange whooshing noise that sounded like a very strong wind. But standing in the colonnade outside the building, Forest could feel no strong wind.

"Arkady, this rain . . ."

"I know," Karapov interrupted. "Don't tell me. It isn't normal." As their eyes adjusted to the darkness, spots of light began to appear in the distance. Candles or flashlights, Forest figured. He inched his way to the top of the steps and suddenly the whooshing sound identified itself. Water was rushing past the building like

a river. Peering into the dark, Forest estimated that the water was at least 2 feet deep.
It had already reached the second step and was
lapping at the building.

A car came around the corner of Maple
Street and, for a moment, there was enough
light to see what was happening. The entire
campus had become a river, which meant that
the entire town was also. The car passed about
100 yards away, pushing a wave of water in
front of it. The headlights illuminating the
water made the car look like some kind of
Jules Verne underwater creature. And then it
was gone. Something, thought Forest, was very
wrong.

Karapov joined Forest at the edge of the
steps. "It's the dam." Forest could hear a note
of hysteria in his voice. "There must be a leak
in the dam. I must get Irena." Before Forest
could stop him, Karapov had rushed down the
steps into the flowing current. The speed of the
rushing water was so great that Karapov's
knees seemed to buckle under the initial impact. But he seemed possessed, drawing on
some inner strength, and stood firm at the bottom of the steps, gaining his equilibrium as the
water rushed by his knees.

"Arkady!" Forest followed Karapov down
the steps until he could see him more clearly.
There was water rising above Forest's feet
even as he stood there. "Arkady, stop! Wait!"
Forest could see Karapov staring into the
darkness, orienting himself, steeling his body
to fight his way home. Deep, deep in the

darkness there came a loud, sharp crack and an ominous rumble. It sounded like lightning and thunder, but Forest knew it wasn't.

The sound seemed to galvanize the professor. His body went rigid and then he plunged into the night and vanished, as if he had been an optical illusion.

"It's the dam, Arkady," Forest called after him. "It's too late. Come back." But Forest knew that Karapov was gone and that he was alone. The rumble of the dam was terrifying and all Forest had to fight it with were the numbers running through his head. The coordinates. Forest decided he would live.

There was another rumbling in the distance and Forest realized that the dam was going to break. He had to find high ground. He waded into the current and was swept off his feet. As he fought to regain his footing, he became aware that he was holding his umbrella above him as if it could keep him dry. His briefcase had disappeared downstream. Forest searched the darkness ahead and then looked back at the looming hulk of the Calder Building. He had no choice. His only chance for survival was to get to the top of the building.

Forest fought his way around the side of the building, thrashing through the now half-submerged shrubs and bushes. He remembered having seen a fire-escape ladder somewhere near the back. He stared upward in the darkness, the rain hurting his eyes as the drops struck him viciously, trying to locate the ladder, but there was nothing there. The rumbling grew louder and the rising water had almost reached his waist. Panic was beginning to set in.

Then he saw it, or rather sensed its shape hanging above him. He waved his arm over his head and felt nothing. The bottom rung of the ladder was too far above him to reach and he could never jump high enough laden down by wet clothes. Reacting by instinct, he snapped his umbrella closed, reversed it so the handle was up, and flailed out above his head. He hit metal, and then the handle hooked a rung and Forest pulled. The ladder didn't move, but Forest's hands did as they slid off the slippery cloth, leaving him face down in the water. Spitting and cursing, he found the umbrella end and yanked again. The ladder came sliding down, almost decapitating him.

Forest climbed for what seemed like an eternity, feeling his way with his hands and trying to keep his footing on the slippery rungs. As he got closer to the top, the intensity of the roar increased, but the pounding of his heart was keeping pace with it. The rumbling seemed to be coming from everywhere and, as he reached the roof, Forest knew he had only moments before the world exploded.

He kicked off his shoes and then started ripping off the rest of his clothes, listening desperately for the change in sound that would mean the dam had broken and the onslaught had begun. He knew he would never see it coming.

And then, between blinks, it happened. It

250

sounded like the air was being let out of 10,000 balloons all at once, and the water was free and running, a giant killer wave devouring the valley.

Forest threw himself flat onto the roof, clutching the slanting slate surface with his fingers and toes, and prayed that the stone building would hold. He could hear the solid mass of destruction careening down the valley toward him, ripping houses from their foundations, snapping great oak trees like matchsticks, and swallowing everything as it came.

The 20-foot-high wave hit the building and Forest was thrown straight up into the air, as if the building had been dynamited from within. As Forest fell to the roof on his hands and knees, he could feel the wave leap around the building, but, just as it passed, his worst fears were realized. The whole building began to wobble like it was made out of plywood.

Forest got to his feet and teetered his way across the swaying roof to the edge. The rasping, grating, tearing noise below told him how quickly the building was disintegrating. Then the building began to buckle and Forest dove out into the churning water, flinging himself as far as he could to avoid being crushed by the crumbling granite walls.

The water was an oily, writhing creature, alive with nameless terrors. Forest sank under the surface and suddenly felt himself sucked forward by the current, hurtling into the darkness. He fought upward and surfaced to find breakers leaping over each other and twisting currents passing him at different speeds, like trains on another track. Forest swam with the current, trying to gasp a breath of air when it would let him.

Over the roar of the water he thought he could hear screams of helpless victims torn from their beds and plunged into a real nightmare. Suddenly the night exploded into fire in front of him. Cars, trees, houses, and a huge pile of rubble that had once been a town, had been caught against a highway overpass 200 yards away, and an oil tank had rammed the debris and exploded. The fire lit up the area for hundreds of yards and revealed a horror greater than any imagination in the darkness could have conjured up.

Forest saw saw debris of every kind bobbing and churning around him. He fended off a piano as it sped by him, and suddenly a hand slapped him in the face. It was a woman. Her arms reached out to Forest like a Siren, pleading to be taken, begging for help. And then, as if she had leaped from a platform, she was upon him, dragging him under the surface. They sank together, her frantic arms preventing Forest from helping either of them. Forest tried to fight her off and finally succeeded by diving under and behind her. He came to the surface and threw his arm over her shoulders and around her head. Then he froze, letting the water carry them along. The woman was dead. It had been the current dashing her against him all the time.

A telephone pole tumbled dangerously near.

Forest let the woman's body slip away and grabbed onto the pole as it went by. He took a few quick, deep breaths and rested for a second, but the telephone pole plunged through the open window of a car. The weight tipped the pole on end and catapulted Forest into the water as it changed direction.

An eight-year-old girl clung to a door. She started screaming when she saw Forest, but no sooner had he started swimming toward her then the door flipped over and then back again. The girl had disappeared into the blackness.

Forest was exhausted. He was cold and, in spite of his swimming stamina, he could hardly lift his arms out of the water. Every second was a fight to keep from being battered by the debris that was rolling and diving invisibly around him. Most were just shapes, but when he brushed against them he could feel the metal of a car or the padding of a sofa, or a bed. But the most terrifying were the bodies. A hairy head bobbed up next to him. It turned out to be a dog. The angry waves were not discriminating.

The screams grew more infrequent. Suddenly Forest was pulled under by another silent current and, with no strength left to fight to the surface he experienced the moment of drowning.

Something wooden slammed into Forest's body from below and shot upwards. Forest held on as he felt the massive hulk launch itself above the surface of the water. He quickly filled his lungs with precious air as the side of a house came back down to the surface, creating its own wake in the midst of all the churning liquid. He held onto the frame where there were no more windows and wondered how long his instant raft would stay on the surface. It didn't follow a straight line, but weaved around slower floating objects, sometimes almost making a right-angle turn. Incongruously, Forest felt for a moment like he was on an amusement park ride.

Forest seized the moment to wipe the water from his eyes and immediately realized he could see flashing lights ahead of him to the left. They were higher than the surface of the water and Forest knew he had to get to them. He had no idea how far away they were, but they weren't moving, so they had to be **on** safe ground.

Forest estimated his raft had to be moving at almost 30 miles an hour and the blinking, flashing lights were getting closer as he rushed downstream. Now he could just make out the silhouettes of several cars. They had to be police cars, he thought to himself, and now, from their size, he guessed they were only 50 or 60 feet away.

At that moment, his raft crashed into something stationary, shattering it and throwing Forest forward into the black water. The splintered lumber rained down around him, but missed him under the surface of the water. He was dizzy from exhaustion and needed energy to reach the lights, but he was afraid he had nothing left.

Then, from below, Forest felt tentacles reaching out and grab him. He couldn't move his legs, and his head filled with visions of giant octopi. But when he swallowed his fear and reached down, he found himself tangled in a spaghetti-like mass of telephone wires. The current was still rushing past him, but he wasn't moving, and he realized that the wires were fastened to something permanent. He held on. It was more dangerous being a still object among the continuous barrage of debris, but Forest knew that if he let go he would surely drown.

The wires seemed to lead in the general direction of the lights and the bank. Forest summoned his last reserve of strength. Hand over hand, he crawled along the wires, pulling himself against the teeth of the current that was trying to rip him from his hold. He struggled over the insane objects that had been captured by the makeshift net—a sewing machine, a bicycle. And then he came to a scene that would live with him forever. A couple—dead—were locked in each other's arms, completely entangled by the wires like lovebirds in a cage.

Forest stared in morbid fascination and only snapped out of his trance in time to duck under a telephone pole spearing its way through the waves. He crawled on, not able to distinguish anything but the lights, and even they were a moving, swaying blur.

He couldn't pass out. Not now. Not yet. As he pulled his body through the wires, trying to keep his head pointed toward the lights, they grew brighter, and brighter. The reflections of their prisms through the waves washing across his face danced like starbursts of fireworks. Finally the brightness made him close his eyes. And then everything went dark. And Forest knew he was dying.

THURSDAY

JULY 13

ARUBA

All he wanted to do was play tennis and maybe lie on a beach.

All she wanted to do was lie on a beach and maybe play tennis.

They had saved for this vacation for over a year. Six nights, seven days. Four hundred sixty-eight dollars and fifty cents per person, double occupancy, unlimited tennis and water sports, chaise lounges, and welcome cocktails. Plus hotel tax and tips. Plus all the pluses. It had been raining from the minute they stepped off the plane. Five straight days of rain and Kenny Blatt was ready to kill.

"Cocksuckers," his foot lashed out at the defective air conditioner. "The tourist brochure said that Aruba's sunshine was almost a cliché among Caribbean travelers." Lucille watched his face grow red with anger as she paced back and forth in the livingroom section of their tiny suite. He angrily enunciated every word.

"Rainfall is so scarce, they said, that an afternoon shower becomes a topic of conversation for days." He shrieked at the ceiling. "Bastards!" Lucille reached out for him across the room.

"Please, Ken, somebody'll hear you."

"I want them to hear me—the fakes, the fucking fakes."

After fourteen years of marriage, Lucille knew his stubborn streak all too well. She told herself there was nothing she could do about it, but the truth was she was always intimidated by his anger and afraid it might turn on her. She resented that truth. Having read every magazine on the island by now, Lucille picked up an old copy of *Cosmopolitan*. She flipped disinterestedly through the advertising and then looked up at Ken, still pacing back and forth and muttering under his clenched teeth.

When had the mystery disappeared, she mused to herself. Images of bathroom doors left open too many times flashed across her mind. The years had thinned their interest and fattened their torsos, and her sexual thrills these days came from reading historical romances like *Love's Wildest Promise* and *Love's Avenging Heart*. Lucille wandered down into the pages of "How To Seduce Somebody Else's Husband." The painful little jokes about their non-sex life crept in between the paragraphs of the *Cosmo* article she had read before.

Suddenly, despondently, faced with the reality of an entire loveless future, Lucille put the magazine down and crossed over to the bar. She poured a double—even more than a double—gin and tonic and, after taking a healthy gulp, walked over and handed the drink to Ken. He'd gone from boil to simmer and was now trying to distract himself with a baseball game on TV. In Spanish.

Lucille then walked deliberately across the room, closed the magazine she had been reading, and continued into the bathroom. She turned on both faucets of the tub so that the water rebounded off the sleek white porcelain surface. Then, searching for an unused bottle of bubble bath, she poured in twice the required amount and closed the door.

"Lucille?" Ken knocked on the door. "Lucille?" There was no answer. "Lucille, what are you doing in there?"

"I'm taking a bath" came the matter-of-fact response.

"In the middle of the afternoon?"

"Have you got something better to do?" she replied through the door.

He pondered the sarcasm, but decided not to reply and went back to the television, and flipped the channel selector back and forth violently between the three channels, hoping to find something to distract his anger. He downed the rest of his drink to avoid looking outside at the rain, the fucking rain.

Some time had passed, but he was not aware of how much, when Lucille's hand reached over his shoulder and replaced his empty glass with a full one, leaving behind a delicate cloud of jasmine. Or was it lavender? He turned around

259

but she was gone. He sat waiting for her return, but she didn't.

"Lucille," he called. Again she didn't answer and that annoyed him. He got up, feeling his gin and tonic, and walked slowly, curiously following the wonderful aroma to the bedroom door.

His mouth opened silently as he sucked in the surrounding air with amazement. There was Lucille, his wife of fourteen years, her legs splayed apart, each foot tied to a bedpost by a silk stocking, and her arms stretched over her, tangled in a similar manner to the headboard. Ken took an unsteady step forward into the room. His mind twisted back and forth between disbelief and the erotic fantasy before him. His eyes memorized every inch of her from head to toe. Long brown hair, always neatly hidden, splashed wildly across the pillows. And her eyes—her eyes seemed larger, emphasized even more by the silver shadow above them. The soft fresh gloss of her lips made him blink. Lucille? A black silk slip he didn't remember floated magically up and down curves he had also forgotten. The slip stopped almost on purpose above her thighs, revealing a hint of hair gathering in the darkness beneath it. And her knees wandered hypnotically from side to side, beckoning him a step closer.

Before he could finish the "doing" in "What are you doing?" he was conscious of an enormous erection, the kind he had only for someone he couldn't have. He placed his drink unsteadily on the night table and sank slowly beside her, unleashing the fantasies and the lust that had nothing to do with the Ken and Lucille of the last fourteen years.

Wonderful minutes, perhaps wonderful hours, had passed before Lucille heard Ken speak for the first time.

"Could you send some champagne to room one thirty-eight please. . . . Just leave it at the door, I'll sign for it later." He put the phone down quietly and rolled over into her arms again. She stroked his face as they exchanged the glow of love both had given up for lost. Tenderly, he kissed the smile on her lips and then her chin and her neck and her shoulders. He nibbled delicately down her throat and across her breasts. Rain fell from the skies and from Lucille's eyes with joy.

CHAPTER TWENTY-SIX

In Washington, Jenny Wells was listening to the morning news on TV with one ear as she got ready for work. She was moving from one room to another, plugging in the coffee, making the bed, putting on makeup and getting dressed, so she didn't really hear the beginning of the news report about the Hamilton Dam disaster. The name would have meant nothing to her, and sandwiched as it was between the rest of the morning's bad news, there was no reason for her to pay any special attention.

But then she heard Forest's voice. She was sure it was his voice and she ran to the TV set. What she saw was a scene of utter chaos: floodlights; police cars and ambulances, their lights flashing; men running back and forth with stretchers; and, in the middle of it all a figure wrapped in a blanket, lying on a stretcher, and a reporter trying to interview him. For a moment Jenny couldn't concentrate on what they were saying. She was staring at the TV in shock, creeping closer and closer to the set, her eyes riveted on the victim. His face was bruised and covered with grease, but it was Forest all right.

The reporter was trying to get him to talk. "You were right in the middle of it, sir. Can you tell us what happened?"

Forest shook his head, trying to clear the grogginess. ". . . Dam broke . . . swimming . . . thought I had drowned. . . ." The exhaustion in his voice was evident. He paused and shook his head again. "I thought I had drowned. . . ."

"Well, you certainly were very lucky, sir. You are one of the very few survivors of this disaster." The reporter obviously wanted to ask Forest more questions but the medics had moved in and were lifting the stretcher, so he turned his attention elsewhere. As Jenny watched, they put Forest into an ambulance and shut the door. She sat in front of the TV set, mesmerized.

The ringing of the phone startled her because she didn't know how long it had been ringing. In a daze, she went to answer it.

"Hello, Jenny? Jenny? Are you there?"

"Forest? Is that you?"

Forest chuckled into the phone. "Of course it's me. How are you doing?"

"Oh, Forest," he heard her wail, and then he heard her start to cry. "I was watching the news and there you were . . . almost drowned . . . on a stretcher. . . ."

"Jenny, I'm all right." Forest interrupted

her with an authority in his voice she had never heard before. "That was filmed last night and I'm fine now. Now listen to me." Forest waited until she stopped sobbing. "I need to come over. Is that all right? I mean, are you alone?"

"Yes . . . please." Forest could hear her trying to control her voice.

"Good. I'll be there in half an hour." He checked the phone book again. "Is this the right address? 3000 P Street?"

"Yes, that's it."

"Can you meet me outside with money to pay the cab?"

"Yes, Forest."

"Okay. I'm on my way."

"Forest . . ." Jenny's voice was tentative.

"Yes, Jenny."

"I love you," he heard her say simply.

"Later, Jenny," Forest answered. And then he hung up. He stood for a moment in the phone booth, drumming his fingers on the glass. He was perplexed. He hadn't been prepared for her reaction at all. Not at all.

CHAPTER TWENTY-SEVEN

So far, so good. Forest's luck was holding. Maybe because of the bruises on his face, or maybe because of the confusion, no one had recognized him when he had been admitted to the hospital last night. He had feigned amnesia and they had bought it. Now he was dressed in a soiled orderly's uniform he had found in a hamper and, amid the arrival of new victims and the clamor of hysterical relatives, no one had seemed to notice him. He walked casually out of the hospital.

He hailed a cab and gave the driver Jenny's address. Ignoring the sparkling grandeur of the fresh Washington morning, Forest sat back in the cab and tried to think. He had called Jenny because he needed to get out of the hospital before he was recognized, and he knew that as soon as the newscast hit the air someone would be on his trail. Jenny's seemed like the safest place to go; at least it was the most unexpected. And he needed Jenny to get into Goddard.

What Forest hadn't been ready for was Jenny's emotional reaction on the phone. Now that he knew that General Wells was involved in Thursday up to his eye teeth, Forest couldn't help but have doubts about what role Jenny played in all this. If she was working with her father, she had to be the greatest actress that ever lived. The tears and the "I love you." Jesus, that was a little strong. And yet, he couldn't imagine the general sending his own daughter to seduce him. That should have been more than any father could have been capable of, but Harlan Wells wasn't any ordinary father and he seemed to be capable of things that wouldn't occur to most people.

So what was Jenny up to? And what was he doing? For all he knew, he could be walking into a trap. Maybe her job was to find out how much he knew, before they did anything about him. Or maybe she loved him. And maybe he loved her. There were too many maybes buzzing in his head. Forest closed his eyes and rubbed his temples. The one thing he was sure of was that he had a hell of a headache.

The taxi lurched around a corner, slowed down, and Forest opened his eyes. They had entered a pretty tree-lined street and the cabbie was looking for numbers. But Forest could see Jenny already, halfway down the block, sitting on the steps of a townhouse. She looked like a little girl sitting there, clutching her money in her hands.

"Stop there," he told the driver. "Where that girl is." The driver grunted and pulled the cab over to the curb at 3000 P Street. As the cab approached, Jenny came to meet it, peering into the back to see if it was Forest. When she saw him, her face lit up and she reached for the door. But instead of waiting for him to get out, she jumped in beside him and threw her arms around his neck. Forest let her press against him for a moment and felt his arms encircle her. They hugged each other in silence.

"You going on from here, or do you just want me to let the meter run?" The driver was watching them through the rear-view mirror, not seeming to care either way. Jenny unwrapped herself from around Forest and handed him the money she had been holding. Forest looked at the bills and could see that they were stuck together and indented from the intensity of her grip.

"We'll get out here," he said, and peered over the back seat at the meter. He separated a ten-dollar bill from the compress and gave it to the driver. The rest he returned to Jenny as he pushed her gently out of the cab. He watched the taxi drive slowly away and then turned to look at the building. It was a four-story, renovated federal house, which had obviously been divided into apartments. Then he looked at Jenny. God, she was beautiful. She was standing still, watching him, her money still clutched in her fist.

"Come on," she said, reaching for his hand. "You look horrible in those clothes. You'll give my street a bad name." She led him through the front door and pulled him behind her as they climbed the stairs. Forest was letting her lead him by the hand again, he realized, and wondered what he was about to walk into.

Jenny opened the door to a bright, airy apartment done in white pine. Bamboo shades covered the windows, but let the sunlight filter through, warming the wood. Jenny led Forest through the living room and to the bathroom, without saying a word. There was a tub of hot water drawn, and Forest could smell the bath salts. He recoiled.

"Jenny, believe it or not, I've seen all the water I want to for a long, long time. I just spent the evening swimming for my life." Jenny looked up at him impudently.

"Ever hear the one about falling off the horse, Forest? Well, it's true. Just take off that disgusting uniform and get into that tub. Trust me, you'll feel better." Forest saw that she was determined, and he was too tired to argue. Besides, the hot water might ease the ache in his bones. He took off the jacket and pants and handed them to Jenny. She was staring at his body.

"Jesus Christ!" She was shocked. "What were you swimming with—sharks?" Forest looked at himself in the mirror and winced. He was covered with scratches, bruises, cuts, and welts, and looked like he had just been released from a medieval torture chamber. Some of the bruises were turning interesting shades of purple. Forest looked at Jenny in the mirror and saw the pain on her face. "Get into that tub, buster," she said, trying to cover her emotions. "I'll be right back."

She hurried out of the bathroom, holding the soiled white uniform in one hand in front of her as if it were contaminated. Forest raised one foot to get into the tub and almost cried out in pain. He was beginning to realize how much punishment his body had taken and how much he really hurt. He inched his way slowly into the hot water, wincing as the water made contact with his cuts and scratches, and finally lay back. It felt good—at last. The warmth was soothing his bones and making him sleepy. Forest looked down at himself. The combination of the tinted water and the colors of his bruises made him look like a coral reef, and his penis floating and swaying in his pubic hair looked like some strange sea creature. He smiled and closed his eyes. He hadn't slept in twenty-four hours and it was catching up with him.

Suddenly he smelled coffee, and then he heard Jenny come into the room. He opened his eyes and sat up as she put a mug of black coffee and a snifter of brandy on the side of the tub. Then she put the lid of the toilet down and sat on it, looking at him.

"I don't know who needs the brandy more, you or me, but you start on it. And drink the coffee, too." She was being very serious and concerned.

"Jenny, you're acting like they just pulled

me out of the water. That happened hours ago. And I've been to the hospital."

"I don't care. I just put you back into the water and I know what you need. They didn't do this for you at the hospital, did they?" Forest shook his head, both answering her question and marveling at the incredible twists of feminine reasoning. "Then drink up," she said. He did, and the combination of brandy and coffee fused in his stomach like a sunburst. By God, thought Forest, she was right. He could feel the inner warmth radiating to meet the outer warmth of the bath. He drank again, waiting for them to balance.

Jenny sat quietly watching Forest, apparently appeased that he was following her instructions and that she was helping cure him. Then she said softly, "Was it very terrible?"

Forest didn't answer for a long time. The events of the night before ran in front of his eyes like a movie, except that everything was out of sequence. Finally, not looking at her, he began to talk, slowly at first and then with greater and greater intensity, until the experience came pouring out of him.

"I don't care how many times you've seen pictures of it . . . or newsreels . . . or thought about it . . . you just cannot imagine how awesome the power of nature is when water gets rolling. It makes you feel like a fly, a pebble . . . like a crouton in a giant world where everything is being tossed around like a salad.

270

"My God, Jenny, there were cars flying through the air, buildings being ripped out by their roots, and telephone poles swirling like matchsticks in a sewer drain. I feel like I've been to hell and ridden down the river Styx. And all around me, death. I was washed over Professor Karapov's home—over him and Irena. And if I weren't such a strong swimmer in such good condition I would have drowned, too. And even then, I did drown at the end. I couldn't swim anymore. My body gave out and I felt myself dying." Forest closed his eyes, trying to shut out the images. "I guess they pulled me out."

Jenny stood up and offered him a hand. "Why don't you let me pull you out, too? You were right. You have had enough water for one day." Forest took her hand and let her help him out of the tub. His legs felt weak and his skin was wrinkled and puckered. He stood still while she dried him and with a big bath towel, patting him gently so as not to hurt him. Then she wrapped him in another big, soft, fluffy towel, and he followed her to the bedroom.

Jenny pulled back the covers and Forest dropped the towel and slid in. Somehow, although Jenny had only recently gotten up, the sheets were crisp and clean and cool. It felt like heaven. Jenny covered him and then lay down on the bed next to him. She sure was taking it nice and easy, he thought. But then again, that was all he could handle at this point. He had to have sleep and then he would deal with the world, if he lived that long. Forest turned his

271

head and found Jenny watching him again. He looked into her face for motives and found nothing but concern.

"What are you doing?" he asked. Jenny smiled a little.

"Just being greedy. I missed your face. And then I thought I had lost you and panicked, so I'm storing some up for later. Just in case." Forest tried to take a swipe at her and missed. "That's not funny."

"I know," she said. She wriggled closer to him and put her head down on the pillow, managing to lie next to him without crowding him or making him flinch. Instinctively, his arm reached up and curled around her head, drawing her golden halo closer to him. He knew he had to make a decision. To trust or not to trust. And he wished his emotions weren't all jumbled up in it. It would be so nice to have a lady again, a friend, an ally. But the general's daughter? Could it be that she didn't know? He squirmed on the bed, caught in his dilemma.

"What's the matter," she whispered into his ear, "do you hurt?" He listened for a false note, for something hidden behind that innocence, and could find nothing. Forest drew her closer.

"No, I don't hurt. It's just that I have a problem and I don't know how to deal with it." There was silence for a moment.

"Is it about me?" Her voice was calm and uninflected and Forest could read nothing in it. He took a breath that moved both their bodies.

"Yes, Jenny, that's what it's about." He could hear the edge in his own voice and he wasn't surprised when he felt her body stiffen. She tried to roll away from him, but he held her.

"It's that you don't trust me, isn't it?" Forest was about to answer, but she went on. "I knew I shouldn't have told you, and certainly not on the phone. Some dumb broad crying over you and telling you she loves you after one lousy date, if you call that a date." She was struggling to get free now and Forest had to hold on tight to prevent her from leaping up and away from him. "I don't know what *she* did to you, Forest. I don't even care. But I'm not her. I'm not any of the others. I'm me. And I don't even know if you feel anything for me at all." Jenny stopped fighting and went limp in his arms.

Forest felt his heart lurch and closed his eyes. "Ah, Jenny. . . ." He moved his mouth closer to the nape of her neck and breathed softly on her as he spoke. "That's the problem. I do care. If I didn't it would be so simple. But I do care." And Forest suddenly knew that he indeed did. Despite himself, he had said it, and peering inside his murky depths he saw there was an emotion shining. It scared him because it made him so vulnerable to hurt, but it also decided him, because he had nothing left to lose and something, at last, to gain. Jenny didn't move, so Forest continued talking, whispering, murmuring to her. Now he needed to talk, and he needed help, and God help them both, she was going to have to be it.

"This is the problem, Jenny my love," he said, snuggling closer to her. "I talked to Professor Karapov last night and learned some very unpleasant truths. It turns out that my theory about the weather was partially right. The only trouble was, I didn't go far enough. It's gigantic. Beyond what I could have ever dreamed. And it's monstrous." Forest was trying to figure out how to tell Jenny the story without mentioning her father, and at the same time tuning his body to hers, testing to feel any vibrations that would indicate that she knew. But she just pressed back against him, warm and firm, and he had no choice but to go on.

"Do you remember that blueprint Arthur sent me?"

"Of course."

"Well, that may have gotten Arthur killed." Jenny didn't move a muscle. "And Karapov." She still didn't move. "And now I'm in danger, and so is everyone I talk to. Do you understand what I'm saying? The reason I don't want to get you involved is because there's enormous danger, even in being seen with me."

Jenny snorted. "That's bullshit, buddy. And you're choking me." Forest let her go and she sat up and crossed her legs on the bed. Her eyes were blazing. "If you don't want me to play, say so. I won't kick you out of bed until you've had your little nap. But don't give me any lame-ass excuses about danger. If you

274

didn't want to involve me, why did you come here in the first place?" She waited for an answer and Forest had none. Goddamn feminine logic.

"All right," he said, pulling himself into a sitting position, "I'll tell you what I can. But," he said, shaking his finger at her mockingly, "don't blame me when you're dead. Remember that I warned you." Jenny grabbed his finger and bit it gently.

"Jenny, I'm serious." He pulled his finger away and Jenny bowed her head and folded her hands in her lap in a good-little-girl position. "Listen," Forest said, lifting her chin in his hand, "what I'm about to tell you is going to be very hard to believe. But it's true. And I have no way to prove it to you yet. So you're going to have to accept it on trust."

"Try me." Her levity was gone and there was icy intelligence in her eyes.

"The blueprint was a plan for a weather chamber. It exists—or existed—until last night when the dam broke. Karapov built it, but now it's gone and so is he."

Jenny nodded. "Did you find out what it was for?"

"Yes. It was the model for a system to control the weather." Jenny's eyes widened in astonishment.

"The system works. Man can control—is controlling—the weather on our planet."

"How?" she said abruptly, but clearly not as a challenge.

"With satellites," Forest continued. "Unfor-

275

tunately, the people who have control of the machinery are using it as a weapon to manipulate the future, and they have to be stopped.

"Who are the 'they'?" Jenny said, without blinking.

"I'm not one hundred percent sure." It wasn't a total lie, but Forest didn't feel like bringing up the general's involvement just yet. "But that's not important now. What is important is that I find some way to prove that they're doing it. I have to find some way to expose them, before they kill me." Forest searched Jenny's face. She hadn't known. He bowed his head for a moment. "And now that you know, before they kill you too."

Forest watched her swallow the information and digest it without flinching. "Okay," she said in a tight voice, "what do we do next?" She raised a small, brave smile. Forest blessed her intelligence, or gullibility, or love, or whatever it was that allowed her to accept what he had said without dismissing him as a lunatic. And it was nice to know that those wonderful tits were being supported by a strong backbone. He was tempted to reach out and hug her, but didn't. He smoothed the sheets instead.

"The only way I can prove what's going on is through the satellites. Karapov gave me their coordinates, but that's all he gave me. I need access to the computer tracking tapes at Goddard. And I need them right away. Using the coordinates, the tracking tapes, the weather records I can expose this . . . thing."

276

Forest looked her flat in the eye. "You work at Goddard."

He didn't turn his eyes away. He had asked the question and he had to see what her reaction would be. But as he scrutinized her face, all he saw was hurt, and then a hardening in her face muscles that revealed what she would look like when she was forty, if she wasn't careful. If she became hard. Forest was puzzled, but he waited, afraid to say anything that would tilt her, letting her emotions churn through.

Finally she broke. The spine that had been holding her erect dissolved and she sagged into a ball of misery. But there were no tears, and when she spoke her voice was muted by a cynicism that matched Forest's years.

"I should have known. Everybody's using somebody, but how far down the ladder can you go? You're not using my body. You're not even interested in my fine Harvard mind. All you fucking care about is where I work. That's why you're here!"

"Jenny?" She wouldn't look up. "Jenny, hear me!" Forest's voice had life again and strength, and the timbre ran through Jenny like a buzzsaw. She bobbed her head, acknowledging, but still avoided his gaze. Forest exploded.

"A minute ago you were begging me to trust you and to let you play. I walked in here, took off my clothes, got into your goddamned perfumed bath and drank your cognac and coffee. And now, here I am sitting naked in your bed

277

and telling you that my life is in danger and that you can help. And you don't think that's trust?" Forest wanted to stop but he couldn't.

"And it's not just about me and you, kiddo, but about something a lot bigger than that. And you think I'm using you? You say you love me? Well, what the hell do you love? This is who I am, and this is what I think is important. And where the hell is your trust?"

Forest stopped, staring at the top of her head, as she absorbed what he had said. He didn't know how she would react and didn't care. And, still, he knew he cared desperately.

At first she stayed bowed, as if the weight were too much for her. But then he saw her fingers begin to wiggle, tentatively, and then her toes. She **had** made a decision and energy was returning to her body. She uncurled her back like a flower rising to the sun, and her face emerged from her hair, shining. An electric current ran through Forest's body. He was excited, sexually excited, for the first time by intellect alone. She had understood.

"Jenny . . ." he said. She was smiling at him now. Her hands reached up to her blouse and began to unbutton it.

"You make me wet, Forest." She was watching her hands exposing her breasts. "I don't know why. You say the strangest things and I . . ." Jenny opened her blouse and let herself free. She shrugged out of the shirt and looked at Forest, puzzling. "It's not so much what you say, I guess," she was rubbing herself gently, her hand being his hand on her nipples, "as why you say it." She stood up on the bed and lifted her skirt. Forest looked up at her pale panties at the end of her little legs and could feel himself throbbing.

"Take them off, Forest." She took a step closer and held her skirt away, so he could reach. She was swaying slightly, almost dancing already. Forest ran his hands up her legs, first the outsides, and then using the back of his hands, inside her thighs, until he reached her joining place. His fingers reached inside the crotch of the flimsy cloth and rubbing gently, as she began to croon, he found that she was liquid for him. He pulled and his hands tore away from her, bringing the cloth with them, and she was open above him.

Forest threw the sheets off his body and lay back, unable to take his eyes away from the unsweeping panorama above him. Jenny could see him pointing at her and sank to her knees over him without touching. She hovered, watching his face, watching the twitching tremors run through his body and feeling them jangle her.

"I love you, Forest," she said, lowering herself an inch and rubbing their screaming exposed sensitivities against each other, but just touching.

"I love you, Jenny," Forest roared, and drove himself upward to meet her more than halfway.

CHAPTER TWENTY-EIGHT

Forest was lying sprawled in Jenny's bed, floating in a half sleep in the warm afternoon sun, when he heard the front door to the apartment click. He opened his eyes and saw that Jenny wasn't in bed with him anymore. He wondered how long he had been asleep.

"Jenny?" he called drowsily. He wanted to catch her before she went out. There were some things he needed her to do for him. There was no answer. "Jenny?" he called again, louder. Still there was no answer, but Forest was sure he could hear her moving around in the living room. What the hell was she doing out there? Maybe she had gone out and had just gotten back. He was about to get out of bed and get her, when the bedroom door swung open and Forest found himself staring into a silencer attached to a gun, attached to a pair of hands. The silencer was pointed at his head and, with the increased perception and absurd attention to detail that sometimes comes just before death, Forest saw the knuckles on the hand starting to grow white as they squeezed the trigger.

Forest flung himself onto Jenny's side of the bed just before he heard the *pffft* from the silenced bullet and felt it hit the bed where he had been lying. He rolled again and hit the floor as the second bullet murdered Jenny's pillow. Forest looked wildly around the room. He was trapped. He was naked. And soon he would be dead.

There was nowhere to go but up a flight of stairs at the back of the bedroom that must lead to the roof. By instinct, Forest grabbed the ashtray on the bedside table and threw it desperately at the figure in the doorway. And then he rolled again and scrambled to his feet, scrabbling, dodging, diving for the stairwell. He ran, feeling his balls slapping against his legs, painfully aware of how exposed he was, waiting for a bullet to smash into his spine. But as he reached the stairs, he could hear the killer's footsteps following him, methodically, as if he were sure he had Forest and was taking no chances. Forest devoured the steps two and three at a time, and he turned the corner just as another bullet chased him, burying itself in the wood behind him.

Forest turned and then turned again, his body beginning to tremble. It was a dead end. The stairs had led to an interior balcony that Jenny was using as a kind of greenhouse. There was no way out. He could hear the killer slowly climbing the stairs, and it was his lack of hurry that frightened Forest most. The man must have known the layout of the apartment. What a fucking setup! It made Forest furious. At himself. At his own stupidity. The man was almost at the top of the stairs and time had just run out.

As the killer turned the corner, he only had time to catch a brief glimpse of Forest swinging what looked like a long green baseball bat at him. Then there was a terrible scream as the long, sharp cactus spikes impaled themselves in the man's face and eyes. The killer dropped the gun, blood spurting from his wounds, and still screaming reached up to pull the plant away from his face. He screamed again as his hands were pierced by the spikes on the other side of the cactus.

His body contorted into a ball of agony, twisting and turning, hopping and kicking, desperately trying to free itself of pain. As Forest watched in horror, he saw the killer totter on the top step and then fall backwards into space, crashing down the flight of stairs, careening and bouncing into silence.

Forest put down the empty plant pot he had been clutching defensively, and picked up the gun. He was shivering. He honestly didn't know if he would be able to shoot the man if he had to. He followed him down the stairs slowly. The man lay crumpled at the bottom, motionless. Gingerly, gun extended, Forest stepped over him and looked down at what he had done.

It was horrible, but Forest had to find out

whether the man was dead. He prodded him sharply with his foot and jumped back. The man didn't move. Still keeping the gun trained on the man, Forest knelt beside the killer and felt for a pulse on his wrist. There was none. He was dead. Using the barrel of the silencer, Forest pried the cactus off the man's face. He had to know who he had killed. Staring up at him, his dead eyes running tears of blood, was Babyface, aide to General Harlan Wells.

CHAPTER TWENTY-NINE

Forest ran for the bathroom and just made it in time to vomit into the toilet. Then he washed his mouth out and rinsed his face with cold water, again and again. God, was he in trouble. Finally he turned off the tap, dried his face, and wrapped a towel around his waist. He felt naked enough. Too naked. He went back into the bedroom and, ripping a sheet off the bed, covered the body of the general's aide. Then he retrieved the gun and went into the living room. He had to think this out.

There was no other conclusion he could reach. It was obvious to Forest that he had been set up. It was all too convenient. Jenny gets him into bed and then she disappears. She notifies her father that Forest has talked to Karapov, knows too much, and she tells him where Forest can be found. Sleeping. General Wells sends Babyface and that should take care of everything. And Forest, like some adolescent kid, goes right along with it, following his cock wherever Jenny leads it. Terrific!

Forest sat there on Jenny's sofa, in Jenny's living room, and felt nothing but anger. But then he put his head in his hands as the pain came. Forest felt as though he'd been kicked in the heart. He had believed her, trusted her, opened to her, and now he was empty again. And alone. And in pain.

But Forest knew he had to shake himself out of this. He was in too much trouble to have time for self-pity. And one thing was very clear: he knew he had to get out of there, and in a hurry. When Babyface didn't report back, the general was sure to get worried and send reinforcements, and Forest had no desire to shoot it out with the whole U.S. Army. But he needed clothes and money, and he had to get to New York. And there had to be other ways to get the satellite information. He'd just have to find a way.

Forest was just about to pick up the phone to call Micky at the TV station when Jenny walked in the door. Her arms were filled with bundles. She smiled at him brightly, and then she saw the gun Forest was holding trained on her.

"Surprised to see me up and about?" Forest's voice was as cold as his eyes. "Sorry to disappoint you. Now drop those packages." Jenny looked at Forest as if he had gone crazy, and she just stood in the doorway, stunned. "I'm not kidding, Jenny," he said, getting up and moving a step closer to her. "Just step inside and drop everything." Jenny moved slowly into the apartment and pushed the door closed behind her. Then she let go of everything in her arms. The packages clattered to the floor.

"Forest, what—what are you saying? What are you doing with that gun?" Jenny seemed genuinely mystified and hurt, but Forest didn't trust her anymore. She was too good an actress. Shit, if she could pretend to make love like that, she could pretend anything. Or maybe she was just surprised and disturbed to see him still there, when he should have been dead and gone long ago.

"I trusted you, Jenny. And you turned me in. You set me up to be killed. You lured me into bed and then beat it, so that goon could get rid of me." Jenny's eyes turned hard, cold, blue flint.

"I did not, you stupid jerk. How dare you accuse me of something so loathsome. What do you think I am?"

"I think you're a Wells, and that blood runs deeper than love, or lust, or whatever you call what we've been doing." Forest waved the gun toward the bedroom. "Just step inside for a minute. Go on." Jenny slowly walked into the bedroom with Forest following her.

"Over there, under the sheet. Take a look." Jenny begged Forest with her eyes not to have to, but he pushed her with the nozzle of the gun toward the blood-stained sheet at the foot of the stairs.

Jenny dragged herself over and knelt down, averting her face as much as possible. She

286

lifted the edge of the cloth and peeked, and then she gasped and looked back again, throwing the sheet off the dead man's face.

"But that's . . ."

"That's right. You sure as hell know him."

"That's my father's aide! That's Eddie Robinson." She turned to face Forest. "What was he doing here?" Forest smiled at her coldly.

"So that's his name. I only knew him as Babyface. Not a very warm person. And for what he was doing here, you know that better than I do. I fell asleep and you called your father and told him what I had found out, and then you cleared out so that Eddie here could kill me. And he almost did, too. You've got some pretty bullet holes in your bed."

Jenny didn't bother to look at the bed. She covered the dead man's face and stood up, confronting Forest, her hands on her hips, leaning forward in anger. "You are a very dumb jerk, Forest Hill. Why would I call my father to send a man over to kill you?"

Gradually, Jenny's eyes widened in understanding, and then in horror. "You don't mean that my father . . . no! I don't believe it. Are you trying to tell me that my father is part of that weather thing? That he sent a man to kill you?" The impossibility of the situation was now racing through Jenny's well-trained mind and boggling it.

"I told you before that I had a problem, Jenny. I didn't know if you knew about all of this, or if you were working for him. I just guessed wrong, that's all." Forest looked at her bleakly.

"You didn't guess wrong about me, buster. And I can prove it." She walked past Forest, completely ignoring the gun. Forest had no choice but to follow her out of the bedroom, the gun now hanging limply at his side. Jenny went to the pile of packages she had dropped and began to unwrap them. She pulled a shoe box out of one bag and opened it, and then dumped a man's pair of shoes onto the floor. Then, almost like a child at Christmas, she frantically began tearing the wrappings off the other packages. Underwear, a suit, a shirt, a tie, socks, all came flying out of the growing pile of papers, until a complete outfit lay strewn about the floor.

"Does that look like I was coming home to a dead man, you prick?" she said. She searched around on the floor until she found her hand-bag, and took out an envelope. Tearing it open, she pulled out a wad of bills and threw them at Forest. "My life savings. I don't see any blood on it, do you?" Her frenzy passed, and she sat back down on her haunches. "I just went out to get you clothes and to get us some money to do whatever we had to."

Forest waved the gun helplessly. "Then how did your father find out I was here? How did he know to send Babyface here, just when you were gone and safe?" Jenny shook her head.

"How should I know? You were on television this morning, weren't you? You were in a hospital. You took a cab here. You have a famous face. Maybe he traced you. And maybe . . ." she said, bowing her head, "maybe he didn't care if Eddie killed both of us." Jenny looked up at him, her face filled with misery. "Did you ever think of that?"

Forest hadn't thought of it, and it floored him. He sat down slowly on the sofa. "You mean you didn't know . . ."

"That my father is a monster? That he doesn't care for any human being? Yeah, I knew that. But not this. Not this." Jenny got up and came over to where Forest was sitting. She reached down and took the gun out of his hand and put it on the coffee table, and then she sat down next to him.

"Are you sure? Are you sure that my father sent him . . . that my father is involved in the weather thing?" Her question was a clinging at hope. Forest could see in her eyes that she knew the answer already.

"I'm sorry, Jen. Karapov told me last night that your father was part of it. He had no reason to lie. And now . . ." Forest didn't know what to do. "Listen, I know how hard this must be for you. If you want to . . ." he paused, looking for the polite phrase, "play it neutral, I'll understand. Just give me time to get to New York."

Jenny's head shot around, her nostrils flaring. "What do you mean, play it neutral? I love you. How can I be neutral? And besides, you almost got shot to death in my bed, and I could have been killed also, and there's a dead man in my bedroom, and my father is doing God knows what to the weather . . . and you want me to play it neutral?" Forest had to admit that she had a point.

"Well, what are you going to do about it?"

"I've already done it, Forest. I was already committed to a side, even before I knew who was involved." Jenny got up and rummaged around in the mess on the floor until she found her purse again. She searched in it, feeling around, until she found what she wanted. It was a scrap of paper. "Here," she said, handing it to him. Forest looked at it. It was just a long series of numbers.

"What the hell is this, Jenny?"

"This is today's code, which enables you to tie into the Goddard computers. You can do it by telephone. You can plug your computer in New York into the computer at Goddard and pick its brains to your heart's content." She looked at him sadly. "You see, as far as my father is concerned, I'm already the enemy."

Forest stared at the numbers scrawled on the piece of paper, and then he stared at Jenny. She certainly was different from any woman he had ever met, and that was for sure. She had just given him the key to Thurday. She had just renounced her father. And, once again, she had given him the opportunity to be alive and love again. And she was just sitting there calmly, as if nothing was happening.

"Do you know what this is?" he asked her, waving the paper. His adrenalin was pumping. "Do you know what this means?"

Jenny smiled. "Yeah, sure I know what it means. I went and got it."

"It means we have a chance. And it means, with a little luck, we can stop them!" Jenny acknowledged his excitement, but she was also looking at him questioningly.

"What?" Forest asked. "What's bothering you?" Jenny suddenly became casual.

"Oh, I was just wondering. You know, this morning, what you said . . . did you mean it?" She was looking away. Forest reached over and took her hands.

"Jenny, I meant it with all my being. I meant it so much I almost died when I thought you had . . ." Her face came around and Forest leaned toward her and kissed her. "I meant it!"

"Good. I'm glad. I meant it too." She pulled away from him and grabbed at the towel around his waist. "Now, would you mind getting dressed, before they catch us in bed again?"

CHAPTER THIRTY

While Forest was picking out clothes from the pile of wrappings and putting them on, Jenny was on her hands and knees, gathering up the money she had thrown. Forest was amazed. Everything fit.

"How did you know what size I am? I don't even know all my measurements." Jenny squinted at him, amused.

"I've tried you on, buster. Remember?" He remembered. Forest finished dressing and Jenny disappeared into the other room, he assumed to pack a bag. It felt good to have clothes on again. She had dressed him well, with expensive clothes that were in good taste. He usually didn't do this well for himself. And even the shoes fit. Forest finished admiring himself and had just picked up the phone to dial Micky when Jenny walked into the room again.

"What are we going to do with you-know-who in there? If we leave him here, he'll stink up the joint." Forest put the phone down again.

"I would guess that we don't have to worry about that. When your father doesn't hear from him, he'll send the next wave. I'm sure they'll clean up. They're very neat." Jenny wrinkled her nose.

"Well, at least he has one virtue, my dad." She went back into the bedroom. Forest watched her go and admired her incredible ability to adjust. And her will power. He remembered that only an hour ago he had been vomiting.

It took Forest almost no time to get Micky on the line. She was, of course, frantic, in her wise-guy, nothing-affected-her style.

"I hear you've been swimming, boss. And for another network." Her voice boomed heartily over the phone. Then, subdued, she asked, "You all right, Forest?" Forest cackled at her evilly.

"Never better, my dear. Now listen, Mick, here's what you have to do. There was a storm over Harrison Dam last night that's supposed to have caused that flood. Track it for me. I want everything you can get. And fast."

"You got it, boss." Forest could hear the relief in Micky's voice that they were back to business as usual. "Do you want to tell me where you are, or whether you're ever coming home again?" Forest calculated quickly.

"No, Mick, I can't. It's better if I don't say. But you better get a stand-in for tonight's weather. You work up the report. I'm sorry to sound so mysterious, but I can't help it."

"Sure, sure." Her sarcastic reply came back immediately. "That's easy for you to say. Okay, will do. Anything else I can do for you, boss?"

"That's it, Mick. I'll see you soon. And thanks." She chuckled.

"Well, do stay in touch, Forest. There are some of us here who care what happens to you." The line went dead.

"Women," Forest muttered to himself, and hung up the phone.

"What about women?" Jenny had just come into the room carrying an overnight bag. "Don't tell me you're still trying to understand us?" Forest shook his head, acknowledging defeat. He looked at the clock over the fireplace and realized that more than an hour had passed since Babyface had arrived and that they were in real danger if they stayed much longer.

"I'm glad you're packed, Jenny. We have to get out of here before your . . . the general misses hearing from what's his name, Eddie." Jenny nodded, but put down her bag and sat next to Forest on the couch. She was plainly troubled about something.

"Forest, I want to call my father." Forest controlled his impulse to interrupt her, and let her go on. "I won't tell him where we are, or where we're going, but I need to know. You can understand that, can't you?" The fact that she was asking for permission made it clear that she was with him, but she was also still chafing at accepting this new concept of her father. Forest knew he had no choice. Unless he let her make the call, some part of her would remain unresolved, and she would be a liability. Yet, once she called, the chase would be on for real. It was a risk he had to take. He wanted and needed Jenny on his side.

"Call him," he said gruffly. "But make it fast. Short and sweet. We're sitting ducks here." Forest got up and began to pace around the room as Jenny dialed the phone. He wished he could hear both sides of this conversation. It was going to be a pip.

"General Harlan Wells, please." She waited. Forest paced. "General Wells, please. This is his daughter." She waited again. "Dad, it's Jenny." She looked up at Forest. "What's the difference where I am?" And then she listened. Forest tried to read her face but couldn't. The general was obviously talking nonstop, uncorking a river. Forest stopped pacing and sank into a chair. Jenny watched him sit, met his eyes, and then looked away. He could see that what she was hearing was hurting her. Finally she could stand it no longer.

"Dad . . . Dad . . . please stop for a second. I hear you. I just need to ask you one question." She was silent as the general erupted again, and Forest turned to look at the clock. The sweep of the second hand was relentless, and he wondered if the general was stalling for time, trying to have the call traced as they talked. He was about to motion to Jenny to cut it off, when she spoke.

"Dad, if you don't let me ask you this question, I'm going to hang up." She looked at Forest to let him know she was hurrying. "Thank you, Dad. Just tell me this. When I got back to my apartment this afternoon, I found Eddie Robinson there." She shook her head. "No, I'm not there now. He was dead. In my bedroom." Forest winced and stood up. "And I found two bullet holes in my bed. Did you tell Eddie to kill me too?" The general must have begun to shout because Jenny pulled the phone away from her ear. Forest could hear his voice on the other end, but he couldn't hear what he was saying. He watched Jenny's face harden into a cynical smile, and then she plugged the phone back into her face.

"Thanks, Dad, that's all I wanted to know." She stood up, and Forest could see the anger rising in her as her body tensed. "You've been a great father and a terrific mother. So long!" She slammed the phone down onto the receiver. Forest had seen Jenny's temper before, but nothing like this. She was on fire. She picked up her bag and faced him, a little, fighting dynamo.

"Let's go," she said, and started for the door. Forest was about to follow when the phone rang. Jenny never reacted. "Come on!" She stood at the door, surveying her apartment as Forest walked out, and then turned to follow him down the steps. The phone rang plaintively behind them, through the open door.

CHAPTER THIRTY-ONE

Without feeling a trace of paranoia, Forest stopped Jenny at the door to the street and checked in both directions. On the way down the stairs, he had explained to her that they couldn't use public transportation to get to New York and that they would have to drive. Forest was certain that the general would have all the airline, bus, and train terminals watched. Now he wanted to make sure that there wasn't someone waiting for them before they even got started.

Forest couldn't see anyone suspicious, but he knew that didn't mean anything. If there was someone there, and he was any good, he would never see him anyway. They ran down the steps and across the street to Jenny's orange Triumph. Jenny unlocked the car, never looking back, and Forest got the feeling that she was saying good-bye to this place forever.

There was no question about who would drive. Jenny slid in behind the wheel and gunned the motor into action. Forest was perfectly content to sit back and let her unravel the intricacies of getting them out of Washington. The car leaped forward, and Forest turned to watch Jenny as she drove. Her teeth were clenched and there was a muscle working in her jaw. She was still very angry.

Forest felt the little car almost literally make a right turn in midair as they turned the corner to head down the sloping hill known as 30th Street. The lights were with them, crossing N and M Streets, but even if they hadn't been, Forest knew it wouldn't have made much difference. Jenny was displaying no interest in anything having to do with the brake.

They hurtled across the little bridge spanning the C & O Canal and swerved under the K Street Expressway, tires screeching. Jenny surprised a line of cars carefully maneuvering their way onto the Rock Creek Parkway by cutting them off and squeezing onto the south ramp. Forest and Jenny were racing along at about 70 miles an hour before Forest finally felt it was safe to take a breath.

"Well?" he asked. "What did he say?" Jenny checked in her rear-view mirror and swerved into another lane.

"He said that you were a lunatic and a clown, and that you were messing around in something that was none of your business. He said not to believe anything you said, and that you were dangerous. He said I should come to his office and that he would explain everything.

to me, but that I should get away from you as fast as possible. I don't think he likes you, Forest." Forest smiled.

"I already got that impression. And I don't think the fact that I'm corrupting his beloved daughter is helping. What did he say about Eddie?"

"Oh, that was terrific," Jenny said bitterly. "He claims that Eddie wasn't sent there to kill you, only to bring you to the Pentagon so you two could have a talk. And it also seems that you are also now a murderer." Forest was stunned. He'd never thought about it that way, but there it was. There was a dead man lying on the floor and a gun on the coffee table covered with his fingerprints. Well, there was nothing he could do about that now. And somehow, Forest couldn't believe the general would leave Babyface there for the police to find. That would involve Jenny, and she was a little too close to home.

"What about you? How did he answer your question?" Jenny glanced at him and then turned her eyes back to the traffic. Forest could see she was hurt as well as angry.

"What he said was that I was his darling daughter and the only thing he had left in the world, and that he would never harm a hair on my head, but . . ." she sighed softly, "if I insisted on hanging around with a dangerous lunatic and clown . . ."

"Will you please stop calling me a clown, Jenny," Forest interrupted.

"I'm not calling you a clown. He is."

"Never mind. Forget it. It's just me. I'm a little sensitive these days. Anyway, if you insist on hanging around, what?"

"He said he couldn't be responsible for what might happen to me. He said he was worried about my safety and that's why I should get away from you. Nice talk from a father, huh?"

"You'll have to forgive me for saying it, Jenny, but I don't think your father is a very nice man." Jenny didn't answer. She was looking in her rear-view mirror and suddenly shifted lanes again, forcing her way in between two cars. Forest looked at her, surprised. "What in hell are you doing, Jenny, trying to get us killed?"

"No. Just trying to see if that ASPD car behind us is following us. And I'm afraid they are." Forest restrained himself from turning around to look.

"And what is an ASPD?"

"Armed Services Police Department. They're like MPs, only better. They're all specially trained. It's a good thing I'm an army brat, I can smell them a mile away." She changed lanes again. "Well, what do you suggest we do now?"

Forest looked out the window. They were passing the Kennedy Center and heading for Watergate. "Your father sure is fast. I should have known he would have given out a description of your car. We'll have to get rid of it. Is there a big garage or parking lot around here? Maybe we can lose them there."

Jenny stomped on the gas, cut across two

300

lanes, and swerved off the parkway under Memorial Bridge. She turned left onto Ohio Drive and into East Potomac Park. The Washington Monument was on their left and at the end of the tidal basin on their right was the Jefferson Memorial. The Triumph wheeled right, past the sign that said "Hains Point Cutoff," went once around the curve, and then turned right again into the Jefferson Memorial parking lot.

Forest looked back as Jenny wove between rows of parked cars, driving deeper into the middle of the lot. The black army car with its gold police sign on the side had stopped at the entrance. Jenny found an empty space and pulled the car in. She stopped the motor.

"I have a feeling we just made a big mistake," she said. "We're trapped." Forest looked around the lot.

"Not yet, we're not. Come on," he said, smiling, "I've always wanted to take a tour of Washington and see all the sights." They got out of the car and Jenny locked the doors. Then she slung her overnight bag over her shoulder like a handbag and they strolled nonchalantly over to join a crowd of people boarding a tour bus.

"My, my, that was inspirational," he said loudly to Jenny, as they wormed their way into the center of the crowd. "I have sworn upon the altar of God eternal hostility against every form of tyranny over the mind of man," he said even louder, quoting Jefferson pompously. "Those are my sentiments exactly." Jenny poked Forest in the ribs, trying to get him to stop, but her eyes were sparkling with merriment. They followed a white-haired couple onto the bus and took seats in the middle. Forest put Jenny by the window and slumped down in his seat. In a few minutes, Forest saw that the bus wasn't going to be full and he closed his eyes to think.

If they didn't stop the bus and search it, they were home free. He turned to Jenny. "Do you have a credit card?" he asked quietly. She nodded. "Good. We'll need it to rent a car once we get out of here." The bus door slammed closed and the driver ground the engine into gear. They were moving. As they neared the gate, Forest and Jenny slipped lower in their seats until their heads couldn't be seen above the windowsill. Forest turned and smiled brightly at the old couple sitting opposite them, and then he grabbed Jenny and gave her a long and passionate kiss. The old couple nodded wisely to each other and ignored them.

The bus passed smoothly through the gate without stopping and when it had reached speed Forest let Jenny go. She took a deep breath. "Whew. You shouldn't do that to me in public places, Forest."

"Sorry, it couldn't be helped." He was grinning.

"Don't apologize. I wasn't complaining. Just warning you." She grinned back at him. Then they both looked back out the window at the parking lot. They could see the soldiers moving through the lot now, systematically searching for Jenny's car. They were going to be mighty disappointed when they found it. The bus turned south on I95 and they settled back into their seats.

Forest felt a hand tapping his arm and turned to see the old gentleman leaning across to him. "Pardon me for interrupting, young man, but do you mind if I ask you a . . . personal question?" The old man winked at Forest.

"Certainly not, sir. What's on your mind?"

"Well, Mom and me couldn't help noticing . . . well, she thinks you're on your honeymoon." Forest looked at the old lady who was beaming at him through her gold-rimmed spectacles.

"Yes, sir. She's right," Forest answered, taking Jenny's hand in his. The old man nodded sagely.

"We've been married almost forty years ourselves, Mom and me. Just wanted to wish you luck." Forest smiled and was just about to thank the old couple when he felt Jenny's hand tighten on his like a vise, almost cutting off the circulation. He looked at her and then quickly joined her horrified gaze out the window. The bus had just crossed the 14th Street Bridge and Forest just had time to see the bus pass under a sign reading, BOUNDRY CHANNEL DRIVE—PENTAGON NORTH PARKING LOT.

"Well," she said sarcastically, "you wanted to see all the sights. You've got it."

"I sure have," he muttered. "I sure as hell have." And then he slumped down in his seat.

"At least they won't be looking for us there," he offered.

"Sure," she answered. "They won't have to look. They'll just trip over us."

"Do you have a scarf with you that would cover your hair?" She nodded. "And sunglasses?" She nodded again. "Well, put them on." Jenny started rummaging in her bag. Then she looked back at Forest.

"And what are you going to do about your face, buddy? Wear a paper bag?" Forest didn't laugh. Jenny pulled a floppy felt hat out of her bag and put it on and then she found her sunglasses. Unfortunately, they were large and definitely feminine, otherwise he would have worn them himself. He looked at her. At least her bright yellow hair was hidden. He didn't know what to do about himself though.

The bus pulled up to the mall entrance of the Pentagon and the door swung open. They were being dropped right on the front steps. Everyone stood up and began to shuffle down the aisle. Forest and Jenny wedged themselves in behind the elderly couple, following them up the steps and into the towering chamber of the concourse. Forest kept his head bent, but out of the corners of his eyes he could see what looked like hundreds of people in uniform.

The group had come to a stop in the center of the main hall and the guide was pointing out the marvels. "The Pentagon stands on twenty-nine acres of land with a center court five acres large. There are thirty miles of access highways and sixty-seven acres of parking lots which can hold ten thousand cars. There are two hundred acres of lawn, six hundred and eighty-five water fountains, seventeen and a half miles of corridors, one hundred and fifty stairways, nineteen escalators, two hundred and eighty restrooms, and thirty thousand employees using twenty-four thousand telephones. The building cost eighty-three million dollars to construct in 1943 and has three times the floor space of the Empire State Building."

Forest stood apprehensively, head down, waiting to hear a shout or feel a hand clap down on his shoulder. Finally he couldn't stand it any longer. "Jenny," he whispered, "we've got to get out of here. My nerves can't take it. When the crowd moves we'll slip away. You must know another exit." Jenny squeezed Forest's hand.

"I've got an idea," she whispered back. "Just follow me. And trust me." Forest cringed at the idea, but suddenly the group was moving forward and Jenny was pulling him sideways and he had no choice. They let the tour pass around them and, overcoming the desire to run, walked slowly down a corridor lined with shops. There were military personnel everywhere, but all apparently concerned with their own business. Forest bent his head closer to Jenny's, but kept walking.

"What's your big idea?"

"We're going out to the South Parking Lot."

"And what are we going to do when we get there?" he asked, a touch of condescension in his voice. Her answer almost stopped him in his tracks.

"We're going to steal my father's car, smart ass." Her momentum pulled Forest forward in an awkward leap.

"You're insane. You know that, don't you?" Jenny kept walking, almost dragging Forest as she went. She talked to him while looking straight ahead, as if on the lookout for any danger.

"I know," she said. "I'm crazy to be following you into all this weather madness. And I'm crazy about you. So now, you be crazy too, and follow me." She abruptly turned right at the end of the corridor and pushed open the exit door leading into the South Parking Lot. The bright sun made Forest squint, but he could still see it was filled with every conceivable type of military transportation, from buses to jeeps to long black limousines.

Jenny got her bearings and then took off like a homing pigeon, weaving between what seemed like infinite rows of vehicles, until she stopped at a Cadillac with two stars above the licence plate. The right front door was locked. As they peered through the window to see if the lock was also down on the other side, the reflection of a uniform loomed in the glass. A 6-foot 3-inch corporal stood facing them as they whirled around.

"Hi there, Miss Wells. You looking for me?" Both Forest and Jenny realized instantly by the innocent smile on the corporal's face that he had no idea of the situation.

"Umm . . . yes, I was, Johnny. My car is in the shop again and Dad said it would be all right if you gave us a lift. This is . . . Mr. Hill. Forest, this is Corporal Kornak. He drives for my father sometimes." Jenny was grinning and Forest realized that he wasn't.

"Pleased to meet you, Mr. Hill." The soldier nodded his head and Forest let the tension flow out of his body. He even managed a smile.

"Maybe I better check with the general to see what time he . . ."

"Oh, he said to pick him up at sixteen hundred hours," Jenny interrupted quickly. Forest gave her a gold star for brilliance. The soldier opened the rear door to the limousine and stood aside for them to enter. Jenny jumped into the back seat and Forest followed her. Johnny closed the door behind them and climbed in behind the wheel.

"Where can I take you?" he asked, looking over his shoulder through the open partition.

"Washington National Airport," Forest answered, before Jenny had a chance to speak. "We're going south for a long weekend." Jenny looked at him in surprise. Forest just put his arm around her and squeezed. If she could play this game, so could he. The driver seemed to notice nothing of their silent interchange and started the motor. As soon as the car was in motion, Jenny pressed a button on the armrest at her side and a panel opened, revealing a telephone. She took the telephone off the hook and closed the panel again. Then she and Forest sat back to enjoy the ride.

307

The trip to the airport was a quiet one, and Forest and Jenny used the time to regroup their thoughts and muster strength for what lay ahead. And it wasn't until the traffic began to congest and slow at the entrance to the airport that the driver spoke.

"Sorry about this, Miss Wells, but it's rush-hour traffic. Happens every day. Which airline are you going to?" Jenny looked at Forest.

"Delta to Key West, Johnny," he answered for her. The traffic was now at a crawl. Forest knew that if the general had men at the airport they would be covering the departure gates, and this was no time to drive up in a general's limo with flags waving. They hadn't yet arrived at the intersection separating traffic for arrivals and departures, and now was the time to move.

Forest looked at his wrist, checking the watch he wasn't wearing, and leaned forward over the barrier. "I'm afraid we're going to miss our flight. Could you stop for a second and we'll jump out and run for it." The driver quickly checked in his rear-view mirror and then pulled slowly to the side. Jenny had the door open by the time the car came to a halt.

"Thanks for the ride, Johnny. And remember to thank Dad for me, will you?" The driver turned and waved as Forest shut the door. Then they began to run for the terminal. Forest led, and Jenny followed him down the ramp to the arrival section. Once they were out of sight of the limo, they slowed to a walk and fought to catch their breath.

"Are we really flying south, Forest?" Jenny finally asked. "That might not be such a bad idea, you know." Forest frowned at her.

"It's a terrible idea. Just do me a favor. Go into the terminal and rent a car. I'll wait for you here. And hurry." Jenny shrugged and turned away without saying a word. Forest watched her disappear into the terminal and then he began to pace.

CHAPTER THIRTY-TWO

Forest and Jenny didn't reach New York until almost midnight. By that time, Jenny had been fast asleep in the front seat for hours. Forest had only slept a couple of hours in the last two days and should have been exhausted, but the closer they got to New York and a chance to plug into the computer, the more excited he got. It was going to be tricky avoiding the general's men if they were here, but New York was Forest's city and he figured he had a small edge on his own turf.

He came into Manhattan through the Midtown Tunnel and headed uptown. Driving up Eighth Avenue, he could feel the energy pulsing in the air. The city that never sleeps. The movie lights blazed on 42nd Street and the hookers and pimps and gawkers and tourists milled in the neon glow. After the empty, silent spaces of Washington, the raucous blare was music. He looked down at Jenny and saw that she was awake.

"We're here."

"I know. You can feel it." She uncurled herself from the ball she had been in and sat up, stretching. "Good morning," she said brightly. Forest smiled to himself; how nice it was that she woke up in a good humor. Forest was cruising slowly, looking for an all-night garage. "And Forest, I have to pee."

"I do too, honey. Just hang on for a minute." Finally Forest spotted a Kinney on 56th Street and pulled in. He stopped Jenny just as she was about to leap out of the car. "Wash your face with cold water. Make sure you're awake." Jenny grabbed her bag and scurried away. Forest turned off the motor and got out, waiting impatiently for the bored attendant to lumber over. At last, with parking stub in hand, Forest also found himself running for the bathroom.

Forest was finished first and stood waiting for Jenny. She was taking a long time. When she came out of the ladies' room he saw that not only had she washed her face, but she had also put on makeup. At least lipstick. She looks wonderful at practically any hour of the day or night, Forest mused to himself.

"Jesus Christ, what a pig sty." She said this loud enough for everyone responsible to hear. Then, walking out of the garage, she asked conversationally, "Can you imagine what it's like to have to do it standing up?"

"Sure. I do it that way all the time. Come on." They walked to Eighth Avenue and Forest hailed a cab. "Go up Central Park West to

Sixty-seventh and take a left," he told the driver. "I'll let you know from there." As soon as the cab started moving, Jenny began to pepper Forest with questions.

"Why did you put the car in a garage? We could have just turned it in."

"Your father would have found out that we didn't take a plane and he'd have checked car rentals. Your name was on the credit card. He can't know for sure where we are until we turn the car in." Jenny thought for a moment.

"Very good. That's right. Now where are we going that you need me so wide awake?"

"We're going to cruise slowly past my TV studio. You say you have radar that can spot an army cop a mile away. Well, this is your chance to use it. I want to know if your father has ABC covered." Jenny was about to protest, but Forest stopped her. They had reached 67th Street and the driver was making the turn. Forest leaned forward and instructed the driver.

"Just drive slowly until we reach Broadway, then head uptown. Okay?"

"You got it, mister," came the disembodied reply from the front seat. Forest took Jenny's hand.

"It doesn't matter, really. Just if you see something, or feel something, let me know." The taxi worked its way across Amsterdam and Columbus and headed toward Broadway. Jenny was sitting as high in her seat as she could, scanning both sides of the street. They passed the main entrance to ABC and Forest saw nothing out of the ordinary. It was well lit and there was a security guard posted outside. Normal. Jenny said nothing. The light was with them and the cab turned into Broadway.

Suddenly Jenny grabbed Forest's arm and squeezed, "There!" He looked out her window, trying to see what she saw, but there was nothing.

"What? Where?" She pointed to a nondescript black car they were just passing.

"That's them. That's the car they use when they're not in uniform." Forest couldn't believe it. He had seen nothing.

"Are you sure?" he asked. It would make a lot of difference if they weren't covering the building. She squeezed his arm again.

"I'm sure. I can smell them. I told you." Forest accepted the information with regret. Plan two. He leaned forward again.

"Okay, driver, now go up to Riverside Drive and take a right on 84th Street. Nice and slow, just like before." The driver didn't answer. He didn't know what kind of games they were playing in the back seat, but he wasn't amused.

The taxi hit 84th Street accompanied by night music from the park, jungle drums bongoing from the darkness. Forest gazed longingly at his building. Jenny was using her infrared. But this time, Forest didn't need it. He could see for himself that there were two cars with soldiers parked across the street from the entrance. So much for home.

When the taxi came to the corner of West End Avenue and stopped for the red light, the driver turned to Forest. "You taking a scenic tour of the city, mister, or what? You want to tell me where we're going?"

"Just take us to sixty-ninth and Park. We'll get out there." The driver muttered something Forest chose not to hear, and set the cab in motion.

"Where are we going now, Forest?" There was a plaintive note to her question, as if she were feeling alone and lost in the big city.

"We are going to visit my friend Roger Moss. I think we need a little help."

CHAPTER THIRTY-THREE

Forest and Jenny had been standing outside Roger's door for a long time. Forest rang the bell again. He knew that Roger was home because the doorman had told him so when he had lied about being expected. Finally the door opened and Jenny found herself staring into the face of the most famous and respected news commentator in the country. His hair was mussed and he was wearing only a pair of slacks.

"Jesus Christ, Forest. Do you know what time it is?" Forest stepped into the apartment, pulling Jenny in with him. Roger was forced to give ground.

"Roger, I'd like you to meet Jenny Wells." Roger looked sheepish, if not embarrassed, but still managed to give Jenny an appreciative once-over.

"Roger, honey . . . I'm waiting," a woman's voice trilled from the bedroom. Roger coughed nervously and Forest fought to control his laughter. He closed the door, taking it out of Roger's hand, and slapped him on the back.

"Why don't you finish up whatever it was you were doing, old buddy. Don't mind us. I need to use the phone anyway. We'll be in the living room." Roger watched them go and stood there for a moment, somehow uncertain about what was going on. Then he went back into the bedroom and shut the door.

All the lights in the living room were on and, while Jenny looked around at Roger's collection of momentoes and awards, Forest dialed Micky at home. As the phone rang he realized that her's was one of the few numbers he knew from memory. She answered on the second ring, but Forest could hear in her voice that she had been sleeping.

"Sorry to wake you, Mick. It's me."

She cleared her throat. "I can tell it's you, mystery man. If you called to wish me goodnight, it's too late. Where are you?"

"I'm in New York, and I need you to do me a favor." Micky groaned. "And don't ask me if I know what time it is," he added quickly, "because I do. It's late."

"Where in New York are you, Forest?"

"I can't tell you that, Micky. You'll just have to trust me." There was a long pause before Micky answered him.

"Well then, you'll just have to trust me, boss, or I ain't playing. Where are you?" Forest thought for a moment before speaking. She was right and he knew it.

"I'm at Roger's apartment, but keep it under your hat. Now, do you have a pencil?"

"Sure," she shot back, appeased and happy now. "I always sleep with one behind my ear. Shoot." Forest read her Roger's number off the phone.

"You got that? Then listen carefully, here's what I want you to do. Go to the studio and find out where they keep the computer. When you're in the computer room, call me back here."

"You mean now? Are you kidding?"

"I'm dead serious, Micky. And try not to attract too much attention going in." He heard Micky whistle softly on the other end of the line.

"Does this have anything to do with those soldiers that have been hanging around? You haven't kidnapped the general's daughter, have you?"

Forest laughed. "Yes, it does. But no, I haven't kidnapped the general's daughter." He repeated this for Jenny's amusement and was rewarded with a smile. "Mick, this is serious and I'm running out of time. Are you going to help me?"

"I'm almost dressed already, your highness. Call you in half an hour." She hung up. Forest went over to Jenny and put his arm around her.

"She'll call as soon as she gets there. How about a drink? I know I could use one."

"That's just what I was going to suggest, old chap." They whirled to find Roger standing in

317

the doorway, now completely dressed, hair combed, but still looking sheepish and trying to hide it. He came over to them and shook Jenny's hand. "Pleased to meet you, Miss Wells. I hope you'll forgive the circumstances but . . ." he shrugged urbanely, "I had no idea you were coming."

Forest stopped him. "No, you'll have to forgive us, Roger. I'm sorry, but it couldn't be helped. You'll understand in a minute. Meanwhile, her name is Jenny and his name is Roger, so let's not be formal. And I would like a drink." Jenny smiled at Roger and he smiled back. He went to the bar to make drinks.

"I think she'll sleep now, so we won't be disturbed. Vodka, Forest?" Forest nodded. "And for you, Jenny?"

"I'll have the same, thanks." Forest and Jenny sat on the couch and watched Roger's back as he poured.

"Anyone I know?" Forest asked innocently. Roger turned and brought them each a glass.

"No. Actually, she's not anyone I know either. But I must admit your timing was consummate. Cheers." They all laughed and drank. Forest waited until Roger had settled himself into his chair and had arranged his face into its professionally intelligent attitude before he began.

"Roger, I've gotten involved in something that's a little sticky . . . and dangerous."

"Does it have anything to do with your . . . rather ghastly appearance?" Roger asked delicately, but not without concern.

"Yeah, in a way it does. But I'll get to that part of it later. Before I give you any details or get you involved, I'd just like to tell you a little story. It's fascinating, it's true, and it won't take long."

Roger leaned back in his chair. "I've got plenty of liquor and nowhere to go, dear boy. Tell ahead."

"It's the story of the eruption of Mount Pelée on the island of Martinique in 1902. Do you know it?"

Roger shook his head. "No, I can't say as I do."

"Well, it was a major disaster that killed over twenty-five thousand people and left the city of Saint-Pierre in total ruins. And the point is, it was a human disaster that could have been averted. You see, more than a month before the fatal eruption the volcano started advertising that it was active again. The disturbances were noted and checked out, and sure enough they found liquid lava being produced on the floor of the volcano. But this vital piece of news was never reported to the people.

"It turns out that there was an election coming up and it was imperative for the government in power, which was white, to keep the white voters from leaving the city." Forest checked to see if Roger was still with him, but he was listening attentively. Jenny had taken off her shoes and pulled her feet up under her on the couch.

"So the news media, which in this case was the local paper, was told to minimize the gravity of the situation. Which it did. But old Mount Peleé wasn't cooperating. Only a couple of weeks later it was shooting ashes and sulpher gas into the sky and birds were dropping in flight like it was a turkey shoot, except that they were dying from sulphurous fumes. But no one moved out of the city. Seven days later the city's power generator and telegraph lines were wiped out by a river of mud that washed down the main street, where once there had been a quiet stream. A crack opened part way up the mountain and destroyed a small village and killed over one hundred and fifty people.

"The following day mud struck again in the form of an avalanche that roared down the slope of Peleé. It was over a thousand feet wide and over a hundred feet high and killed hundreds of field workers on its way to the ocean, where it created a reverse tidal wave that smashed back onto the city causing more death and destruction. By now, the heat being generated by the volcano was driving snakes and poisonous insects down the mountain in waves. But there was no evacuation of Saint-Pierre.

"On the following day, volcanic debris began to fall. The cinders and ash were so thick that houses began to collapse. The governor had the city blockaded by soldiers to prevent an exodus and he finally had to come to the city personally to reassure the population.

"Twenty-four hours later it was all over. It took only three minutes and four incredible belches from Peleé to destroy the city and annihilate more than twenty-five thousand people. What the volcano had disgorged is called a *nuée ardentée*, which is dust, gas, and steam in an incredibly hot cloud with temperatures that reach over nine hundred degrees. The hot gasses killed when they were breathed in, but the major cause of death was boiling. It was so hot, the blood boiled until it became steam. The corpses were strewn like split, over-ripe melons all across the countryside, but their clothing never burned. The wave had traveled so quickly it killed them without setting their clothing on fire."

Jenny's face was a picture of horror and disgust. "What a perfectly gruesome story, Forest." She shuddered. Roger didn't flinch, but he did down the rest of his drink.

"I would have to agree, old man. I do hope there is a point to this?"

"Of course there is," Forest said, disappointed that Roger didn't immediately understand. "We are on the verge of disaster of a far greater magnitude. The warning signs are as clear as the rumbling of a volcano. The people have to be warned. But there is a group that, for political reasons, doesn't want this warning to be given."

"I see." Roger eyebrows went up slightly. "Or rather, actually, I don't. Do you think you could be a little more specific about this?"

Forest shook his head tiredly. "No, Roger, I can't. It's too complicated and it would take too long to explain. And there's no point in getting you involved in it if I don't have to."

Roger twirled the ice in his empty glass. "How can I help you then, dear fellow?" He sounded indifferent, but Forest knew he was disappointed at being excluded from the story.

"We need to stay here tonight. I need to use your phone. Micky's going to call me here from the studio and I need to do some work." Roger contemplated his ice cubes for a moment, and looked back at Forest.

"Well, certainly. It's perfectly all right with me. But without sounding rude, why here? Why not your home or the studio?" Forest looked at Jenny for support. This was going to be the hard part. But Jenny was also fascinated to know how Forest was going to explain this.

"Ah, yes . . . you have a good question there." Forest was trying to figure out how little he could tell Roger and still sound credible. "It's like this. One of the gentlemen who doesn't want me to tell my story is General Harlan Wells."

Roger almost choked on the ice cube he had been chewing. "You mean this young lady's . . . er, father?"

Forest nodded helplessly. "I'm afraid so. And he's made it inadvisable for me to go home or to the studio for the moment. That was the dangerous part I was telling you about." Roger got up and went to the bar.

"I see. Perhaps just one more drink might help, then," he said, with his back to them.

"Not for us, Roger. We have to work tonight." Roger poured himself a drink and composed himself. When he returned to his chair, his face was noncommittal again. He studied Forest seriously over his glass.

"I certainly don't disbelieve you, Forest. I've known you far too long for that. But could it be that you are overreacting slightly? Perhaps the general is only upset about your relationship with his daughter. Father's sometimes do get like that, you know."

Forest was shaking his head vigorously. Roger tried another tack. "Or . . . could it be," a twinkle appearing in his eyes, "that you are pulling my leg? Just the teensiest bit? You're not trying to get old Roger involved in a PR stunt for the show, are you?"

Forest slammed his drink down on the table. "Goddammit, Roger, I told you I was serious. I am. Now how about it?" Roger said nothing. He sat there sipping at his drink, and Forest could see that they were at an impasse.

"Roger, honey. You didn't tell me we were having a party." Roger was saved the embarrassment of trying to answer Forest by a new embarrassment. His date was standing in the doorway to the living room, swaying gently. She was an artificial blonde of about forty, who probably had been pretty once. She was dressed in a towel that barely covered her ample body, and she was obviously drunk.

"How about a drinky-poo for little ole me?" She made her way carefully across the room and Roger rose, as if to catch her should she fall.

"Forest and Jenny, this is Lila." He put his

323

arm around her. "The party's over, dear. We were just saying good-night." Roger turned her around so she was facing the door. "Make yourselves comfortable. You know where everything is, Forest. I'll see you in the morning."

Forest and Jenny had averted their eyes. "Thanks, Roger," Forest called after him. "I appreciate this."

"It's nothing, old boy," Roger's voice trailed from the other room. "Ta Ta." They heard the bedroom door slam. Forest looked at the empty doorway, picturing Lila, and then turned to look at Jenny. His heart went out to his friend Roger. Jenny seemed to know what Forest was thinking.

"You're damn right you're lucky, mister. And don't you forget it."

CHAPTER THIRTY-FOUR

The phone rang. Forest catapulted himself across the room and managed to get to it before it rang a second time.

"Forest?"

"Yeah, Mick, it's me. Are you in?"

"I'm in and I'm scared. It's lonely here and I feel like a spy." Forest could hear the apprehension in her voice.

"Don't worry about it, hon. You'll be home and in your own little bed in less than an hour. Now here's how we'll work this. I'm going to put Jenny on the phone and she'll tell you what to do. All you have to do is follow her instructions."

"Who's Jenny?" There was instant jealousy and antagonism in her voice.

"Come on, Mick. She's General Wells's daughter and she's a computer analyst. She'll talk you through all the steps. Okay?"

"Sure, loverboy." Micky sounded bitter. "Put your girlfriend on." Forest sighed. He didn't have time to placate her now. He handed the phone to Jenny. She sat down at Roger's desk and put the phone to her ear, staring into space, trying to visualize the set up and the sequence of steps that were automatic to her.

"Hi, Micky. This is Jenny. Is there a computer terminal . . ."

"A what?" Jenny realized that she would have to describe everything.

"Sorry. Find what looks like a large electric typewriter with a small TV screen on top of it."

"Oh, that," Micky answered instantly. "Got it."

"Good. Now, there should be two switches on the lower-lefthand side. Turn them both on." Jenny turned to Forest. "That will give us a printed computer readout as well."

The tension was beginning to get to Forest. "Yeah," he said grimly, "if we're lucky enough to need one."

"It's on," Mickey reported. Jenny frowned and closed her eyes, concentrating.

"On the right-hand side of the terminal there should be a phone and a carrier, a horizontal cradle for the receiver to fit on. That has two switches also. Turn the top one on. A green bulb should light up."

"Done. The light is on."

"Good. Now pick up the phone and listen for an electronic tone, like a dial tone. When you hear it, you're going to have to dial a number." They waited while Micky carried out the instructions and then reported back in. Jenny looked up.

"We're ready to plug into Goddard. You have that piece of paper?" Forest reached into his pocket and found the paper. When he handed it to her, their hands brushed and Forest felt a tingle of electricity.

"Hang on, Micky," Jenny said, smoothing the paper in front of her. "Dial 202-975-0001. You got it? Okay, now put the receiver on the carrier and hit the return key on the typewriter." There was excitement in Jenny's voice.

"Hey," Micky was excited, too. "It works. The screen says, TYPE IN PASS CODE. What do I do?"

"Here's the pass code. I'll read it for you twice. You type it on the terminal just like on a regular typewriter. SKY 44B–F2F–7–13. The first numbers are the plug-in code and the last ones the day code until eight A.M. tomorrow. Are you ready?"

"Ready. Just read nice and slow."

"SKY space, Four, Four, B dash, F, two, F dash, Seven dash Thirteen." Jenny heard a whoop over the phone and smiled at Forest.

"It worked again, Jenny. The letter lit up on the screen and then the machine exed them all out. Then it printed READY underneath it. And then this amber light came on."

"Micky, that's fine. That means the signal's been accepted. We're in." Jenny looked relieved. "At least my part worked," she said to Forest. "Now let's see if there's anything on those tapes that we can use." She spoke back into the phone. "Micky, type the word *LOAD*." Jenny paused, and then went on. "Now type *SYNCH*, that's S,Y,N,C,H. Now *SAT TRACK*. You got that? Micky, are you there?"

"Yeah, I'm here. Okay, go ahead. It says READY." Forest moved behind Jenny's chair and picked up a pencil. Bending over her, he wrote the coordinates Karapov had given him on the paper in front of her. Jenny nodded.

"Type the word *LIST*, then *TRI*, then *VERTEX*. Now type *83D, 58D* and *39D,* and then the word *RETURN*. Now we wait," she said to Forest. He stood behind her, his hand squeezing her shoulder gently, but she could sense his nervousness. What if there were no satellites at those coordinates? Jenny could picture Micky sitting listening to the computers chatter to each other, staring at the empty screen, waiting for something to appear.

Finally the wait was too agonizing for Forest and he went and sat down. Jenny sat listening, tapping her pencil on the pad in front of her. Then her head came up as she heard something, and she beamed at Forest.

"Micky says, and I quote, 'Holy Mackerel'!" Forest leaped out of his chair. "How many lines of numbers do you have, Micky?" Jenny waited while Forest circled her like an animal. "She says about twenty, Forest."

"Hot damn! Hot fucking damn!" Forest didn't know whether to laugh, cry, or shout. He got down on one knee, next to Jenny's chair, and hugged her to him. "We've got it! It was right there, just like the professor said it would be. Jenny, we have proof!" Jenny wrestled herself free, trying to hear what Micky was saying over the phone.

"Hold on a second, Micky. We have a small celebration going on here." Forest sank back on his haunches. He was suddenly very tired. But Jenny was still all business. "I'm back, Micky. Sorry. Now I want you to read the last two columns of numbers on the right. In the next-to-last column are dates, and there should be numbers like eleven, nine, sixty-one. In the next column are latitudes and longitudes.

"Sorry about that, kids," Micky said dourly. "My last column of numbers is dates. I don't got no longitudes and latitudes." Jenny looked down and bit her lip in frustration. Forest was immediately alert.

"What?" he asked.

"All we have are dates. No locations. Shit." Forest had dismay written all over his face, but Jenny was thinking. She ignored Forest's unspoken questions and returned to Micky. "Listen, Micky, I think I have an answer. Try this. Press the button marked 'hold' and keep your finger on it. That's important. Don't let go. Now type *LIST ORBIT LOCO dash RETURN*. Got it? All right, you can let the button up now." Jenny refused to look at Forest as they waited, and finally he could stand it no longer and got up to pace again.

"Well?" Jenny asked.

"Nothing yet, Jenny. The machine is just clattering. Hang on. . . . Bingo! Here comes the lats and longs." Jenny expelled a breath she felt she had been holding for hours and tried to unclench the death grip her hand had on the telephone. She looked at Forest, stopping him in his tracks, and nodded. Forest hid his face in his hands for a moment and then looked back at Jenny, haggard with exhaustion.

"Thank God," he muttered. Then he sank onto the couch.

"Micky? Good. I want you to read me the numbers, starting at the top, from the last two columns. First the date, then the location. Go." Forest watched Jenny record the numbers and resisted the temptation to run across the room and tear the paper out of her hands. All he knew was, it was almost over. With the dates and locations, he could put the whole picture together. Tomorrow. His eyes were closing. He had to sleep.

Jenny had finished writing and was instructing Micky on how to shut down the computer. "And, Micky, remember to tear off the printout that the machine typed. Take it with you. I want to see it tomorrow." Forest struggled to get his eyes open.

"Tell her thank you for me, Jen. Tell her I love her," he said. "I can't move." Jenny relayed Forest's message, hung up the phone, and came over to the couch. She sat down next to Forest and put the pad of paper in his lap. Forest picked it up and forced his eyes to focus. "Thank you, Jenny," he said. "Thank you

ever so much." He stared at the jumble of
numbers.

12 14 64	12 23' 15" N	108 57' 10" E
11 14 70	26 14' 5" N	65 41' 37" E
06 28 71	40 5' 56" N	127 58' 37" E
01 03 72	38 21' 13" S	73 18' 2" W
06 09 72	44 41' 25" N	103 50' 19" W
07 09 72	39 44' 15" N	117 6' 7" E
09 04 72	41 58' 20" N	29 18' 56" E
11 19 72	53 2' 17" N	157 39' 13" E
10 16 73	20 15' 58" N	9 18' 22" W
10 16 73	12 18' 29" N	31 6' 42" E
11 12 74	52 11' 32" N	81 2' 29" E
01 06 76	48 13' 48" N	85 31' 6" W
01 22 76	46 55' 14" N	79 33' 43" W
02 17 76	41 8' 30" N	73 3' 57" W
04 11 76	19 7' 32" S	50 51' 18" W
04 22 77	72 16' 11" N	71 2' 19" E
08 77	39 26' 10" N	74 31' 47" W
06 16 77	35 17' 39" N	106 2' 11" W
07 05 78	38 12' 17" N	95 56' 2" W
07 12 78	38 59' 12" N	77 21' 6" E

The numbers began to swim and blur, and in
spite of himself, Forest's eyes closed. He was
asleep.

FRIDAY

JULY 14

PITTSBURGH, PA.

The air in the ghetto wasn't any worse than
the air the whities were breathing, it just felt
that way. Especially today.

On the third floor of a building nobody gave
a shit about, in a room nobody hardly went
into, Mary White lay on her bed, gasping. She
couldn't even cry for help, not that anybody
would have answered anyway. The television
was blaring something about the air being
unacceptable . . . and inversion, but all Mary
knew was she couldn't catch her breath. Mary
was fifty-seven years old. Then she was dead.

CHAPTER THIRTY-FIVE

It was noon before Forest opened his eyes. At first he had no idea where he was, but then he recognized Roger's living room and it all came back to him. He had passed out last night in his clothes. Jenny must have undressed him because he was lying on Roger's couch in his underwear with a blanket over him.

He sat up and saw Jenny sitting in the middle of the room, cross-leged on the rug, with a pile of papers and books spread around her. "Hi," he said, trying to rub the sleep out of his eyes.

"Hi, yourself." Jenny got up and went over to Forest. She sat down next to him and kissed him on the cheek. "I thought you would never wake up. You were sleeping like you were dead."

"I guess I was tired. Thanks for undressing me." Forest looked around the room. There was only one couch. "Where did you sleep last night?" Jenny snuggled closer to Forest, and he put his arm around her.

"Oh, I slept on the couch next to you. You forget, I am a very little person. And I do like to cuddle." Her warmth was tempting and Forest had an urge to pull her back under the cover with him, but as he became more fully awake he realized that time was a factor now and they had to get going.

Jenny seemed to read his thoughts. "It's just about noon, Roger is gone, and I've just about finished tracking down the locations from the latitudes and longitudes. It's very interesting, Forest. And confusing." Forest stiffened.

"Let me see them," he said, getting up.

"Not so fast, buster. You go take a shower and shave. By the time you're done, I will be too, and you can look at the whole picture." Forest gazed longingly at the pile of papers on the floor, but decided he owed her that much. She had gotten up early and gone to work; she deserved to finish. "And by the time you're dressed, I'll have coffee for you, too." Forest kissed her on top of her head and went into the bathroom.

Fifteen minutes later, a cup of steaming coffee in front of him, Forest sat staring at the lists of dates and places Jenny had compiled. She was right, it didn't make sense. Certainly, not in terms of triage alone. Forest could see immediately that the time span was about right—from 1964 and Vietnam, to the day before yesterday. He went to the end of the list first. The last entry was Wednesday, the twelfth

335

of July, and the location was northwest Maryland. That had to be Harristown Dam.

Working backward, Forest found what had to be Garnett, Kansas, and Los Alamos, New Mexico. He recognized the dates and locations even without weather descriptions. So he had been right. But why? It made no sense for Thursday to cause damage inside the United States, unless it had something to do with an economic or political maneuver. Forest searched in vain for a date that corresponded to Arthur's plane crash, but it just wasn't there. And somehow that bothered him. The rest of the locations were all over the world, and meaningless, without knowing what the weather had been like.

"Interesting and confusing aren't the words for it, Jen. It's weird. But there's no way we can tell what the hell's going on until we find out what weather they created over each location. And for that, we need back issues of *CRUMB*."

Jenny giggled. "What's *CRUMB?*"

"*Climatic Research Unit Monthly Bulletin.* It's a magazine that lists the world's weather on a day-by-day, place-by-place basis. I have them at home, but that doesn't help much."

"The library?" Jenny suggested.

"Nope. I think it's time for the fraternity of weathermen to start helping each other. I think I'll call my friend Joe Walters at CBS. He should have them."

"Isn't that like Macy's talking to Gimbel's?" Jenny asked, as Forest went to the phone.

336

"Something like that," he admitted. "But I won't tell if you don't." Jenny watched Forest transform himself into a totally different person as soon as he got on the phone. He joked, teased, and bantered as if he didn't have a care in the world, and in a few minutes he had persuaded Joe to let him use his research library. Yet the moment he hung up the phone, he was himself again.

"Okay," he said seriously, "we got it."

"You know, Forest, it's scary the way you do that. Put on that other face." Forest looked startled. He hadn't even been aware that he had changed roles, and it bothered him that he had gotten caught doing it.

"Yeah," he said morosely, "it's one of my great talents. If I didn't get paid so much for doing it, they'd probably lock me up for being a schizo. Anyway, today is my last day. From now on, I'm going straight." Jenny didn't understand, but she saw that it bothered him and let it pass. She began to clean up Roger's apartment. Forest watched her for a moment and then, without saying anything further, started picking up books from the floor and putting them away. They were done in a few minutes and let themselves out of the apartment.

Joe Walters, himself, came to the security desk to escort them to his office. He was blond, boyish, and good-looking, and could have passed for Forest's younger brother. And he was friendly; it always amazed Jenny when celebrities acted like people. She was also surprised that he didn't question Forest or rib him about having to borrow his library. Maybe they had gotten that out of the way on the phone, or maybe, Jenny mused, he was just a gentleman. After winding through a maze of gray corridors and back stairwells, they arrived at Joe's office. He showed Forest the bound, back issues of *CRUMB* and left them alone.

The magazine was easy to use. You looked up a date and a location and *CRUMB* told you what the weather was that day. After they discovered that the date the satellites had been over an area sometimes didn't produce weather until one or two days later, the work went quickly. They divided the list in half and worked in silence, except for an occasional "Jesus Christ" or an incredulous "I don't believe it!"

When they were finished they exchanged lists. Forest was still puzzled. A lot of the incidents still just didn't make sense. Some of them were self-inflicted, but possibly they could be explained as internal maneuvering, like Karapov's reference to Nixon making rain on a demonstration. Some were clearly against non-triage countries, but possibly could be explained by a foreign policy of aggression and harassment. But there were some cases where it looked like nothing had happened; there was no disaster, no major storm.

Forest shuffled the papers distractedly, searching for an explanation, looking for a pattern, but there was none. It was clear that the satellites were being used to create weather, but it was also obvious that Karapov hadn't had all the information. Forest picked up the phone and dialed Micky at the studio.

"Micky, it's me."

"I know that. Now where do you want me to go?" Forest could hear the edge in her voice and realized that she must be exhausted.

"Micky, my love, please forgive me for not thanking you last night for going into the studio, but I was passing out at the moment."

"I've told you that you drink too much," Micky snapped back without missing a beat.

"Well, anyway, thank you. What you did was invaluable."

"Forest, for Christ's sake, please stop thanking me. I'm only doing my overworked and underpaid job the best I know how, even if I have no idea what I'm doing or what's going on. What do you want?" Forest thought for a moment.

"Set up a screening room for me at four o'clock, but don't use my name. Get one on another floor, near a kiddie show or a soap. Next, in a minute I'm going to read you that list from last night, with dates and locations. I want you to pull news footage from the library and have it edited or marked so you can find the sections that discuss weather." Forest paused, trying to figure out how to get into the studio without being seen.

"Is that all, boss? I should tell you I don't do windows."

"No, that's not all, Mick. I want you to send

339

a prop van to pick me up at Fifty-seventh and Tenth Avenue at three-thirty. You meet us at the carpentry entrance at three forty-five and let us in."

"And with my other hand . . ."

"With your other hand, pick up a phone and call Roger. Ask him to meet us in the screening room at four. Tell him it's very important that he be there. You got all that?"

Micky snorted. "Sure, I got it. Whether I can do it or not is another question. You don't, by any chance, want me to work up tonight's weather report also, do you?"

Forest cackled madly into the phone. "No, my dear, I don't. Just do everything I told you and tonight's weather report will take care of itself. Now here's the list."

CHAPTER THIRTY-SIX

The driver of the closed, paneled prop van backed onto the sidewalk at the rear entrance of CBS at 3:42. He had no idea what the two people were doing in the back and he couldn't care less. He was just making a delivery. Forest and Jenny sat on the bare metal floor and waited for Micky to unlock the corrugated sliding door so the driver could back all the way in. But they were early and she wasn't. They waited anxiously as they heard the driver get out of the cab and walk to the entrance. He banged on the metal door loudly, and then they heard it slide up and open.

"Hold your horses, you goon." Micky's cutting voice had never sounded sweeter. "This fucking door isn't made of tissue paper."

"Sorry, lady," they heard the driver answer. He got back in the van and slammed the door closed. One of the reasons why Micky was so efficient, Forest realized, was because it was almost impossible to argue with her. That is, of course, unless she was in love with you.

The van slid back into the loading area and Forest heard the big door close. Then Micky opened the back of the truck, and they were out. And they were in. But Forest knew they weren't safe yet. He led Jenny and Micky at a run through the carpentry shop, past the prop department, and into one of the many makeup and costume rooms that were scattered throughout the studio.

"What are we doing here, boss?" Micky panted, as she finally caught up with them. Forest was already pawing through a coat rack of costumes.

"We are about to get into costumes, at least Jenny and I are. We're going to disguise ourselves so those nasty soldiers leave us alone." He looked at Micky and winked. "By the way, it's nice to see you again."

"Yeah," she said, trying to scowl and failing, "it's nice seeing you too, even if you're not as pretty as you used to be." Forest turned back to the rack and finally found what he was looking for. He pulled two clown costumes off their hangers and gave one of them to Jenny.

"This should be about your size. Try it on. Fitting, don't you think?" Jenny heard the sarcasm in his voice but refused to be intimidated by it.

"Absolutely," she said.

They put the costumes on over their clothes and sat down in chairs in front of the makeup mirrors. Patting his bruises gingerly, Forest quickly and professionally began putting on a clown face while Micky helped Jenny. With whiteface, lipstick, and red noses they would be difficult to recognize. The clown hats would make them invisible.

For the first time since they had entered the studio, Forest felt safe. "Where's the screening room?" he asked Micky.

"Second floor, in the back. Room 2114."

"Terrific. Go on ahead of us. In fact, go up to the third floor by elevator and come down again by the back stairs. We'll meet you there." Micky appraised Forest and Jenny for a moment, her hands on her hips.

"Sure, boss. But I hope somebody tells me the plot of this spy movie before it's over."

"Somebody will, Micky," Forest answered, "as soon as somebody knows. Now get out." Micky left, and they waited. Forest had to hold himself in his chair to keep from running after her. He was so close to the end, so close to seeing what it all meant.

"Are you really going to expose the story tonight, Forest?" He was startled by her question. He had been elsewhere.

"I haven't got much choice. How long do you think we can hide from your father? He's got men all around now. And even if I can't piece it all together for tonight, we've got enough right now to stop them. I can prove that weather control is not only possible, but that it's being practiced. I have satellite tapes with the dates and locations where Thursday caused disasters. And I'm going to have the ears and

eyes of thirty million people. After tonight, at
least, they won't dare harm us. And that's a
big start. The rest will take care of itself."
Forest couldn't wait anymore. He got up.
"Let's go," he said.

They walked slowly through the corridors,
mingling with actors dressed as cowboys, policemen, doctors, and animals. Trying not to
flinch as they passed soldiers in the halls,
Forest wondered whether the other actors
thought the soldiers were actors, too.

They made it to the screening room without
being stopped and Forest saw Micky already in
the control booth. He waved and she waved
back. Roger wasn't there yet, so they took seats
near the front and waited. While the video
machine was warming up, Forest scanned the
list in his hand.

12 14 64	Vietnam	Rain
11 14 70	Pakistan	Cyclone
06 28 71	North Korea	Hot?
01 03 72	Chile	Hot?
06 09 72	South Dakota	Rain
07 09 72	China	Earthquake
09 04 72	Turkey	Storms?
11 19 72	Kamchatka	Tidal Wave
10 16 73	Sahel	Drought
10 23 73	Sahel	Drought
11 12 74	Russia	Cold
01 06 76	U.S. Northwest	Cold
01 22 76	U.S. Northwest	Cold
02 17 76	U.S. Northwest	Cold
04 11 76	Brazil	Rain

04 22 77	Russia	Cold
08 77	U.S. Northeast	Storms?
06 16 77	New Mexico	Storms
11 19 77	India	Cyclone
07 05 78	Kansas	Tornado
07 12 78	Maryland	Rain

It was obvious which events fit into Thursday's triage program, but the ones that didn't were driving Forest crazy. Somehow it wasn't enough merely to expose the fact that weather control existed, he wanted to show how it was being used. And that's why he had asked Micky to set up this screening. Forest hoped that in the news reports of the events he would be able to find some clue as to what they were up to, some pattern, some political implication he couldn't see yet.

Forest looked around the room, hoping to see that Roger had arrived, but saw only Micky standing patiently in the control booth. He wanted to review each of the events and they were running out of time. He couldn't wait any longer. Forest waved his arm and Micky dimmed the lights.

"December 14, 1964, Micky," he called out staring at the screen in front of him. It remained blank, and then he remembered where he was. He pressed the intercom button next to his right hand. "Let's start from the beginning, Mick. December '64, Vietnam." The screen flickered a few times before them and then they sat face to face with Chet Barkley, the long-time anchorman for ABC before Roger had arrived.

Chet spoke in deep, resonant tones. "United States military operations in South Vietnam were brought to a halt today when torrential rains from Typhoon Iris flooded more than five million acres in the Mekong Delta. News reports say that approximately five thousand people have died and almost a million have been left homeless. Heavy rains from a typhoon just last month, over the same area, had raised all water levels to capacity, saturating the ground and leaving it incapable of absorbing any more moisture." The screen went black.

Forest turned to Jenny. "They were just experimenting then. That's just one of a long list I picked as a sample. Vietnam, Laos, Cambodia, no wonder the war went on so long." Jenny shook her head, looking anything but comical in her clown costume. Forest punched the intercom.

"Run the next one, Mick. November, 1970. Pakistan." Forest knew what was coming. It was an event impossible for a meteorologist to forget, and his adrenalin was pumping in anger. The light on the screen flicked on, followed by an electronic beep-beep, and they saw Roger sitting behind a desk, deadpan as always. Jenny's first thought was how young Roger looked and Forest's how stiff he seemed, and neither of them noticed him slip into the room behind them.

"Shortly after midnight, on November 13,

the worst hurricane of this century struck the shores of East Pakistan. With winds of over one hundred miles an hour, the storm passed over the mouth of the Ganges, carrying tides ten to fifteen feet above normal. The waters surged over thousands of offshore islands, washing away every trace of human habitation."

The picture suddenly cut to footage shot from a helicopter which flew low over the endless misery of the flooded lowlands, over the tips of houses, tops of trees, and miles and miles of floating debris. It was a scene of strange and incongruous quiet, where once there had been the cacophony of hundreds of thousands of people.

"The scope of the devastation is difficult to conceive. Five hundred thousand dead; a million acres of rice, ready for harvesting, washed away; and a million head of livestock drowned." Roger's voice continued narrating as the screen showed bodies of men and carcasses of cattle hanging from the trees and then boatloads of refugees weeping in anguish. "Thirty-foot waves washed away complete villages on the three largest islands of Shabbazpur, Dakhim, and Hatia, leaving no trace that they had ever been inhabited."

"Enough!" Forest barked into the intercom, and Micky pulled the cassette. Forest just stared at the blank screen until he felt Jenny touch his arm.

"Does that mean . . ." Jenny whispered, "that Thursday was responsible for Bangladesh?"

"Of course it was!" he spat, his voice too loud in the empty room. "Another five hundred thousand people died from starvation and disease before the government at Karachi got around to sending aid. And by the time East Pakistan rebelled to establish the state of Bangladesh, there were another hundred thousand dead from fighting the civil war." He took the clown hat off his head and placed it carefully beside him on the floor. He ran his fingers through his hair. "A million less mouths to feed, give or take a few." His voice was quiet and cold. "A pretty effective method of triage . . . if you have the stomach to do it."

Forest fought to control his anger. This was just the beginning, the easy part. Now they were coming to what he didn't understand. He checked the list in his hand in the muted half-light and pressed the intercom. His premonition was so strong that he knew he was hoping against hope.

"The next two, Mick, were in '71 and '72, North Korea and Chile. All we could find out was that it was hot. Was there anything in the news?" Micky's answer came all too fast.

"Nothing."

Forest slammed his fist onto the arm of his chair. The next entry on his list was rain in South Dakota in 1972, and he was sure of what that was. It was Rapid City. But he still didn't know why. He looked at the list again.

"Okay," he said, his weariness showing, "skip the next one. What have you got for July 9, '72. China." The open intercom crackled while Micky shuffled tapes. Jenny snuck her hand into Forest's and he squeezed it, unaware that he was doing it.

"Nothing, boss . . ." but there was a quiver of delight in her voice. "However, I did find something on July 26 about China. You want to see it?" Forest closed his eyes, maintaining.

"Yes, Micky," he said spacing his words, "I would like to see it. If you don't mind."

"Nice piece of investigating, eh?"

"Run it!" Forest bellowed.

The conscientious face of Roger Moss illuminated the screen once again. "After seventeen days of silence, Chinese officials have officially admitted that at least twenty square miles in and around Tangshan City were completely leveled by what is estimated to be the worst earthquake in China since 1556. Spokesmen were unwilling to admit how many were dead, but did not deny published reports of six hundred and fifty-five thousand." Jenny gasped, but Forest was shaking his head.

"Just before the first tremor at three forty-two A.M. it was reported that the sky lit up like daylight, and that multicolored lights, mainly red and white, could be seen up to two hundred miles away." Forest's finger found the intercom button, but before he could say anything, Micky pulled the tape. Forest turned to Jenny.

"It doesn't make any fucking sense." He sounded like he was thinking out loud. "China's not a triage country, unless you're really pushing the concept. So what the hell are

349

they doing killing off half a million people?" Jenny gazed back at him in misery, wishing she could supply an answer. And when Forest turned away from her to stare at the papers in his hand, she felt even more alone. She so desperately wished she could help him. If only she knew what he was trying to prove.

Forest stabbed the button. "I don't suppose you found anything on the next one either?" Micky's answer was slow in coming. She had been watching him from the booth.

"Sorry . . . there was nothing on Turkey."

"And the next one, Kamchatka?" He asked the question expecting a denial.

"That one I got. But it's twenty after five, Forest, and if you're going to do a show . . ." Forest stared ahead numbly. He knew he would never care about doing a show again. There was only this show.

"Please run the tape, Micky," he said.

She pressed a button and Forest recoiled. He wanted to turn his eyes away, but couldn't. There he was on the screen, oh so many years ago, crew-cut, intense, too skinny in a wide-lapeled, double-breasted suit, painfully and obviously preaching the gospel of the weather.

"A fascinating phenomenon in the world weather watch happened early this morning." He was so sincere. "The highest tidal wave ever recorded washed over the southern tip of the Kamchatka peninsula, reaching a height at Cape Lopatka of over two hundred and ten feet. Don't ask me who stayed around to do the measuring . . ." Forest turned his head away, disgusted at this early manifestation of his other personality. He sat staring at the clown hat on the floor until the film ran out and there was silence once again.

Jenny stirred beside him, but waited an eternity before she spoke. She was afraid to touch him now. "Forest, I'm confused. What does it all mean?" He turned his head slowly toward her, forcing himself to recognize her, showing her his red rimmed eyes behind his already sadly painted mask.

"I don't know, Jenny." He looked down, and then struggled to lift his eyes up again. "It doesn't make sense." She saw defeat in his eyes, and the will power he was using to continue to face her. "It's there. I know it's there. The pieces are all on the table, I just don't know how to put them together. And there isn't any more time."

A voice rang out from the back of the room, shattering the intimacy of their despair. "Could it be, dear boy, that you're trying to fit the pieces into the wrong puzzle?"

CHAPTER THIRTY-SEVEN

Forest and Jenny whirled in their chairs to see Roger, an amused expression on his famous face, leaning against the wall at the back of the room. He ambled down the aisle toward them, and as soon as Micky saw him she raised the lights and came scurrying out of the control booth, a sheaf of papers clutched in her hand, as if she were afraid to miss any of the conversation.

"My, my, my," Roger commented dryly, "are we going to a costume party, or has Forest Hill come up with a brand-new way to wrinkle the weather?" Roger had no idea how much Forest welcomed his appearance, sarcasm and all.

"It's about fucking time you showed up, you bum. I said four o'clock. How long have you been standing back there? How many of the clips did you get to see?" Roger draped himself in a chair a row behind Forest and Jenny, and Micky slid into one next to him.

"I saw enough," he sighed, "to witness the

fact that we're not getting any younger."
Forest was too impatient for small talk.

"What did you mean, we're trying to fit the pieces in the wrong puzzle?"

Roger shrugged and leaned back, making himself comfortable. "Well, dear boy, since you haven't seen fit to let me in on your little theory, I can only view these events as an . . . educated observer. I have no idea of who you think is doing what to whom, or for what purpose, or what . . . triage . . . has anything to do with it. I can only tell you what I know about the events in terms of their broader ramifications, and perhaps that would shed a little light on them for you."

Forest knew that Roger was intentionally being smug, taking his revenge for the one thing he couldn't bear, being excluded. But he had no time for niceties now. "You are a wise and learned man, Roger," he said humbly. "Now, will you cut the bullshit and get to it?"

"All right," he said, now completely serious, "let's take Pakistan. The reason that the Pakistani government didn't send aid immediately to the flood victims in the east was because that money had already been earmarked to buy a nuclear reactor from the French. And the real tragedy was that that money could have been used to save thousands of lives, because the United States pressured the French into reneging on their agreement to sell."

A gleam came into Roger's eye. "Now, if one wanted to play a came of coincidences, and I assure you it's only that, you could connect the

353

earthquake in China to this tragedy." Forest had no intention of arguing the point; he just wanted to know the connection.

"How? How are they tied together?" he asked earnestly.

"Well, the Pakistanis looked elsewhere for their nuclear reactor and, after a year and a half of negotiations, they were able to tell the French that the Chinese would sell them one if the French didn't. But, unfortunately, they never got their reactor from China either because the factory that manufactured the components was totally destroyed . . ."

"In the earthquake at Tangshan City!" Forest said, finishing the sentence for him. "Fascinating," he breathed to himself. He didn't know where this was leading yet, but at least the pieces were starting to connect. "What about the hot weather in North Korea in 1971?"

Roger looked at him in astonishment. "Excuse me, old chap, don't you pay attention to anything besides the weather? Don't you read the newspapers?"

"Roger . . ." Forest growled.

"Your hot weather over North Korea was a drought that destroyed more than half of their rice crop. It was quite an incident, actually. South Korea became terrified that the North would have a famine and attack them. Big scare in the military—secret mobilizations and whatnot." He paused, recalling the event. "Now this I wouldn't expect you to know, but the United States was instrumental in having large supplies of rice pumped in to avert another war."

Forest was beginning to see that he had been looking at everything too narrowly, taking each event as an isolated occurrence. He remembered now what Karapov had said about Chile.

"I suppose then that the hot weather in Chile in '72 was also a drought?" Roger nodded. "But there was no danger of a war there."

"Of course not. But it was equally damaging. It caused enough civil unrest to depose Allende after we wouldn't sell him any of our surplus wheat." Forest got up out of his chair and went to lean against the wall.

"Politics. It's all political," he said, thinking out loud. "Okay. Let's assume that Karapov was totally wrong and that none of this has to do with triage. Where does that lead us?" He looked at the list in his hand, studying it as if he could make something new appear.

Suddenly Jenny turned to Micky. "Let me see those computer readouts, please." Micky shuffled through the papers in her lap and then handed them to Jenny.

"What about that storm over the Bosporos? What do we have in Turkey?" Forest had just had an idea.

"There's a NATO base on the Black Sea," Roger answered casually. "Depending on the storm, it might have caused quite a bit of damage."

"And Kamchatka?" He came and kneeled on his seat, facing Roger. "What's there?"

"Russia's eastern radar defense system. But I don't see . . ."

"War!" Jenny screamed. "It's a war! We're having a goddamn Weather War!"

CHAPTER THIRTY-EIGHT

There was a stunned silence in the room.

"Weather War?" Roger asked incredulously.

Jenny was staring at the sheet of computer data, her hands trembling. "Look!" she said, leaning over the paper. Forest and Micky leaned over her to see. "These aren't all the same satellites. The prefixes are different. TS stands for the American ThorStar satellites, and the ORB prefix must be the Russians'—the Orbita satellites." She looked at Forest as if she had failed him. "I'm sorry," she said in a little voice, "I should have looked at this before." But Forest was already in another world.

"Weather War?" Roger asked again, his mind not being able to compute the information.

Forest leaped to his feet, clapping his hands together and pacing rapidly. "Of course!" He looked like he was leading a cheer. "How could I be so stupid? So naive. Why should we have assumed that we were the only ones who knew how to do it? No wonder it didn't make sense."

"It's all here, Forest." Her excitement was building. "We did everything in Vietnam." Her finger ran down the page. "And we did do Pakistan ..."

"Because we didn't want them to have the bomb."

"But Russia did the earthquake in China ..."

"Because she didn't want them to have it either," Forest interjected. "And it was also a great way for Russia to slow China down."

"And Russia did North Korea because we're committed to South Korea ..."

"So we must have done Chile, because we didn't want them going Communist." Forest was almost beside himself as he saw the pieces falling into place. "They attacked our NATO base in Turkey and we answered by blitzing their radar station in Kamchatka."

"With a two-hundred-and-ten-foot tidal wave?" Roger was looking at them as if they had gone mad, and Forest realized that their clown costumes weren't helping their credibility. He motioned Micky back into the control booth.

"Run everything you've got, Mick, in order, until I say stop." She got up and went, without saying a word. But then Roger began to rise also. Forest leapt at him, grabbing him and holding him in his chair, on his knees as he clutched him. "Please, Roger. Just tell us the political and economic repercussions ... even if you think I'm crazy."

Roger looked at his watch pointedly. "Forest, I've got to get to makeup. We're on in twenty minutes." He was avoiding Forest's imploring eyes.

"Roger, please..."

Suddenly the room went dark and Roger was on the screen. "Over four hundred thousand people are said to have already starved to death this year in Ethiopia as the drought which plagues the Sahel regions continues..."

"Russia," Jenny said, reading from the computer chart.

"Haile Selassie was deposed because of the unrest the drought caused," Roger said resignedly, speaking over his own voice on the screen, "and the Russians supported the new military government. They finally got their foot in the door in Africa. But they lost it last year when they were kicked out of Somalia. They also lost a key naval base at Berbera in the Gulf of Aden."

Forest held onto Roger with one hand and leaned forward to reach the intercom button. "Next," he shouted.

"November 12, 1974," Jenny said, reading from the chart. "That's us. Heavy snows over the Russian steppes." Roger appeared on the screen again, dressed in a different suit.

"The Russians have asked the United States to sell them an unprecedented one hundred and seventy-five million metric tons of grain as a result of a sudden, early snow which has frozen almost three-quarters of their usual fall harvest . . ." Roger again interrupted himself on the screen.

"Control of the international grain market gave America the greatest economic power it had ever experienced, including the period right after World War II. It was a tremendously profitable year for farmers."

The screen had gone blank, leaving only a reflected white light to illuminate the room. Forest held up a hand, signaling Micky to wait, and picked up his list from the floor where he had dropped it. Roger sat stolidly in his chair, unmoving, even without Forest's restraining hand.

Forest found what he was looking for and turned to Roger. "January and February of 1976. Intense cold over the northeastern United States. What did it do?" Roger passed a hand over his face and then rubbed both his eyes. He spoke as if from rote.

"Almost two hundred inches of snow fell over the Northeast. Many major cities were shut down. Transportation and shipping were disrupted. America lost all the economic superiority it had gained in the grain monopoly of 1974. Our energy reserves were drained and we were put at the mercy of the OPEC nations. When they raised the oil prices, we were . . . up shit's creek." He bit off the last three words.

Forest couldn't understand Roger's attitude. He seemed so disinterested, almost hostile, while Forest's blood was racing at the incredible magnitude of the story that was unfolding before them.

"Forest?" He looked up to see Micky peering out of the projection booth. "Should I run the next one? It's getting late." Forest waved her on and squatted at Roger's side, watching the screen. Roger's face appeared, looking more tired and worn than usual.

"Most of the lights in New York City," he intoned, "are back on tonight. Only a few sections of the Upper East Side and Jackson Heights are still without power, thanks to the lightning storm that crippled the nation's largest power company..."

Jenny gasped. "My God, that was the blackout!"

Roger stood up abruptly and Forest rose with him. Ghostlike light and dark images played over their bodies as they faced each other. Forest waved his arm and Micky instantly pulled the tape, plunging the room into silence. He waved again, pushing upward with his hand, and she gave them light.

"It's ten minutes to air time, Forest, and they've got to be in a panic in the control room." Forest searched his old friend's face and saw nothing but distrust and aversion. They looked at each other for what seemed like an eternally long time, and then Roger looked away. Forest knew that Roger was feeling used and excluded, but Forest couldn't help it. Roger was too good a journalist to accept all this on face value, and there just wasn't time to explain it now. Their friendship would have to carry them until later.

"All right, Roger," Forest said quietly. "Thank you. Thank you for your help. As it turns out, I could have never done it without you." Roger glanced tentatively at Forest and saw him smiling. He drew himself up and extended his hand. Forest took it.

"Congratulations, dear fellow. I think you've finally turned the weather into news." Then he turned and left the room.

CHAPTER THIRTY-NINE

Micky burst out of the control room, a jar of cold cream and a box of tissues in her hand. She stormed down the aisle in a fury. "That's fucking outrageous!" Forest couldn't help but smile at her indignation.

"It sure is, Mick."

"You mean I froze my ass off last winter, and my heating bill was doubled, because someone was playing political games with the weather?" Forest nodded. "And they rained out my sister's garden wedding . . ."

"Wait a minute," he said, stopping her. "We don't know if they did or they didn't. And that's the problem. You never know if it's them or nature." Micky seemed stunned.

"That means every time it rains . . . or snows . . . or anything . . ."

"You got it, Mick."

"Forest, they can't do that. It's got to be stopped."

"Believe it or not, Micky, that's precisely

what I'm trying to do," he shouted in exasperation. "If I could just get a little help. Now, take Jenny with you and set up the big board in the studio. And get a globe—the big one. Steal it from Phil Kenner's office." Forest took Jenny's hand and squeezed it gently. "Now get out, you two."

They started up the aisle toward the door. "And, Micky . . ." Forest called, "would you mind leaving the cold cream and tissues?"

She put them down on a seat. "Sorry, boss," she said sheepishly. Then she grabbed Jenny's hand and they ran.

It was ten minutes to six. Forest went on at 6:20. That gave him half an hour to organize his information. Using the glass of the projection booth as a mirror, he smeared cold cream over the wide red lips and white eyes of the clown's face. It was an image he would erase once and for all tonight.

There would be no antics tonight. He would control every move to appear serious and scientific. Otherwise—and deep inside himself he still feared that the possibility existed—no one would believe him. It was ironic: his clowning made it possible for him to get on the air, and it might be the very thing that would undo him.

As Forest scrubbed at his face, he started composing his speech. First he would tell the people that they weren't crazy. Yes, there was something wrong with the weather. Then he would explain about weather control. He could draw a diagram of how the satellites worked. That's good, he thought. It's simple and clear.

Forest's face emerged from under the makeup. He wiped away the last of the white and started peeling off the clown costume. Next he would explain that weather control could be used for good or evil, to feed people or to kill them. And that as it was being used now, without our knowledge, it was the world's most powerful weapon. Its power was greater than any bomb ever invented and, because it was weather, it was invisible. Truly the ultimate weapon.

Forest straightened his tie and with his hands tried to press the wrinkles out his jacket. It would have to do. He had so much to tell and so little time. He had to explain about the Weather War and the disasters it had created. And he had to name General Wells and the Thurday group. He smiled. It would be silly, and dangerous, to forget that.

Forest looked at the clock. He had ten minutes. It was frightening, he thought, how big this was. Until now, wars had been fought by soldiers, and the military had sustained the majority of the casualties. That was the basis for the Geneva Convention and for the war crimes trials in Germany after World War II. But now there was a third World War, being waged by the military entirely against civilians. And no one even knew that we were at war.

Forest looked at himself in the glass and smiled. He liked what he saw. He was tired and bruised, but he wasn't beaten. His life had meaning now.

"They're going to have a chance to know," he said aloud. "They're going to know." He looked at the clock. Five minutes. He ran out of the screening room.

CHAPTER FORTY

Roger Moss was just finishing a story about pushcart peddlers in Central Park when he was handed a note. For the first time in his long career on national television, his face registered shock and dismay.

"Now, standing in for Forest Hill," he read, "is Tex Austin with the weather.

According to Tex Austin, it was a perfectly normal, hot July day.

THURSDAY

AUGUST 17, 1978

GUANTANAMO BAY, CUBA

Ensign First Class Alvie Evans lay face down in the water as a small navy launch drew slowly alongside him. Three men leaned over and hoisted his body into the boat, laying it gently on top of a pile of what turned out to be forty-two of his buddies. When the exception of the masts and top decks of a few ships peeking out of the calm waters of the bay, you could hardly guess from the clear blue sky that a hurricane of unrecordable force had passed through here only two days ago. The naval base at Guantanamo was all but totally destroyed.

FRIDAY

AUGUST 25, 1978

ZHITOMIR, SIBERIA

Tvardovsky was doing his best to make a home in Zima Junction. He had a small farm near Lake Baikal. Actually, the lake was more like an ocean to him because you couldn't see across it. After being deported to Siberia for setting his landlord's house on fire, Tvardovsky quickly lost his revolutionary inclinations. That was thirty years ago.

As he pulled another potato out of the earth, he blinked a couple of times toward the giant Ural Mountains growing straight up out of the plain. Something glistened in the distance, and he stared harder as if he could see farther that way. A thin, glistening line spread across the entire floor of the valley. He rubbed his eyes and stared again. Lake Baikal was moving toward him. He stood in his potato field, frozen with uncertainty, as the water crept around his legs and through his house and over his land, flooding the entire valley.

The phenomenon was put down to a sudden and rapid thaw in the mountains. The fact that the underground missile silos at Zhitomir were completely flooded never made the papers.

THE END

According to *The New York Times*, the United States, the Soviet Union, and twenty-nine other countries meeting in Geneva, signed a treaty that would prohibit modifying the environment for military purposes. The treaty was concluded after three years of negotiation.

A similar treaty had been signed by the United States and the Soviet Union in 1977, and earlier, in 1972.

KILLSHOT...
MORE THAN A GAME.

Killshot:

"When one player, by virtue of perfect execution and precise coordination, drives the handball in such a fashion so it strikes the front wall low to the floor, allowing his opponent no possibility for a return shot."

THE ARTE OF HANDBALL
By S. O'Dwyer
Dublin, Ireland, 1815

But there is a second kind of Killshot:

"When a certain breed of renegade player attempts to hit his opponent with such force so as to maim or otherwise injure him...for life."

The ultimate novel of life and death.

Coming in January, 1979 from Pinnacle Books